I've travelled the world twice over,
Met the famous: saints and sinners,
Poets and artists, kings and queens,
Old stars and hopeful beginners,
I've been where no-one's been before,
Learned secrets from writers and cooks
All with one library ticket
To the wonderful world of books.

THE FORTUNATE MARRIAGE

Everyone said it was a fortunate marriage for Rowland Dynham, second son of an impoverished baronet, when he secured the hand of beautiful and vivacious heiress Caroline Caynnes. But when Caroline's orphaned cousin Louisa went to live at Rosewell Abbey in North Cornwall some eight years later she soon discovered that it had not turned out to be a happy one. Caught up in the increasingly violent battle of wills, Louisa's own life was dramatically changed.

MERIOL TREVOR

THE FORTUNATE MARRIAGE

Complete and Unabridged

ULVERSCROFT
Leicester

First published 1976

First Large Print Edition
published May 1980
by arrangement with
Hodder & Stoughton Ltd.
London
and
E. P. Dutton, New York

British Library CIP Data

Trevor, Meriol
  The fortunate marriage. — Large print ed.
(Ulverscroft large print series:
  historical romance).
I. Title
823'.9'1F   PR6039.R52F/

ISBN 0-7089-0455-6

Published by
F. A. Thorpe (Publishing) Ltd.
Anstey, Leicestershire
Printed in England

I

THE CAYNNES HEIRESS

1

WHEN her mother died, after a long decline, early in the year 1797, Louisa Pierce was only seventeen and had not a notion what she was going to do. Small' as were their lodgings near the Hot Wells in Bristol, she did not know if she could afford to continue to live there beyond the month's end, even had it been proper for a young woman to live alone. Besides, she had always hated those narrow rooms, which reminded her of the sick, tired woman who had hardly seemed the same person as the mother she wanted to remember, so full of gossip and reminiscence.

"Oh, Louie, it is a pity you cannot recall your grandmother," she had often said. "Even after she left the stage she had the looks and manners of a queen. Well! My sister Emma certainly had the looks, but not the dramatic talent and I never had either. Nor have you, my love, except that perhaps that romantic fancy of yours comes down from her."

Louie's head was indeed filled with dreams and imaginations, and as her mother's prolonged illness had cut her off from social entertainments she was shy and inexperienced in comparison with her late school friends, the only people she knew well there.

No relations had come to the funeral; in fact, Louie was uncertain if she had any, beyond one cousin. Her father, a merchant officer, had deserted them long since, and his own family had cast him off even before his brief excursion into matrimony, so that she knew nothing about them. He was the reason Louie was left so poor, for he had married Sarah Watson for her dowry, most of which he had squandered before taking himself off.

Poor Sarah never had much sense, said her elder sister Emma, who had done very well for herself, years ago, in catching a rich and noble widower when he was trying to cure, at Bath, the effects of a life devoted to pleasure. Lord Caynnes was an old rake, but when he died not long after his second marriage, he left his widow very well off, and with one child, a daughter, who, though she could not inherit his title, became the heiress of considerable estates. Emma sometimes brought this girl, who was ten years older than Louie, to stay in Bath, and Sarah and her daughter would drive from Bristol in a hired chaise, and stay grandly at the White Hart.

This cousin, the Honourable Caroline Caynnes, had seemed a kind of goddess to Louie, a princess from another world, who had everything she could possibly want, and was so beautiful and high spirited that no one could refuse her anything. Carelessly generous, she had enchanted her little cousin, but though there was sometimes talk of "going to stay" somehow it never happened—not until Caroline's marriage, eight years ago.

Louie wrote to Caroline when her mother died, a conventional little letter, for since that summer of 1789 she had not seen her, and after Aunt Emma's death had scarcely heard of her. No reply had come before the funeral, but about a month later a long scrawl arrived from north Cornwall, where the original home of the Caynnes family was situated. A much finer house in Hertfordshire had been sold to pay Lord Caynnes's debts, at the time of his death; his brother, who inherited the barony, had refused to pay them, having quite enough of his own. When he too died, the title lapsed for lack of male heirs. It had been conferred at the Restoration by a grateful Charles II, who had borrowed considerably during his wanderings from the Caynnes of the day, and had found the son an amusing companion in the pleasures of the town. The family, notorious for charm and beauty, remained favourites at court so long as the court was gay; in staider times they found a place with the smartest set in town. None of them had ever done anything noteworthy, except to employ such good stewards that each generation enjoyed a rich inheritance.

Caroline Caynnes apologised for her delay in writing; Louie's letter had been sent on from London, down to Rosewell Abbey. "Indeed, I have been banished from town this long while, my dear Louie," she wrote in her large, rapid hand. And after some regrets for her Aunt Sarah, and laments that she had not seen them for so long, came a paragraph which seemed to Louie to start from the page.

Dearest Cousin, I hope you will come and make a long stay with me here at Rosewell. Why should you not make your home with me, indeed? You could help to teach the children, for I abominate the whole tribe of governesses, and yet Mary Anne will soon be seven, though she is as stupid as possible. Adrian is sharp enough but he is a naughty fellow and will not do as he is told. Now do come, for I am dying of *ennui* here alone and Dynham is always in London, though he forbids me to go there. Come, Louie, come at once. I will send Hannah Colwill in the carriage next week, to assist in the packing and bring you here.

She assumed that Louie would not refuse her invitation; what orphaned girl could? To be offered a home, and with the cousin who had always represented for Louie the very image of beauty and womanly power—it was something she had never imagined possible, too good to be true. Certainly, since Aunt Emma's death, which had happened suddenly, after the birth of Caroline's first child, they had heard very little from herself, though an annuity had continued to be paid regularly, through a certain Mr. Pendry, by the direction of the Honourable Mrs. Dynham. Louie had wondered, when her mother died, whether she would still receive it. But to go and live with Caroline herself was an infinitely more exciting prospect.

She put the letter down, took it up, read it again. There was no mistake. But she had to talk to someone about it, so she hurriedly put on her black mourning cloak and ran across the street to the friend who lived nearest to her, and in Susie's excitement and congratulations her own sense of good fortune was confirmed.

"Only think, Louie, your cousin will certainly take you up to town, you will meet men of fashion—why, you may marry a lord yourself!" said red-cheeked dark-eyed Susie, whose mind ran on love and marriage.

Louie's imagination had not leapt off to London like that, and the thought of *Town* simply alarmed her; she was shy and unsure of herself and it was not her ambition to shine in society. It was Rosewell Abbey she was thinking of, as she told a disbelieving Susie.

"Oh, but it is the most beautiful place in the world, an old house and near to the sea."

"And miles from anywhere else, I understand," said Susie. "I don't wonder your cousin suffers from *ennui*." For of course Louie had showed her the letter from Caroline. "I wonder why her husband forbids her to go to London," remarked inquisitive Susie.

8

"That is just Caroline's manner of talking," said Louie. "She expresses herself very forcibly. He may have sent her down there for her health. It is his own country too, for he was brought up at the Dynhams' home there, Brentland House. They are a very old family too, but not well off. It was Caroline who had all the money, and estates."

Louie had made only one visit to Rosewell Abbey, when she was a child between nine and ten, for her cousin's wedding, but she had never forgotten it.

When her mother had heard of the engagement she had been disappointed. "I thought Caroline would marry a Duke at least," she had said. "But here's this Captain Dynham, who seems to have nothing but good looks to recommend him. His brother will be a baronet, and has married a banker's daughter, but this Rowland will not come in for anything, and I suspect him of making his fortune by turning Caroline's head before she has come out into society. I told Emma it was mistaken to delay that event, but she was so much afraid of Caroline's wilfulness—and now see what has happened! I wonder Lady Caynnes had not put her foot down and forbidden the match."

Lady Caynnes was the widow of George, the brother of Caroline's father Adrian, who had briefly held the barony, though the effects of a life as dissipated as his brother's had carried him off a few years later. He had married late, and for money. Maria Warstowe, sister of a rich merchant banker of London, was no beauty, nor much endowed with wit or charm, but very substantially endowed with thousands in the Funds. The marriage proved childless, but Lady Caynnes held firmly to the position she had won and regarded her husband's family as her own. She owned one great house in Mayfair where she lived, and another in Wiltshire, which she liked to say were destined for Caroline's children—until Caroline's choice of a husband had so annoyed her.

"Rowland Dynham has done very well for himself in securing Caroline," she said to Mrs. Pierce, when they met at Rosewell before the wedding. "Yes, for a younger son, of no means, it is a fortunate marriage indeed! He carries off an heiress who must be one of the most beautiful girls in the country. But I believe he has always been an ambitious young man, and jealous of his elder brother."

It turned out that, much to her annoyance,

Lady Caynnes had been instrumental in their meeting each other, for Rowland Dynham's elder brother Mark had married her niece, Mary Warstowe, and Lady Caynnes had invited Caroline and her mother to stay for the wedding. She considered it quite proper for Mark Dynham, who would be a baronet, even if a poor one, to marry her niece on the banking side; far otherwise when it came to Rowland Dynham's proposing to the Caynnes heiress.

"But Caroline is a most self-willed girl, she carried her weak mother quite with her," said Lady Caynnes, not caring in the least that she was addressing the sister of the weak mother in question. "I declare, Mrs. Pierce, your sister has always spoilt that girl. I am sorry I was not in a position to forbid the match."

But when they met Captain Dynham Louie at least was not surprised that Caroline wanted to marry him. For he was a very tall, lean and handsome young man with aquiline features, active and energetic in his smart uniform, always impeccably turned out, and with a fine, if slightly formal courtesy of manner which soon won the admiration of Mrs. Pierce.

"They certainly make a handsome couple,"

11

she had said one day, looking from a window at the pair as they walked round the paths of the garden enclosed by three sides of the house, at the back.

In the middle of the paved place was a small fountain, and this had been set in order to play for the wedding of the heiress, but the jet was slightly crooked, so that the stream of water fell to one side. This disturbed Captain Dynham's orderly mind; he walked up to the edge of the bowl and stood on the rim, stretching out a foot to try to push the jet straight. In spite of his long legs and excellent balance he could not reach it and Caroline, standing by in her white dress with its long tight sleeves, her beautiful glossy brown hair uncovered by any cap or bonnet, laughed at him.

"It is no use, Dynham, you would have to wade," she said.

Captain Dynham was wearing very fine Hessian boots and did not choose to subject them to the water.

"I'll get Beer to fix it," he said.

"I beg you will not!" cried Caroline. "That would upset old Prust, who already feels his province has been invaded from Brentland. Keep your Beers in check, if you please!"

12

Louie, standing at the open window, watched them intently, and retained the memory long after, so that it was clear in her mind as she packed her belongings to leave Bristol.

Hannah Colwill proved to be a small wiry woman of indeterminate age, with dark, sloe eyes and a secretive look. She was not talkative and Louie thought she despised her mistress's poor young relation.

"You are not the least like madam, in looks, miss," she observed. She did not speak with a broad accent.

Louie was a slender girl with a small rounded face, softly brown in complexion, the mouth wide and thin lipped; her large brown eyes shy but watchful. Her dark hair was straight and she had trouble putting curls into it; curlpapers irritated her at night; curling irons, applied before going out, were a source of anxiety. Hannah Colwill seemed to divine all this at a glance.

On the long journey down to North Cornwall Louie was thinking much of the last time she had been there, for the wedding in 1789. A number of Dynhams had come for the occasion—the old General, stiff-backed, with a brisk, barking manner, and his tall, pale,

13

composed wife: both had died since, and so had the eldest son, killed in the war which had begun with France in 1793, so that he had never become a baronet after all. The only child of his marriage to Mary Warstowe, who had not long survived the shock of his loss, was now Sir Miles Dynham; a child of seven, he lived with his banking uncle, Frederick Warstowe, in London, as Louie discovered from Hannah Colwill.

"And a poor sickly little creature he is," said Hannah. "They say he won't never live to grow up. I daresay that would suit Colonel Dynham all right, for then he'd be master of Brentland and Sir Rowland, and more the equal of madam."

In the war in which Mark Dynham had died, his brother had reached the rank of Colonel.

"Why doesn't the child live with his Dynham uncle, rather than the Warstowes?" asked Louie. "Especially as Brentland is not far from Rosewell."

She remembered the Dynhams driving over from Brentland, which was high on the moor inland; remembered, too, Lady Caynnes remarking with a snort on "those old names they take, because there were

Rowlands and Joscelins among the Dynhams of the middle ages, though everyone knows the principal family died out then, and these are descended from some obscure minor branch. Why, Brentland was hardly more than a farm till Sir Oliver gave up the Stuart cause and put a new front on it—not that it is much of a place now, nothing like Rosewell."

Still, however scornful Lady Caynnes might be, Louie could not but feel impressed at the thought that the Dynhams' ancestors were Norman, that their name came from "de Dinan" and that, for generations they had fought in the British army. The baronetcy had been conferred, again by Charles II, for military services, but unlike the Caynnes family, the Dynhams had never greatly prospered. Yet it seemed strange that the young heir should live with his banking relations in London, and not with his Dynham uncle.

Hannah Colwill sniffed. "Those London people don't think our family suitable," she said.

"Suitable!" repeated Louie, astonished that Caroline, the daughter of a Lord, could be considered unsuitable by London bankers. "What do you mean?"

15

"Well, miss, there's been a deal of trouble since the Colonel came back from the war, and madam's fine house in town has been given up. Some thought things would be better after Colonel Dynham left the army and went into the Foreign Office, but I doubt if it is—well, madam would hardly have come down to the country, would she, if all was right?"

Louie gathered that all was not well in her cousin's affairs but she did not like to question the maid, and Hannah Colwill did not volunteer information; although she had been with her mistress in London she retained her secretive Cornish character.

Louie brooded on the hints she had received and at night she re-read Caroline's letter, noticing her remark about her husband's forbidding her to go to London, though he lived there himself. It certainly did not sound as if that marriage had turned out as well as it had started. Yet Louie could still hear her mother saying, as they drove away, "Well, that was the prettiest wedding I ever did see!"

It had been a very simple one, the whole party walking up a grass path from the garden to the little dumpy church. The youngest of the Dynham sons, an ungainly giant of a youth, had been much teased at the wedding breakfast because when he had sat down in church the old bench had given a loud crack in protest. Poor Joscelin jumped up in confusion and shambled to the back, standing with the bell ringers under the squat tower, and later taking part in ringing a peal for the bridal pair.

In Louie's memory Rosewell Abbey lay perpetually bathed in bright June sunshine, with roses breathing sweetness, people laughing in the old house and Caroline, queen of it all, tall in her white dress, smiling and bountiful, loading her little cousin with presents.

But now, at the beginning of April, when she came there eight years later, the weather was cold. The sky was low and grey, the chill light made even the new growth of green in the hedgebanks look cold and pinched. The greyness took the life and colour out of the spring and made the old house itself look almost grim, when Louie had remembered it as mellow and golden.

Her childish memory had retained some images vividly, but she had not then seen the place in perspective. Now she noticed that the approach was by a mere lane, turning off

17

the coastal road which was not itself either wide or well kept, and in fact ran a mile or two inland, away from the high cliffs. She saw how the valley opened out in flat meadow bottoms towards the sea, with a small full stream winding through, how the tiny village, merely a few cottages, clustered round the small church with its square tower, close by the house—so clearly once a religious house, now that she knew more of such things. The shape of it still stood in the three walls of a cloister, the fourth pulled down to leave the formal garden with a view of the country. The front had been rebuilt in the seventeenth century and nothing much had been done to it later, since the Caynnes family had lived so much in London and in their Hertfordshire house, now sold.

Rosewell Abbey was well placed, behind a shoulder of hill as the coombe turned seaward, sheltered from the Atlantic gales, but now Louie could observe—what she had forgotten—how near the sea was; the dull grey wall of it rose up between the headlands like a triangle, rimmed against the softer grey of the huge, hanging, cloudy sky.

Louie became aware, as she had not been eight years ago, of the isolation of the place, hidden away in this remote valley on the western edge of England—hardly England here, she reflected, but Britain, the ancient island of the Druids. Louie's head was full of legend and story.

Yet once inside, all was civilised and comfortable; the rooms, many of them wainscoted with wooden panels, and with polished boarded floors, were not too big to keep warm, and any modern alterations had been to increase comfort. And the Caroline who came quickly and gracefully to greet her with a kiss was wearing a fashionable gown with her sash tied high and certainly did not look in the least countrified. In fact, Louie was a little overwhelmed by her cousin's splendid manner, though her embrace was warm enough.

"Little Louie, a young lady!" she said, surveying her. "Yet not so very grown up, cousin, after all."

Louie was indeed small beside her. Caroline was tall for a woman and carried herself with a proud grace, her superb figure at its best when she was in movement. Vivid energy seemed to infuse body and soul in a restless, impulsive way. Her colouring was brilliant, her eyes a dark bright grey, glancing with quick-changing moods. Louie was once

19

more, and instantly, cast under the spell of Caroline.

They were still in the hall when a door upstairs opened and a little boy came rushing headlong down the staircase shouting, "How do you do, Cousin Louis*ah*!"

It was Adrian Caynnes Dynham, five and a half years old, and behind him, slow and timid, came Mary Anne, soon to be seven. She was a solid child with a round rosy face, large blue eyes and fair straight hair fanning out on her shoulders. Adrian was charming, Louie thought, as she kissed him. He was alive with restless energy, his grey eyes, with dark flecks in them, bright and inquisitive, his soft dark hair falling in thick curling waves.

Louie had brought little presents with her from Bristol and it was fun unpacking them and watching the children's delight. It was many months since they had been in London and to them their town life seemed already distant. They were still playing with their new toys when Louie came downstairs again, after changing out of her travelling dress. Black, which she wore in mourning for her mother, did not suit her, and she felt plain and dowdy beside Caroline.

Adrian was running round the hall, flying his paper bird behind him on its string, looking round at it, and dodging the table and heavy chairs that stood in the middle.

"Oh, Adrian!" Mary Anne was saying anxiously. "Mind the table! Oh, Adrian, look out, you'll tread on Mop's puppy."

"Well, you pick him up then," said Adrian impatiently, and the girl, blundering after the fat, wobbling puppy, collided with her brother, so that they ended in a heap on the floor, Adrian laughing and Mary Anne, for a moment, nearly crying. The puppy yapped excitedly.

"Heavens, what a noise you children make!" said Caroline. "Go upstairs if you want to play, or come with us and be rational."

The children came into the drawing-room but Adrian soon tired of grown up talk and ran off, his sister presently following. Although the younger, he was plainly the leader.

Caroline, associating her cousin with youthful visits to Bath, began to ask her what was doing in that town, and was quite surprised to hear she had not been there for several years and knew little even of such people of fashion as came to try the Hot Wells in Bristol.

"However, I never could understand what people see in Bath," said Caroline. "Life is a great deal more entertaining in London. I do believe that if Dynham persists in his refusal to take a house in town again I shall be driven to stay with Aunt Caynnes—though heaven knows it's hard enough to entertain oneself under her auspices, and she flatly refuses to receive most of my friends."

"Why don't you stay with your friends, then?" asked Louie, innocently, surprised that someone as rich and well-born as Caroline could not do as she pleased.

Caroline, who had walked to the window, laughed and turned round, glancing at Louie for a moment as if uncertain what to say. Then she remarked casually, "Oh, I could not stay with my friends—either they are in bachelor lodgings or immured with their impossible families. Besides, I don't know what Dynham would do—though it might be interesting to find out."

While Louie was hesitating, uncertain how to reply, Caroline came back to the fireplace and leant her elbow on the mantelshelf; the warm light of the flames played upwards on

22

her lovely face and bosom, on the graceful rounded arms. She really was the most beautiful creature, Louie thought, and was suddenly reminded of a print of their grandmother in some theatrical rôle, queenly and grand.

"Dynham is a very stiff, conventional man—I suppose you hardly remember him?" said Caroline. "I imagine he intended me to be a stiff conventional wife, such a woman as his mother was, never betraying an atom of feeling or caring for anything beyond formal visiting and ruling her family. But it bores me to death, that respectable life, especially since Dynham became a clerk in the Foreign Office. The officers were most of them stupid, but at least they had some go in them, whereas the diplomats—oh, I cannot stand pompous talking men, for ever taken up with politics."

The next moment her attention veered back to her cousin.

"Let us not talk of Dynham's notions of behaviour! What fun we are going to have together, Louie! I declare, we shall amuse ourselves very well without any tiresome men to interfere with our pursuits. I am sure you are better at music and drawing than I am.

And we will go out riding together."

When Louie was forced to confess that she could not ride, Caroline assured her that she would soon learn. "And we will teach the children together every day. You will be the greatest help to me, Louie, I know we shall get along excellently."

And Louie felt her welcome was genuine, even if conditioned a little by the loneliness of her present situation.

2

IT was lucky that Louie took to the children, for she soon found herself spending much of her time with them. Caroline had talked of teaching them every day but she soon tired of it. She was not a good teacher; impatient and careless, she made Mary Anne, who was a slow learner and over-anxious, cry with her hasty criticisms, and she laughed at Adrian's antics instead of correcting him.

"Oh, I don't know the answers myself!" she would cry, flinging down the book. "What does it matter? Let's go for a ride."

She was fond of riding and an excellent horsewoman but far too impatient while Louie, eager but nervous, began to learn. Caroline left her to an old groom and rode off, quite often alone, without even a stable lad. She did not care what people said.

As Caroline did not like taking walks with the children and Louie wanted exercise and to see the country, she often went with them, usually with Lizzie Jewell, the Devonshire nursemaid, in attendance. With the children she explored the woods inland and discovered the seashore, so much wilder than anything she had ever seen before. Huge waves curled and smashed on a bank of smooth grey stones, heaped by the tide between the headlands; at ebb, wet lanes of sand were laid bare between long ridges of black toothed rock that ran out in bars towards the sliding wash of the unresting water.

There were no boats on this coast; fishermen lived in the Cornish coves southward, and round the corner of Hartland Point on the North Devon shores of the Bristol Channel; here, it was too wild. The only boats were wrecks and there was a battered bulkhead of one remaining on the rocks which fascinated Adrian. He always ran to it and climbed up to sit astride, imagining himself sailing the seas, voyaging to Newfoundland far beyond the horizon.

Mary Anne hunted for marine treasures and found several curiosities. She had a collection of pieces of wood, rubbed smooth and into odd shapes by the pummelling of the waves; but she rarely found shells. They were ground to pieces by the ceaseless crashing of water on rock.

Caroline hardly ever came this way. "I hate

the sea," she said once. "It is so melancholy. It shuts one in."

Louie felt just the opposite; to her that vast turbulent expanse was a liberating vision. She had never felt so much alive, so free, as roaming on the shore, or standing on the short turf on the cliff above, gazing to the gleaming horizon. The everlasting rush and withdrawal of the waves sounded in her ears like breathing, not like sighing.

Caroline took her rides inland and one day she came back with a stranger in attendance, both of them laughing and talking, evidently familiar friends. He was in his middle thirties, a man who ten years earlier must have been extremely handsome; he was still good-looking, but the lines of his face were growing a little too soft and sagging and his figure showed the effects of good living, the curves not disguised but rather emphasised by his close fitting smart town clothes. His hands were white and his face pale, his soft dark curly hair beginning to look a little thin. He had an easy manner and a frequent laugh. Caroline introduced him as Jack Caynnes Ridgway, without further identification.

"You haven't yet told me what brings you down here, Caynnes," she said, as she offered him a glass of wine, still in her habit, though she had pulled off her hat. "It cannot be for my sake."

He laughed and raised his glass to her. "Your health, my dear! You look as lovely as ever. The country air suits you—I must allow that point to Dynham."

"You need not," said Caroline. "I would far prefer the air of Newmarket."

He smiled. "You're not still chafing at that? It's done your reputation a world of good, my dear. Everyone is now on your side—even those who were suspicious before. Dynham is voted a brute—as we know he is, though it does not always appear."

"Here's my cousin staring—she doesn't know what we are talking about," said Caroline. "Last autumn, Louie, I escaped my virtuous husband's vigilance and went to the races with Caynnes and some of my friends."

"And Dynham came and carried her off—in chains, as it were," said Caynnes Ridgway. "Stalked up as stiff as a poker and led her away like a runaway pony. We did laugh, Caroline, when you had gone."

"It was no laughing matter to me," said Caroline. "I went because I did not choose to battle it in public, but I've been down here in

28

disgrace ever since, after that one week mewed up with Aunt Caynnes, who kept on talking of impropriety and making myself notorious, in the most tedious way. Why didn't you come to see me then, Jack?"

"My dear, Lady Caynnes hates to acknowledge my existence, you know that."

Caroline, perched on the arm of the sofa where he sprawled, laughed aloud. "I know you don't give a fig for that," she said. "You would charm Aunt Caynnes soon enough, if you wished. No, you were afraid of boredom in that house, admit it."

"I don't deny it, my dear. Besides, I hate to see that splendid place wasted. What wonderful evenings one could spend there, with the right people! It should be yours, anyway."

Caroline shook her head. "No—have you forgotten, Jack? It was Aunt Caynnes's dowry which bought that house, those useful plebeian thousands—it never was in the entail. However, she has sworn she will leave it to Adrian, all the same, because she thinks he's more like a Caynnes than a Dynham."

"Lucky little devil, he'll scoop the lot," said Ridgway, drinking his wine. "Well, I wish his papa would make way for him as soon as possible, but since he's left the army I fear that's unlikely. He's made of iron, like all the Dynhams. It takes a cannon ball to carry them off."

Caroline made no comment on his wish that her husband's life might soon be brought to an end. She smiled as she put down her empty glass. "Will you stay to dinner, Jack? Do! Amuse us with the latest gossip from town."

"Well, it seems too bad to dine with you in riding boots, Caroline, but yes, I would like to stay," said Ridgway. "It's confounded dull with the old man, and after all, he's not going to die this time."

It appeared that his father was the family solicitor, in Monkhampton, and that it was a sudden heart attack which had brought the son down from London.

Mr. Ridgway was certainly an entertaining dinner guest, though Louie presently began to wonder if every married person in London had a lover, so complex were the shifting relationships among the people he talked about so amusingly. A certain Lord Walter's affairs seemed to interest Caroline most, though she wanted to know whether Lady Walter was still pursuing a foreign ambassador.

"I must have Hester happy, or I shall be

30

angry with Walter," she said. "Perhaps I am angry with him anyway for letting Dynham march me off so tamely. But Walter has no heart; no memory, either, the selfish fellow."

When Louie discovered that this noble pair were the brother of a Duke and the daughter of an Earl, it seemed to make their wickedness less real; one expected immorality among the nobility.

Having exhausted the activites of Lord Walter Chervill and his wife, Caroline presently asked, "Have you seen my cousin Hilary Tollington, lately?" And she added, "The son of my Caynnes aunt, Louie—he's my only near relation, that side."

"Oh, poor Tollington, haven't you heard? He's lost his bride!" said Caynnes Ridgway, with a laugh.

"Why, I thought the wedding was fixed in a week or two," said Caroline, "after this long engagement—for surely Julia has put him off before."

"Oh yes, the wedding was fixed, and the ravishing Miss Whichcote has accepted some very valuable gifts, but this time she has not put off the date, she has run away with someone else—that handsome fellow, Grant."

"Eloped with Grant! She's a fool then,"

said Caroline, "for Grant has nothing but Hilary has inherited Woodford St. Petrock from his uncle Tollington, as well as the Caynnes money he had from his mother, my aunt."

"But Grant has expectations, I understand," said Ridgway. "And if you put him beside Tollington . . . well!"

Caroline laughed. "Poor Hilary is certainly nothing to look at," she said. "Well, he will have to marry his cousin Henrietta Tollington, so that she can go back to her old home as mistress again. Her sister, Lady Hayford, has always wished it. And Henrietta would make a good wife for an M.P."

"Little Miss Henrietta is as cool as they come," said Ridgway. "I hear she has refused several offers already. I don't fancy cousin Hilary will satisfy her ambition, M.P. though he is."

"Did he come to your wedding, Caroline?" Louie asked.

"Oh yes, he came," said Caroline. "He was at Oxford then. If you remember a small willowy creature with rabbitty teeth, that's dear Hilary. The teeth belong to the Tollingtons, not to us, thank goodness. Henrietta has them too."

"But she contrives to look very charming with them," observed Caynnes Ridgway.

"Oh, you will call any woman charming who laughs at your chatter," said Caroline. "As for Julia Whichcote, she must have taken a great fancy to Grant to run away with him. I must say, I think a woman cheapens herself by an elopement."

"Maybe she does," said Ridgway, indolently. "But I can see why she felt unable to face the future with you little cousin, my dear, with his delicate health and his unfortunate teeth."

Caroline did not disagree and began to talk about other acquaintances, while Louie found herself remembering not Hilary Tollington but his cousin Henrietta, then a little girl like herself, a year or two older but no bigger, a neat small creature with golden curls and, yes, slightly prominent, though tiny, white teeth. Henrietta had been interested that Louie went to school. A sociable child, she longed to go to school but said her father would never let her, for he was afraid of her catching something and dying; he had lost several daughters between the eldest, grown up at the time of Caroline's wedding, and Henrietta, who was the youngest. There were no sons; that was why Hilary had inherited the family home, in the Torridge Vale, on the way to Bideford in Devon. Louie could remember the old man too, small and spry in his old fashioned coat and wearing a powdered wig: Mr. Tollington of Woodford St. Petrock.

Caynnes Ridgway stayed late, saying he could ride home to Monkhampton in the dark—could do it with his eyes shut. When he was leaving Caroline said, "Of course you'll come again, Caynnes. Come when you like."

"Thanks, my dear, I will."

To Louie's surprise, he kissed Caroline's cheek as he took leave of her.

"Don't be shocked, Louie," said Caroline, smiling at her startled face, as she turned back from the door. "Caynnes isn't my lover. He's my brother."

"Your *brother*!"

"Wrong side of the blanket, as they say," said Caroline. "My father, you know, never had a reputation for virtue. Old Ridgway, the family lawyer, had a pretty wife—childless till she became acquainted with my father . . ." Caroline laughed. "Mr. Ridgway agreed to call Jack his son, but father sent him to Eton and Cambridge. He's a barrister, but he don't work very hard, I'm afraid. He's a good fellow, is Jack, knows everybody, and knows how to work things if one wants some cash."

She yawned, stretching her arms and shaking her fine mane of hair.

"Poor Jack! If he were legitimate he'd be Lord Caynnes and own this place and all the rest of the property. He's surprisingly fond of me, considering our relative positions."

"Did you always know about him?" Louie asked, full of curiosity.

"Oh no—not till we met in London when Dynham was off at the wars," said Caroline. "He came along to find me out, and introduced me to his set. I owe Caynnes a lot of fun, one way and another."

After that evening Caynnes Ridgway seemed always to be coming to Rosewell. He advised Caroline on a phaeton she wanted, so that she could drive herself about the country; she went to Monkhampton, the nearest small town to the south, to see about it and came back in high spirits. She had met a friend of Ridgway's, a gentleman whose house was not far away, called George Godfrey.

"I've heard Dynham talk of the Godfreys," she said, "I think his brother Mark had a fisticuffs fight with this one, when they were boys; apparently the Godfreys were their great enemies. Well, I never do agree with Dynham—I thought Mr. Godfrey a good-looking fellow, fair, somewhat high-coloured perhaps. I hope he'll come here soon, for I'm bored to death in this place."

"Perhaps his wife will invite us to their house," said Louie, who had often wondered why they never called on any neighbours or received any calls.

Caroline laughed. "Oh my dear girl! Don't you realise what a reputation I've got? Why, I shall be very surprised if Mr. Godfrey tells his wife he has met me!" She threw herself down on the sofa, putting her arms behind her head. "I wonder if I shall take Godfrey for a lover? It would annoy Dynham so much—I might do it just for that."

Louie stopped her drawing and stared at Caroline.

"Oh, now I have shocked you, my poor little cousin!" said Caroline, with a slightly self-conscious laugh.

Louie certainly was shocked but she was young enough not to wish to appear too innocent. "I suppose you are joking," she said cautiously.

"Oh yes, I am joking," said Caroline, carelessly. "George Godfrey does not greatly take my fancy, Louie. But I am very dull here. I like to be among friends, all enjoying ourselves together at routs or at the races. I daresay you think my London acquaintance very wicked. But I assure you my name has never been coupled with any one man's." She laughed suddenly. "When Dynham came back, he did not know which to be jealous of!"

Then her mood changed. She sat up and said earnestly, "How you stare at me, Louie, with those great brown eyes of yours! But you don't know what I have endured. Dynham is such a hard man; he is without feeling, without heart. A wife is merely a possession to him, his exclusive property. He never has cared in the least what I feel. It was Rosewell he wanted, so as to be greater than his brother at Brentland, and play a part in the world of affairs. Because he is handsome himself my looks mean nothing to him; I daresay he would have preferred me to be plain and meek. But as I am not, he suspects me every time I speak to another man. Yet it is not because he cares for me himself; it is just that he cannot endure another to have what is his.

37

He would like to keep me down here till I am old and ugly but I won't stand it. No, I will not!"

She jumped up again and began to move restlessly about the room.

"People don't realise what he is like, because he is so self-controlled," she went on. "But underneath that civilised manner there's a Dynham temper all right—oh yes! He can be ruthless. He can be cruel."

Louie felt quite frightened, by the intensity of Caroline's feeling, and the picture she drew of her husband. She remembered Rowland Dynham's formal manner and his correctness, his love of order, unusual in so young a man; it was the idea of this rather cold convention as a mask for a cruel temper which was so alarming. She felt sorry for her brilliant, high-spirited cousin, linked for life to an unyielding tyrant.

Caroline gazed at her broodingly. "Take care whom you marry, Louie. Do not be taken in by handsome looks."

Louie could not help smiling. "Why, it is not likely that I should attract a handsome lover!" she said. "One has to be a beauty or an heiress for that, or both, like yourself, cousin!"

Caroline smiled too, casting off her melancholy. "Do not imply that you are plain, Louie, for you have so much charm, if only you would lose that childish shyness. But I don't want you to blossom out too soon and run away to get married. What should I do without you?"

Louie was flattered that Caroline should be fond of her after only a few weeks; she herself was so fascinated by her beautiful cousin that she did not believe her hints about lovers in town. Any husband might well be jealous of such a lovely wife and Caroline could not help attracting men. But from the critical way she talked of them, Louie felt that she did not think very highly of any.

But when Caynnes Ridgway brought Mr. Godfrey to spend an evening and stayed late, Louie was sent to bed. "They have taken something too much of wine after dinner," Caroline whispered to her. "I do not care that you should stay, Louie. I can manage them—I am used to it."

But from her room, listening to the laughter below, Louie heard her cousin's voice as often as the men's. She felt she could understand why Caroline was unlikely to be invited by ladies like Mrs. Godfrey.

"But it is her high spirit," thought Louie lying in bed. "She means no harm."

Caroline had to live like a queen; she had to be free.

3

ROWLAND DYNHAM was coming down for a brief visit, to include Mary Anne's birthday at the beginning of May, and because Louie had heard something of Caroline's feelings about him, and felt that he must be a hard, tyrannical man, she was embarrassed at the prospect of meeting him, as if he could read her thoughts. It is one of the disadvantages of youth to imagine that everyone is probing one's inmost being, when very often the stranger's attention is fixed elsewhere. In the event, Louie's own feelings were almost blotted from her mind by the feelings of others, to which she became an involuntary witness.

Colonel Dynham had written to name the day of his arrival; he was travelling by the mail to Exeter and then by short stage to Okehampton, where he would hire a chaise. At least one night would be spent on the road, but he had timed the journey to bring him to Rosewell during the afternoon. Mary Anne went off in tears for her walk with the nurse-maid, for fear she would miss his arrival.

Caroline too was going out; she had arranged to meet Caynnes Ridgway and visit a moorland farm. Ridgway senior was getting old and so was Pendry, the agent, and Caynnes was not averse to advising Caroline on the family property when he could do so personally.

"If Dynham comes before I return, it can't be helped," Caroline said to Louie as she went out to mount her horse.

She was wearing her favourite scarlet habit and a crisp white stock, with a plumed hat pinned jauntily on her glossy brown curls. She had already mounted when the hired chaise turned in at the gate.

Rosewell Abbey had no drive, merely a gravel sweep in front of the house. Rowland Dynham opened the door of the chaise himself and jumped out, walking across towards Caroline, hatless and with his long travelling coat swinging open. The weather was fresh and windy, the sun shining out between hurrying puffs of cloud.

Louie's memory was of a tall young officer in uniform; now he was a man of thirty, very well-dressed in civil clothes. He certainly was tall, unusually so, with a spare lean figure and hard-cut aquiline features. His brown hair, which had a dark reddish tinge, grew thick and close to his head, giving it a crested look.

"Well, Caroline!" he said, glancing up at her. "You look in excellent health. Have you been for a ride?"

"No, I'm just going out," she replied.

"I said I would arrive this afternoon," remarked Rowland Dynham, with a slight frown.

"But I have something better to do than to wait for you to come," said Caroline. "The children are gone out for their walk. I shall see you at supper time."

She turned the horse's head, making to leave. Rowland put his hand on the bridle.

"What, must you be off at once?" he said, in a tone of somewhat forced amusement. "Stay till I have changed and I will come with you."

Caroline looked down at him. "Why should you suppose I wish for your company, sir?" she retorted, with resentment.

At this rebuff he looked hard at her for a moment and then said, "Surely you cannot still be angry because you are not in town? In this weather, it is much more pleasant at Rosewell, I assure you."

"Why should I care for the weather?" said Caroline, impatiently. "It is the company of my friends I miss."

"Your friends seem to do very well without you," he observed dryly.

"That is exactly what I should expect you to say," said Caroline. "However, the lack of their company does not incline me to yours, so take your hand off, sir, and allow me to proceed."

"You are unreasonable, Caroline," he protested, not releasing the bridle. "I hope you do not intend to battle it with me now, if only for Mary Anne's sake."

"For Mary Anne!" said Caroline and laughed angrily. "Yes, you would like me to be as meek as Mary Anne, for whom you can do no wrong. But it astonishes me, Dynham, how you can come down here expecting the prisoner to rejoice at the sight of the gaoler."

"Such nonsense!" he retorted sharply. "It is better you should stay here than that the lot of us should be in the debtors' prison."

"How can you talk so, as if I were a criminal?" cried Caroline furiously. "You know I never lost a third of what Lord Walter lost at those confounded races!"

"I daresay, and we do not have a third of Lord Walter's income," said Rowland, in a tone of sarcasm.

"We!" said Caroline scornfully. "What would you have now if you had not married me? Married Rosewell, I should rather say. Do you think you can bully me here, sir? In London you could hold the threat of the country over my head, but now there is nothing more you can do. So take off your hand, for I am going."

She urged the horse forward so that Rowland had to step quickly aside. He stood there, watching her ride out of the gateway and along the lane, a proud figure in her scarlet habit, unconquered. Louie thought his face, set hard, looked grim. But he did not seem to feel defeated.

The next moment he called to his man, one of the Beers from Brentland, to bring in his bags, and turning, saw Louie on the threshold.

"Why, it is little Cousin Louisa!" he said, apparently not caring that she should have witnessed the scene with Caroline. "I beg your pardon, cousin, for not greeting you

45

sooner, but you see how it is—I have annoyed Caroline by coming before she expected me."

Louie felt that he regarded her as scarcely more than the child who had been at his wedding years ago. But she was observing him with different eyes, as he walked into the house and threw off his overcoat, greeting the housekeeper who came forward at his entrance. Although Rowland Dynham was no longer in the army he carried himself very upright and moved with a deliberate and controlled ease which suggested that he was still accustomed to regular physical exercise and did not spend all his time at a desk in the Foreign Office. His clothes, too, were cut to exactly the right fit, though there was nothing in the least foppish about them.

"Something of a formidable person," thought Louie, standing by, watching. "Invulnerable."

Presently Rowland Dynham turned to her. "Do you know which way the children have gone? I should like to go and meet them. Perhaps you would come with me, Cousin Louisa?"

And soon afterwards she found herself walking inland up the stream with this stranger, who seemed to expect her to think of him and address him as a cousin straight away. It was sunny and windy, the springy turf damp and glistening, with clumps of primroses in the banks. The hawthorns were coming into flower, thick and white; the strange heavy scent was blown towards them in waves, as they passed.

"How do you like this country?" Rowland asked her, looking round at the rough hillsides with evident pleasure.

"I like it very much," said Louie. "It is wild—and romantic."

Rowland smiled. "Romantic? But here are no mountains," he said. "Are not mountains essential for romance?"

"These cliffs are as rugged as mountains, I am sure," said Louie. "But then I have never seen a mountain, sir."

"Cousin Rowland," he corrected her, smiling. "For now you are part of our family. Indeed, I wish I had known sooner how few you had about you in Bristol. Somehow I had imagined there must be others of Caroline's family there, more relations of the Tragedy Queen."

Louie glanced up in surprise and caught an ironical smile on his lips; the corners turned slightly down, rather than up.

"I don't mean Caroline, but her grandmother, the actress," he added quickly, guessing her thoughts.

Louie laughed and Rowland went on, "Sometimes I feel that what Caroline wants is a stage—she could let off her feelings to more purpose then."

It had not occurred to Louie that Caroline dramatised her feelings and she could not accept the suggestion without an inward insistence on her cousin's sincerity, but as she thought of her riding away from Rowland with her chin high, she could not help realising that there was some truth in his observation.

"I think she feels lonely here," she said at last. "She has welcomed me very kindly."

"I am glad to hear that," said Rowland. "It will be better later, when more people will be down here. I can't say I think very highly of Caroline's cousin, Hilary Tollington, but I daresay he will bring a party of friends to Woodford St. Petrock when Parliament adjourns."

It sounded reasonable enough, Louie thought. Caroline had made it seem as if her husband were punishing her with a virtual exile from all good company.

"It is just the set she associates with in London—Jack Ridgway, the Chervills and their friends—that I cannot allow her to associate with," said Rowland Dynham and immediately Louie's judgment was swayed against him once more. Cannot allow her! It was such a magisterial pronouncement.

Then they saw the children returning with their nursemaid Lizzie Jewell, a bloom-cheeked Devonshire girl with a soft high voice. Mary Anne was picking flowers, Adrian running ahead, waving a stick and shouting. But it was the girl who saw her father first. She came running helter skelter along the path, calling out, "Papa! Papa's come!"

Rowland caught her up and kissed her and then Adrian reached him and was swung high in the air, laughing excitedly.

They turned back and walked all together, Rowland with a child on each hand, Adrian telling incoherently about Mop's puppy and Mary Anne begging to know what her father had brought her for her birthday.

"But that must be a surprise," he said. "You have real May weather for the great day, Mary Anne. What a lucky girl you are to be living here, while I see nothing but pavements in London."

"I wish you would stay here, Papa, and let those foreign people look after their own office," said the little girl seriously.

Rowland Dynham laughed and glanced at Louie. He had very clear, keen grey eyes. "We can't let the French take over the Foreign Office, can we?" he said. "Much as they would like to, I've no doubt."

Louie had been surprised to see his children run to him; from the way Caroline had talked she had imagined him a man without feeling. But though he plainly demanded a high standard of behaviour it was evident that he was proud of his children, even fond of them. As they walked home he asked what they had been doing and soon discovered that Louie had been giving them regular lessons. His gratitude was real and expressed immediately.

"Caroline cannot stick to a plan," he said. "And will not employ a governess, so that I came down wondering what was to be done, if they were not to grow up a couple of little numskulls."

"Numskulls!" shouted Adrian, liking the

word, and executing a hop, skip and a jump which landed him in a puddle.

The children spent some time in the drawing-room before they went up to the nursery for their supper and bed. Caroline had not returned when Louie, in her evening frock, came downstairs to find Rowland, also changed, sitting reading. The supper hour was approaching and he took out his watch, remarking that he was hungry, having had a hasty and early dinner on the road.

At last Caroline came in, still in her riding habit.

"I thought you would have begun," she said. "I must go and change."

"You are very late," said Rowland coldly, watch in hand.

"I've been up on the moor with Caynnes Ridgway, visiting Venn farm," said Caroline. "And we met George Godfrey, just by the inn there."

She gave him a challenging look, but Rowland picked up his book again.

Caroline went out of the room.

There was a pause and then Rowland remarked, "Venn was one of our farms once."

Louie, who had expected him to comment

on Caroline's companions, was surprised. She realised that Rowland Dynham still thought of Brentland as his home, rather than Rosewell.

He insisted on waiting for Caroline, who took a long time making her toilette but then appeared in the gown she had worn all the week and with no elaborate hairdressing, so that Louie wondered what she could have been doing.

Supper was a constrained occasion. Caroline would not ask anything about London and though Rowland made inquiries on local affairs she pretended she knew nothing about them and answered in a bored tone.

Rowland, though he continued to address her with courtesy, became noticeably colder as the evening wore on. There was something intimidating about him in this mood, Louie thought; she felt that his chill reserve was a mask for deep resentment. Although Caroline's defiant hostility rather shocked her, she could not help thinking it needed courage thus to dare Rowland Dynham's anger.

She escaped early from the drawing-room but she was still on the stairs when Caroline came out a moment later, speaking so loudly to Rowland through the doorway that Louie could not help hearing, and suspected that she was meant to hear.

"I had the bed in the Rose Room made up for you, Dynham," Caroline said, with such emphasis that Louie felt she wanted her husband to know that even her young cousin must realise that she did not want him in her own room.

Louie fled upstairs, embarrassed and uncomfortable. She was made a witness to the quarrel between Rowland and Caroline whether she liked it or not, forced to participate in a passive, negative way, for she was not in a position to give her own opinion, far less advice, to either. Indeed, she was uncertain what her opinion was; her views fluctuated from day to day.

Caroline seemed determined to make her husband's visit as unpleasant as possible, no doubt in revenge for his keeping her in the country. And she knew exactly how to provoke him. As Louie had already realised, he was a man who liked order; he hated wasting time, he was punctual, methodical, planning ahead, and in personal habits fastidious almost to a fault, always neat, always dressed correctly, always self-controlled.

Caroline was impulsive and careless but not usually to the degree she now assumed, on purpose, Louie was convinced, to annoy Rowland. She would say one thing and do another; she was late for every meal, did not trouble to change her dress, interrupted the children's lessons, took them out late, or promised them some expedition and then forgot it. Mary Anne was in tears several times a day and Adrian became wildly excited and unmanageable.

Worse still, from Louie's point of view, Caroline would choose some moment when she was present to launch into one of her grievances against her husband. On these occasions, the more impassioned Caroline became, the more cold and ironic Rowland appeared. He never lost his temper and often put an end to the scene by walking out of the room. Caroline found this frustrating in the extreme. As she once said, furiously, it was like kicking an iceberg. She made no impression and only hurt herself.

"But then why do you do it?" Louie burst out. "Surely you must see that it's the very worst way to get him to do what you want?"

"What do you know about it?" retorted Caroline, still angry. "Besides, I don't want

anything except for him to admit that it's unjust and cruel to shut me up here, just
because I lost some money at the races. After
all, the money is mine."

Louie thought this was the only cause of
trouble between them, till one morning when
Rowland was in the library writing a letter
and Louie colouring plant drawings, when
Caroline came in like an avenging fury.

"Dynham! You have been prying into my
private accounts! How dare you!"

"If your accounts are private, why do you
let Pendry make them up?" said Rowland
coolly. "I was going through things with
him, as I told you in my note."

Caroline had a sheet of paper in her hand.

"Yes! And why write me a note?" she
cried. "Heavens! Am I to be brought before a
court of law?"

"Let us not inflict our differences on
Cousin Louisa," said Rowland stiffly.

Louie rose, anxious only to get away, but
Caroline said, "Stay, Louie! I want you to
know how I am overlooked and restricted."
She slapped the note with angry fingers.
"Here I am taken to task for a loan from a
neighbour, from a friend."

"Mr. Godfrey is no friend of mine," said

Rowland. "How can you possibly want that much more money, Caroline?"

"I needed another horse for my phaeton, and the coachbuilder was pressing for payment, too," said Caroline. "If I am to be buried down here, at least I must be able to get about."

"You have a perfectly good carriage," observed Rowland.

"But I like to drive myself and I do not see why I should not," said Caroline. "If you were not so mean I could have asked you. But I knew Mr. Godfrey would not refuse me."

"No doubt he likes to have you his debtor," said Rowland, dryly. He was still sitting at his writing table with his chair half turned towards her. "I suggest you sell your phaeton and pay him back."

"You cannot be serious! As if I could do anything so humiliating! And then he might feel he should give me the phaeton."

"And why not?" said Rowland, ironically. "It comes to the same thing in the end."

"Oh, you are intolerable!" cried Caroline. "If he did, you would demand why I allowed him to give me expensive presents—as you did about Lord Walter's presents."

"You mistake, Caroline," said Rowland, in

his dry way. "My complaint was that as Lord Walter Chervill had omitted to pay for his presents, we could not sell them for ready money but had to return them to the shop."

"Was there ever any man so mercenary?" Caroline demanded furiously. "I declare, Louie, I believe he would sell me, if such a thing were possible."

"My dear Caroline, it will take me the rest of my life to *buy* you," said Rowland. "It does not assist if you are continually raising the price."

He spoke with an ironic smile and Louie felt a sudden desire to laugh which she had to suppress because she saw that Caroline was very angry.

"Louie! You hear how he despises me!" she cried out, walking restlessly about the room. "And yet Rosewell is mine—mine! It is not yours, Dynham."

"It is for Adrian," he said seriously. "Come, Caroline, think of his future. The estate is overburdened as it is. Allow me to sell this phaeton, which in any case I do not at all like you driving, and pay back this loan at once to Godfrey."

"You don't like my driving alone because you don't trust me," said Caroline. "You suspect me with Mr. Godfrey, I've no doubt," She looked at him tauntingly.

"I leave your relations with George Godfrey to your conscience—and to your taste," replied Rowland coolly, looking straight at her, his grey eyes bleak as the sea outside. "What I distrust is your ability to drive yourself safely."

"Oh! This is unbearable!" cried Caroline, incensed, her cheeks flaming. "But you would not be so cool if you did think you had cause to blame my conduct with Godfrey. That was not your attitude when you came back from the Low Countries and made me the laughing stock of the town with your suspicions and your jealousy."

"That was now two years ago," said Rowland. "Let us not embarrass Cousin Louisa with our happy memories."

"I am glad Louie should know how little you care for me, how you despise me!" said Caroline passionately. "She will take care, when she marries, not to choose a man who thinks about nothing but money and loves nobody but himself."

"I imagine that Louie will be in no hurry to marry at all, after being the involuntary witness of our felicity," said Rowland, with his ironical smile.

Caroline, perhaps realising that she was not going to win this bout, rushed out of the room, and indeed out of the house, for they soon saw her walking quickly through the garden outside, the wind fluttering her light muslin gown, for she had not stopped even to pick up a shawl, let alone put on a pelisse.

Rowland got up and stood looking out of the window for a moment watching her and then turned round.

"I must apologise to you, Cousin Louisa," he said. "It is unseemly that a young girl like yourself should be dragged into our domestic quarrels. But I assure you it was not on account of Caroline's behaviour at the races that I gave up the house in town, but because it showed that she had still no notion of the magnitude of the debt with which we are already burdened, through her folly when I was away, and what I can only call the unprincipled encouragement of some of her friends. Caroline has no more idea of the value of money than Mary Anne—rather less, for Mary Anne will lay out her sixpences with great care, to ensure that her dolls have the proper complement of hats and stockings."

Somehow this final remark gave a touch of comedy to the scene that had just passed, so that Louie smiled as she went to get ready for dinner, but she had an uneasy feeling that he was not as indifferent as he seemed. She thought he felt more anger than he would show, and that it was not coldness but iron control that refused to counter Caroline's passion with his own.

The day after the quarrel about the loan Caroline put on her scarlet riding habit and went out alone. Time passed and she did not come back. The dinner hour, early in the country, arrived, but no Caroline. Rowland told the servants not to wait and sat down with Louie and the children. They had finished by three and as it had turned out a blowy day, with squalls of rain, they did not go out, but stayed in the drawing-room. Rowland had a fire lit and Mary Anne brought her dolls, Adrian his soldiers, from upstairs.

Mary Anne was a devoted doll-keeper, and no new favourite was ever allowed to displace the old. Rowland was much amused when she presented to him an old rag doll wearing a smart frilled hat which came down almost to the mouth sewn smiling on her stuffed face.

He laughed so much that Mary Anne said in pained tones, "But Papa, La Belle *must* have the new hat. She hasn't had one for years."

"But let us give the poor creature a view," said Rowland, and he stuffed the hat with a piece of paper, so that it sat on top of her woollen hair, much to Mary Anne's delight.

"What did you say her name was?" Louie asked.

"La Belle," said Mary Anne seriously. "Papa christened her. It's a longer name, really. What is it all, Papa?"

"La Belle au Bois Dormant," said Rowland solemnly. "I brought her back from abroad and as she always goes to bed with Mary Anne, it seemed appropriate. As she is such a beauty."

"It's French," explained Mary Anne kindly. "Papa can talk French."

"I daresay Cousin Louisa can talk French too," said Rowland. "It is an accomplishment shared by many."

Adrian, his soldiers at last drawn up in two separate companies facing each other, sat back on his heels.

"There! Now let's have a battle. You can have the blues, Papa."

"What, those old fellows with only a leg or

two between them?" said Rowland. "And you've given me the oldest field gun, too."

Adrian looked up at him doubtfully. "We could change guns half way," he suggested.

Rowland laughed. "What would the French generals say if we offered to do that in our war?" he said. "No, you keep your new gun, Adrian, but watch out. I daresay the old blues are not bad marksmen."

He was soon quite as absorbed in the mock battle as his little son, firing pellets with a very good aim, so that the smart red-coated soldiers fell right and left.

Louie sat by the window with her sewing, but watching the scene, and helping Mary Anne who was making a curious garment for La Belle which she insisted was going to be an opera cloak. The afternoon was wearing towards evening when they heard a crunching of wheels and Mary Anne, looking out, said, "Oh, here is Mamma back in a chaise, with Mr. Ridgway and another gentleman."

Rowland, who had been sitting on the floor, at once got to his feet and was standing when Caroline came in, still in her red habit, with Caynnes Ridgway and George Godfrey in tow, both slightly the worse for drink. Caroline herself was so exhilarated that Louie wondered if she too had not taken a little too much.

"Dynham, you know George Godfrey, of course," she said. "I stayed to dinner with Caynnes in Monkhampton and Mr. Godfrey has kindly brought me back in his carriage."

"I thank you, sir," said Rowland in a cool voice. "I fear you will hardly get home before dark."

"Good God, Dynham, the horses won't stand it," said Caroline. "Of course they must stay the night."

"Perhaps we can lend you a pair of horses, Godfrey," said Rowland.

He evidently did not intend the gentlemen to stay ten minutes, let alone for the night.

George Godfrey looked slightly sheepish but Ridgway remarked coolly, "I told you Dynham would turn us out, Caroline. I am sure he thinks you should have ridden home in the rain, so that his dinner should not be spoiled."

Caroline swept across the room, the skirt of her habit scattering the toy soldiers. She did not even glance at them, but looked only at Rowland.

"You cannot be so boorish as to throw my

friends out, without so much as offering them a glass of wine."

"It seems to me they have had quite enough wine already," said Rowland dryly. "Godfrey, will you kindly come with me to the stables and we will see what can be done."

"I beg you will do no such thing, Mr. Godfrey!" cried Caroline.

George Godfrey stood uncertainly, red in the face.

Caynnes Ridgway laughed and stretched himself on his favourite sofa. "Now for the championship fight!" he said. "Odds are on Ramrod Dynham but I'm not sure I don't back the game Scarlet Lady."

The children had been staring at this unexpected scene. Now Adrian suddenly let out a loud laugh.

Rowland turned to him. "Go upstairs to bed, Adrian. You too, Mary Anne."

"Don't want to!" shouted Adrian excitedly. "Are you really going to have a fight?"

"Of course not," said Rowland, annoyed. "Louie, would you be so good as to take the children upstairs?"

It was easier said than done. Mary Anne came obediently to Louie's side but Adrian ran about the room, shrieking with excitement, cheered on by Ridgway, till Rowland made a sudden grab and caught him, handing him over to Louie. Although he was a strong little fellow, he was only five years old and Louie was able to drag him, protesting loudly, towards the door.

Caroline, her colour high, said, "He is sending you away, Louie, so that he can say what he likes to me."

"Caroline," said Rowland in a freezing voice, "there is nothing to prevent you going out of this room yourself."

"I am not going to be ordered about my own house," retorted Caroline.

George Godfrey suddenly roused himself. "Now look here, Dynham," he announced belligerently, "I won't stand by and see you bully your wife like this."

"You're drunk, Godfrey," said Rowland. "Come out to the stables with me and we'll find you horses."

He went up to take Godfrey's arm but Godfrey, fuddled and pugnacious, hit out at him. Rowland caught the blow on his arm easily enough but Mary Anne, from the hall and looking back over her shoulder, let out a piercing shriek.

"Oh Papa!" Frantic with alarm she broke away from Louie, and ran back into the room. "Go away,you horrid man!" she screamed at George Godfrey.

Caynnes Ridgway, lying on the sofa, was laughing helplessly.

It was, Louie supposed, in some ways a comic scene but somehow it aroused in her a feeling of disgust.

Rowland picked up his daughter and carried her out of the room, across the hall and straight up the stairs, while she clung to him, sobbing on his shoulder. He stroked her fair hair and when he reached the landing, gently pinched her round pink cheek.

"Now, no more crying, my Mary Anne. Mr. Godfrey's not himself and he is very soon going to be on his way home, so you must forget all about it."

"Why was Uncle Caynnes laughing at you?" asked Adrian, not crying but excited.

"Because he finds other people's difficulties amusing," said Rowland grimly. "I desire you not to call Mr. Ridgway Uncle Caynnes, Adrian."

He put Mary Anne into the old nursery basket chair and said to Louie, "I must apologise for this stupid scene, Louisa. Jack

Ridgway has always been a very bad influence on Caroline. He has no conscience and dislikes other people to have any. However, we'll soon get rid of him now, and that idiot, Godfrey."

"But can you manage both of them at once, Cousin Rowland?" Louie asked anxiously, going out of the nursery with him.

"I'll fetch Noah Beer," he said.

His man Beer came from Brentland and had been with him in the army; indeed, it had surprised Louie that a man so fastidious about his clothes as Rowland Dynham should not employ a typical valet rather than the tough, silent Devonian, who looked as if he would be more at home with horses than houses. However, in an emergency like this, Noah Beer was certainly the right man for the job.

In spite of Beer's assistance, Godfrey evidently took some getting rid of, for there was a good deal of noise and swearing below, and more laughter from Caynnes Ridgway. Louie shut the children in with Lizzie Jewell and went out to the landing, peering down into the dim hall.

She heard Caroline's voice. "You see how he treats me, Godfrey!" she cried hysterically. "Caynnes, how can you lie there and laugh?"

Caynnes's voice, chuckling, slurred, answered her. "My dear, I don't intend to get my face punched. I told you what would happen. Don't blame me."

Eventually Godfrey was frog-marched out of the front door, Ridgway following, buttoning up his long overcoat. He waved his hand to Caroline as he went out, rather unsteadily, into the gloomy evening twilight.

Caroline stood in the hall, her hands clenched. Then she suddenly turned for the stairs and Louie fled, retreating into her own room. She felt she could not face her cousin at that moment. Nor Rowland Dynham. She stayed up in her room till bedtime.

4

THE next day was Mary Anne's birthday. A few days earlier Rowland had said to her, "Choose what you would like to do on your birthday, Mary Anne."

"Anything? Can we do anything I like?" the little girl asked, amazed.

"Short of going to the moon," said her father, smiling at her fair round face.

"Then I would like, if we can, to go and see your own home, Papa."

"Brentland? Would you really like that?" he said.

"It is all shut up—we can't go there," said Caroline."

"Couldn't we have a picnic there?" asked Mary Anne, wistfully.

"Of course we could," said Rowland. "The Hickmans are there to look after the place, after all."

"Oh! I've no doubt Hickman will do anything for *you*," said Caroline crossly.

Hickman had been General Dynham's soldier servant and had married his children's nurse, a Devonshire woman whom Rowland still often referred to as Truscott, her maiden name. It was a favourite game of Adrian's to ask, "What did Truscott say when Uncle Josce fell in the pond in his Sunday suit?" or, "Did Truscott smack you when you were naughty, Papa?" As far as Louie could tell from the stories that ensued, the Dynham boys had been known for miles around as a regular gang, for village lads had been enrolled in their band. Joscelin Dynham was the comic character of these exploits, always the one to fall in, fall out, or fall off, and be caught by irate farmers or the angry General. Rowland's elder brother Mark was the ringleader, but had to face a certain amount of opposition, it was clear, from Rowland himself. Rowland had never been cut out to play second-in-command.

Uncle Mark was well known to the children in story but they could not remember him. He was not as tall as Rowland, but perhaps even more tough physically, strong-willed, hot-tempered but hard-headed; he went all out for what he wanted, and always knew what he wanted.

"Why wasn't Uncle Mark 'Sir Mark'?" Adrian asked, on the drive to Brentland.

"Because father was still alive when he was killed," said Rowland, who was driving them in an old gig. "He died not long afterwards—had a heart attack."

"But why is Miles 'Sir' and not you, Papa?" Adrian pursued. "You're much older than he is."

"But he is the son of the eldest son," said Rowland. "It's always the eldest son who inherits any title, and usually the property too. If I had anything, you would get it."

"Shall I have Rosewell?"

"Of course—but it is your mother's."

Caroline was not with them. She had not appeared at breakfast and had sent Hannah Colwill to say that she did not feel like a long drive that day. It was all too plain that Mary Anne's pleasure was not spoiled by the absence of her mother.

Brentland House was some fifteen miles by the carriage road, which ran down to Monkhampton, the nearest small town, and then looped inland through the large village of Ashworthy. But it was less than ten miles direct across the moor and this was why they had decided to go in the gig, bumping over small side roads. It was a fine spring day and larks sang overhead, so that Mary Anne sat

71

with her head back staring and staring, looking for the soaring pinprick from which that high song trilled.

She wore a pink sunbonnet, looking, as her father observed, like a large sweet-pea. For the picnic they wore comfortable clothes; even Rowland, usually so smart in dress, was wearing fustian trousers, tucked into country half-boots, and an old brown shooting coat. True, his neckerchief, however loose and unlike a cravat, was of fine linen, and his round hat well brushed, but still in this get up Louie could imagine him as he must have been on holidays at Brentland before his marriage. And he seemed in holiday mood, relaxed and ready to enjoy everything on this domestic expedition. Generally, in spite of his hard good looks and courteous manner, he seemed to Louie so reserved as to be lacking in charm. But today she felt she could understand why Caroline had married him eight years ago, in spite of warnings from her family that it was her property attracted him, rather than herself.

Brentland was in origin an old farm house, set unusually high in a fold of moorland, so that they saw it long before they reached it. Rowland had told Louie that one of the

72

reasons why the Dynhams had not prospered like the Caynnes family was that they had remained Catholic till the time of the Forty-Five, when Sir Oliver Dynham had conformed to the Established Church. He had celebrated his new standing in society by putting a new front on his house, classical and pedimented, with rows of sash windows. This side of the house commanded a long view southward and inland over the wide-backed hills and sunk, wooded coombes. But the drive from the lane curled to the old front of the house, belonging to an earlier era, of stone with mullioned windows, some timbering above and a roof with eaves. It was an odd effect, like two houses jammed together, neither very big. There had never been enough money to rebuild the whole in modern style.

Because the house stood high there was little in the way of gardens, just a lawn divided by flagged paths in front of the classic façade; a flower garden was enclosed in high walls and tucked away next to the kitchen garden.

"We get all the winds that blow, up here," said Rowland.

He jumped down and lifted the children out and gave his hand to Louie. A plump smiling woman came running out to them.

"Oh my dear life, Mr. Rowland, sir, how good to see ye once again," she said, in her soft, cracky Devonshire voice.

"Truscott, you get younger every year!" said Rowland, and kissed her cheek. "As I get older."

His old nurse then embraced the children and exclaimed over them. "But neither of them favour their papa, I'd say," she remarked. "Little Miss has your own mamma's hair, Mr. Rowland, sir, but in other ways she's not like."

"Mary Anne is a great deal more soft-hearted than my mamma," said Rowland, smiling. "Adrian is said to resemble his namesake, Caroline's father, but I hope he will not resemble him in character."

"If he has Caynnes looks and Dynham character, he should do well, sir," said the old nurse.

Now Hickman, her husband, came out, a stringy elderly man who saluted Rowland like an old soldier. "Well, sir, can't seem to get used to having none of the family in the service no more."

"I'm a Colonel of Militia," Rowland said, with a smile.

Hickman's expression was eloquent of his opinion of the Militia.

They went into the house, which still felt shut up even though the Hickmans had hastily opened the principal rooms for them.

"We didn't take off the covers, sir, since you said not," Mrs. Hickman. "But it don't seem very homely, to be sure."

Mary Anne was staring round, holding her father's hand. Adrian ran to the windows of the drawing-room, which was on the classical side of the house and looked, beyond the lawn, over the green sunny fields to the backs of the hills. Only the first coombe was visible, a chasm of trees.

"And how is poor little Sir Miles?" the old nurse was asking. "Not long for this world, they say. What a shame to be cooped up in London! Why don't you have him down here, sir?"

There was a perceptible pause before Rowland answered and his voice was constrained as he said, "It has not been possible, Truscott."

Louie realised that he resented the circumstances which forced him to leave the education of his nephew to the Warstowe family. In this house she already had a strong impression of the Dynhams, proud, impoverished generations of soldiers. In the hall and in the dining-room there were portraits of tall craggy men with bushy eyebrows and grey eyes staring out in uncompromising fashion, as who should say, "Take care how you cross my will."

Rowland Dynham, though his features had a more aquiline cast than most of those ancestors, certainly had the grey eyes, clear and keen. Seeing Louie staring at a large canvas in a heavy frame which hung in the hall, he remarked, "That's our grandfather, Old Noll we used to call him—Sir Oliver, who had the sense to see that the Hanoverians were here to stay and went foxhunting instead of swashbuckling abroad on behalf of those tiresome Stuarts. He's the fellow who altered the house—the only one who could afford to do it."

"Prosperity did not improve his figure," observed Louie.

Sir Oliver Dynham was of massive proportions.

"If Josce ever settles down, he'll look like that," said Rowland. "My youngest brother, Joscelin."

"What has happened to him?" Louie

asked, thinking of the young giant at the wedding, who had cracked a bench in the church.

"Nothing has happened to him," said Rowland dryly. "He knocks about the world like a tramp."

"He didn't go into the army, then, like you and your elder brother?"

Rowland smiled. "No. There was a terrible row with father. Josce said he didn't want to kill people. Father thought he was soft in the head. Perhaps he is. He's converted in the opposite direction to Old Noll—become a papist."

"Why did he do that?" asked Louie, in surprise. There was no advantage to be gained by such a choice, as there had been for the grandfather in his.

Rowland shrugged his shoulders. "Likes the music better in their churches, I daresay," he replied. "Josce has always been a poetic fellow, though you wouldn't think it to look at him."

Mary Anne tugged at his hand. "Papa, where did you sleep when you were a little boy?"

"Up in the attic," he said, and they had

to climb the stairs to the top of the house to see it.

The great bare attic room, with old beams in the roof, had four beds in it, one in each corner.

Adrian ran and jumped on the nearest. "Was this yours, Papa?"

"No, Uncle Mark's—he had control of the door there. That's mine, by the window."

"You wouldn't fit on it now, Papa," said Mary Anne seriously.

Her father laughed and then walked over to the dormer window and stared out. "You could see the sea from here," he said, narrowing his eyes in the sunlight. "Yes . . . there it is."

"Where? Where?" Adrian had to be lifted up; the window sill was above his head.

"It's far away," he said, gazing out. "Not like at Rosewell."

"Who slept in the fourth bed?" Mary Anne wanted to know.

"Our cousin, Cary Vyner, from Hartleigh Court, further up in North Devon," said Rowland. "He was sent here for his holidays while his father was," he hesitated and then added, "ill. You must have heard me speak of him."

"I remember!" shouted Adrian. "You had a fight with Cousin Cary and you won, papa, but you said I was never to fight anyone smaller than me, because I might hurt him worse than I meant, like you did."

"Oh, Papa, I'm sure you didn't hurt him unfairly," said Mary Anne, looking up anxiously.

"Yes, I did, I am ashamed to say," said Rowland, and Louie noticed, to her surprise, a flush rise in his face; she had never seen him discomposed before, not by any of the quarrels with Caroline. "I told Adrian about it to warn him against the family temper. It can take you unawares; you can utterly lose your head, not realise what you are doing."

"But you never are angry, Papa," said Mary Anne, wonderingly.

"I was then," he answered. "Cary was a couple of years my junior and attacked me for mocking at Joscelin. It wasn't easy to get the better of Cary, who was thin but wiry and quick, but I was in such a rage I went on hitting him after he was down and hurt him so much they had to send for the surgeon from Monkhampton. I thought he was going to die. It was a terrible lesson. Of course I was much older than you are now, Adrian, about fifteen or more, but I don't want you to have to learn that way, to control yourself."

Louie was more struck by the story than the children, who presently ran away through the empty attics, bouncing on the beds and calling to each other. Like Mary Anne, Louie found it hard to believe that Rowland Dynham, always so controlled, had ever been carried away by rage, even as a boy.

He stood by the window, looking out, silent.

"Is that cousin of yours dead?" she asked, at last.

"Cary?" His thoughts had evidently turned elsewhere. "Not so far as we know, but he went abroad after a row with his grandfather, Sir Brandon Vyner, and hasn't been heard of since."

He turned from the window with a sigh. "Will Adrian bring his children here one day?" he said. "Life does not look so long as it did from this window, twenty years ago."

Louie felt that life had somehow disappointed his expectations and yet, by his marriage, he had achieved the Caynnes estates, so much greater than Brentland. But she felt that he loved this place, bleak and abandoned, much better than Rosewell; that he took a pride in these soldierly Dynham ancestors that he did not take in the Caynnes courtiers.

He was telling his son about them as they went downstairs, passing the portraits, and remarked that in the Middle Ages there had been a Lord Dynham living at Hartland, some miles to the north, where the Bristol Channel opened into the Atlantic ocean.

"Mamma says I ought to be a lord," said Adrian suddenly. "Lord what?"

"Lord Caynnes," said Mary Anne. "Like grandfather Caynnes."

"She would like to get the barony revived for you, Adrian," said Rowland.

"Wouldn't you like it?" asked Adrian, looking up at his tall father.

"I doubt if it's worth the trouble and expense," said Rowland. "You are a Dynham— that's good enough for me."

"My lordship," said Adrian thoughtfully.

Rowland laughed and swung him up in the air.

"Will your lordship condescend to a picnic?" he said.

The picnic was really a cold meal set on the table in the dining-room, since the Hickmans would not hear of their eating out of doors. "It's much too windy, sir."

"Hickman, I am entirely of your opinion," said Rowland. "I hate picnics. Now, let's go down to the cellar and see what's left of father's wine."

He came back with a pair of dusty bottles and the picnic became a merry one. Rowland was more agreeable than Louie had yet known him, teasing Mary Anne with a straight face, while she gazed up at him taking every word literally.

But the meal was not over before Caroline arrived, driving herself in her new phaeton. And immediately she came, the atmosphere changed.

She arrived full of resentment that nobody had come to enquire after her, when she had sent down her message that morning.

"I take it very ill, Mary Anne, that you should not come to see your mamma on your birthday."

Tears popped up in Mary Anne's blue eyes.

"I thought you had a headache," she whispered nervously.

"Do not blame Mary Anne," said Rowland. "I told the children not to disturb you, Caroline. And I am glad to see you look so well, after the long drive."

The irony of his tone was unmistakable and annoyed Caroline still more.

"It is so much more pleasant in the phaeton," she said. "But still, you may give me a glass of wine."

Rowland opened the second bottle for her. He had called in the Hickmans earlier, to drink Mary Anne's health, but he had added water to the children's wine, so that one bottle had sufficed.

Caroline proceeded to drink several glasses rather quickly, eating little, and the wine, restoring her spirits, exhilarated her. She filled Adrian's glass.

"That is too much for him," said Rowland, reaching for the water jug.

Adrian, grinning wickedly, quickly swallowed a large mouthful and began to choke. His father put out his hand for the glass, but Adrian, excited by the antagonism between his parents, clung to it, peering at him over the rim with bright defiant eyes.

"Adrian, give me your glass," said Rowland, rising.

"Shan't," said Adrian, taking another, but smaller sip.

"It won't do him any harm," said Caroline. "Your health, Adrian!"

Rowland went and stood behind the child's chair. "Give me the glass," he said, so sternly that Louie thought it quite courageous of the little boy to defy him, as he did by silently clinging to it with both hands, though he was glancing out of the corners of his eyes, wondering what the result of his boldness would be.

Caroline laughed.

Louie thought her connivance irritated Rowland more than Adrian's disobedience. He lifted the boy out of his chair and the wine splashed over the table. Adrian gave a yell of alarm.

"Don't be such a bully, Dynham!" cried Caroline.

Rowland did not answer. He carried his son out of the room. Adrian was struggling and the glass fell and smashed on the floor.

Caroline jumped up but as she went towards the door she glanced out of the window and stopped. "Oh, he has taken him outside," she said.

Louie and Mary Anne both got up to look. Through the open window they could hear Adrian's frightened bawling as Rowland car-

84

ried him along the path between the lawns, away from the house. He sat down on a bench with his back to them and stood the little boy in front of him.

"Oh, he is only going to lecture him," said Caroline, going back to the table and cutting herself a slice of ham. "I would not have stood it, if he had beat him. What a great fuss about nothing! So like Dynham; he must ever exert his authority."

Mary Anne, a slow eater, was bidden to finish her luncheon. When they went outside some time later they found that Adrian, overcome with wine and emotion, had gone fast asleep, lying curled up on the bench, with his head on his father's thigh. The wind blew his long soft dark hair this way and that, as it was blowing the grass in the meadow below the ha-ha.

He woke up when Caroline sat down on the bench, for she moved his feet out of her way. He lifted a sleepy face, rosy as a baby's, blinking in the sun. The next minute he had jumped up and began to run races with Mary Anne round the paths. The struggle over the wine glass seemed to be forgotten. Nor did anyone else refer to it.

Caroline began to talk about Brentland. "It

may come to you after all, Dynham," she said. "Everyone says poor little Miles won't live to grow up. He's like his mother—I never could understand what your brother Mark saw in Mary Warstowe, sickly, mousy creature as she was, poor thing."

"You can never tell with these delicate children," said Rowland. "Hilary Tollington was a miserable little goblin, always going down with something, but he's survived to become an M.P. Miles may do the same."

"He may, but I doubt it," said Caroline. "And I am sure you think the place ought to be yours, since you look after it. I know you and Mark always quarrelled."

"We certainly fought like cat and dog," admitted Rowland "But Mark's son is the heir."

Mary Anne, who had paused by them to get her breath, asked "Which were you, Papa? Cat or dog?"

"Cat!" said Rowland, with a laugh. He stroked her straight fair hair.

Then Adrian came rushing up and pulled her away to jump the paths with him, pretending they were streams.

Caroline would still pursue her thoughts

aloud. "If Miles were to die and you got Brentland, you would be . . ."

"I don't need Brentland," interrupted Rowland. "Adrian will have Rosewell, and that is enough. Besides, if I had it, Warstowe would make me raise a loan on it, to pay off the Rosewell debt."

"You can never let me forget my crimes, can you?" cried Caroline, her resentment once more flaring up fiercely. "As if you cared anything for the land itself! All you care for is power, climbing the tree in London. Well, if you had let me make the right friends, I could have helped you on your way."

"Thank you, I have no desire to rise by means of my wife's bedfellows," said Rowland coldly.

"How can you say such things in Louie's presence?" cried Caroline.

Louie was sitting on the grass behind the seat, watching the children.

"I beg your pardon, Louie, I did not know you were there," said Rowland, but he did not sound much discomposed that she had overheard him.

But having invoked her cousin's youth and innocence, Caroline could not go on to quarrel to her heart's content and presently she got up and walked over to the children. Louie, thinking it hardly proper to remain alone with Rowland after what had just been said, went after her.

Exploring the enclosed garden, she and Mary Anne lost sight of the others, and when it was time to leave, Caroline and Adrian were not to be found. Nor was the phaeton in the yard behind the house.

"Mrs. Dynham has taken the little boy to Ashworthy, to buy him a top," said Hickman.

Rowland frowned but said he supposed they would catch up with them. Goodbyes were said, the Hickmans congratulated on the condition of Brentland, and they set out for home, this time taking the carriage road by way of Ashworthy.

No phaeton was visible in that village, nor did they see it in Monkhampton, and imagining that Caroline would be at home by now, they went on. But when the gig reached Rosewell, late in the afternoon, she had not returned.

Louie could see that Rowland was not only annoyed but anxious. He could not stay in the house but kept walking out into the road to see if they were coming. Mary Anne went too. Louie, who had changed her dress and put on her thin slippers, was sitting in the drawing-room, but at the open window from which she could see the gateway.

She was therefore a witness of the incident which occurred when Caroline returned, driving fast along the narrow lane, with Adrian beside her, excited and shouting. Mary Anne was on the bank picking flowers and jumped down when she saw them coming. The new mare shied, the tall vehicle lurched dangerously and Adrian was swung to one side, almost flung out. Indeed, he probably would have fallen into the road if Rowland had not jumped to the side of the phaeton, up the step, and caught him. The next moment he had pulled the child out altogether. He jumped back into the road, set him on the wall near the gate and then ran to the nearest horse's head.

Caroline was crying out, with anger as well as alarm.

A groom came hurrying from the stables and Rowland left the excited mare to him, going back to take Adrian from the wall and collect Mary Anne, who was standing in the road, for once too frightened to cry. He came back into the drive just as Caroline descended from the phaeton.

"Caroline, I told you that mare was dangerous," he said.

"We should have been all right if Mary Anne had not jumped down the bank in that silly way," said Caroline.

"You are not safe in that phaeton, and I forbid you to take Adrian out in it," said Rowland.

"Don't order me about in that vulgar way," retorted Caroline.

Rowland turned to the groom. "Tom, see that the children never go out in the phaeton," he said abruptly, and walked away from Caroline without looking at her.

She followed him at once into the house and into the library, and though he shut the door, her voice could be heard through it, shouting at him in a passion of rage.

"Mamma's angry," said Adrian, listening, wide-eyed.

"I hate it when she does that," said Mary Anne. "I hate her screaming voice." She shivered, shifting closer to Louie, who put her arm round her.

She herself was startled; she had not before seen Caroline in one of her tempers, though the servants had hinted at such storms.

Through the shut door she heard furious scraps. "I will not have you order my servants to disobey me . . . Adrian is my son as well as yours . . . What will he have from you? It is the Caynnes heritage, not yours . . . How dare you speak of me before my cousin as you did today—and without the smallest evidence, you jealous devil! . . . I don't care if everyone in the place hears, let them know how you provoke me . . . You're worse than a gaoler, you are a tyrant, Dynham! It pleases you to torment me, don't dare to deny it . . . "

Louie took the children into the drawing-room, but they sat silent, listening to that distant, frenzied voice. As for Rowland, if he spoke it was so quietly that his words did not sound through the shut door.

At last they heard the door open and Caroline run upstairs, weeping. She ran into her room, slammed the door and locked it.

"Finished," said Adrian, with a sigh of relief.

He climbed down off the window seat and began to spin the top Caroline had bought him, not in Ashworthy but in Monkhampton.

Presently Rowland came across the hall.

He seemed perfectly calm, unnaturally so, Louie thought, after such a scene.

"It's time you children went to bed," he said. "And I must change for supper." He held out his hand to Mary Anne, who took it and went out with him. Adrian pocketed his top and ran after them.

It was not long before Rowland returned, immaculate in his evening dress, not a hair out of place.

"I hope you will not object to sitting down to supper with me at once, Cousin Louisa," he said. "I do not think Caroline will come down again this evening."

They sat decorously at the table and until the servants left them to their dessert Rowland made merely formal conversation. It occurred to Louie that he must make a good diplomat.

But when they were alone he said gravely, "I am very sorry, Louie, for the scenes you have been forced to witness in this house, but as you see, I cannot control Caroline. I daresay she will behave better when I have gone back to town, for my presence seems to cause her extreme irritation."

Louie looked up at his impassive face and

then down at her plate. She felt embarrassed, even if he did not.

"I hope you will stay on here, all the same," he went on. "The children are already fond of you and it will be a relief to know there is someone sensible looking after them."

"Of course I will stay," said Louie, and then, screwing up her courage, she added, "I think Caroline is lonely here."

"You will be good company for her," he replied, carefully extracting a walnut from its shell.

Louie could hardly say what she thought—that hers was not the kind of company her cousin longed for. But she ventured to say, still without looking at him, "If you allowed her to return to London, perhaps she would promise not to bet again at the races."

She felt he was looking at her, with those piercing grey eyes, though she dared not lift her own. But his tone when he spoke was dry and ironic.

"My dear Cousin Louie, allow me to observe that Caroline would never so lower herself as to *promise* anything to *me*. She must always act as she pleases, and she considers I have no right to complain if she wastes her inheritance."

Louie knew this was true. She said nothing.

Rowland was silent some time, turning his wine glass in his hand. Then he said, "That scoundrel Jack Ridgway led her into extravagance and worse when I was away at the wars—it is his fault. She once had spirit and intelligence, but it has all been wasted."

Louie, glancing up, thought how stern he looked. Yet it was hardly unjustified, considering how badly Caroline had behaved during the whole of his visit.

"You look at me with those innocent doe's eyes," said Rowland suddenly, "as if you thought me very cruel. Do you think so?"

Louie was taken aback. She felt her heart hammering.

"N . . . no," she stammered. "She has been very . . . wild. I see that."

"Perhaps I am too harsh," said Rowland meditatively. "I do not think I understand women very well. We had no sisters, you know. And then, Caroline glories in being a child of nature. But in my opinion nature needs the discipline of civilisation, if it is not to become a mere wilderness of conflicting passions."

It occurred to Louie then that it might be just his own civilised control which goaded Caroline to such outbursts of passionate fury. But although she now felt some sympathy for Rowland Dynham, especially after seeing him today in his old home, Louie did not dare to discuss his marriage with him.

Nor did he seem disposed to further communication. He excused himself to her when they rose from the table and went into his study, which opened out of the drawing-room, taking the newspaper, which had arrived while they were out.

After playing a little while on Caroline's pianoforte, Louie felt she ought to go and see her cousin. She went upstairs and found the door now unlocked. Caroline was lying on a couch by the window, in a pretty dressing gown, though her hair was hanging dishevelled about her shoulders. In spite of her angry tears an hour or two ago she looked as beautiful as ever. She had great vitality and resilience.

"Oh, it is kind of you, Louie, to care about me—no one else does," she said, as Louie came and sat on a low chair near her.

She began to ask what Rowland had said of her, embarrassing Louie, who finally disclosed that he had remarked that he did not understand women.

"That is quite true," said Caroline with satisfaction. "He expects us to behave like men, only unnaturally docile men. It's his mother's fault. She was a female general. Well, I'm not!"

Louie could not help laughing. This was the old Caroline, whose charm was at least equal to her temper. "But Caroline," she said, "I fear he does not trust you to behave with circumspection in town. He blames Mr. Ridgway for everything, but he no longer trusts your good sense."

Caroline gave an angry laugh. "Oh, I know he hates Caynnes! Because it was Caynnes who showed me that I need not live mewed up just because my husband was at the wars. Dynham has never forgiven me for not living as a widow for his sake." She brooded, frowning. "Yes, he was not so cold then. That was when I discovered that he had the famous Dynham temper after all. Hannah had told me that everyone down here knew it, that he half killed a cousin of his when they were boys, but I could never believe it, for you know how stiff and correct he always is. But then, once, I saw it myself. I can't even remember what I said to rouse his anger, but Louie, I thought he was going to kill me. He took hold of me and threw me against the wall. Yes, if Hannah had not come into the room, I don't know what he might not have done. He seemed like someone gone mad."

Louie stared at her; surely she must be dramatising again? In spite of having heard, or perhaps just because she had heard of the fight with his cousin from Rowland himself, she could not imagine him in the sort of violent passion which Caroline herself had recently indulged in.

"You don't believe me," said Caroline, watching her face. "You think that because he is so cold towards me now, it was always so. But I assure you, it is only since then that he has come to despise me."

"Oh no, Caroline, he did not speak as if he despised you."

"He does," insisted Caroline. "He despises me for acting from feeling. He despises feeling. He worships reason and order, cannot understand what is not laid down in his stupid traditional code." She made an impatient gesture. "Oh! Let us talk no more of Dynham. I hate him!"

"I don't think you do," said Louie, with a

sudden flash of insight. "You are angry because he doesn't love you any more."

"You horrid creature!" cried Caroline, furious. "Go away! How can you understand anything about it? Go away and leave me in peace."

Louie fled. But she was not at all sure she had not hit on the truth of the matter.

5

AS soon as her husband left Rosewell, Caroline became more reasonable. She resigned herself to staying in the country and began to speculate as to who might be coming down in the summer.

A few days later Caynnes Ridgway came to dinner, driving himself in an old gig, much to Caroline's amusement.

"Why, in town you would not be seen dead in such a thing!" she said. "Caynnes has a very smart curricle, Louie, in which he challenges comparison with all the famous whips."

"And which I shall soon be driving again," said he, and so she discovered that he was going back to London. It quite put her out of temper.

"It is heartless of you, Jack—I shall have no one to gossip with, if you desert me."

"My dear Caroline, do you expect me to miss my chance of carrying off an heiress of thirty thousand pounds, in order to gossip with you?" said Caynnes Ridgway, indolently. He did not attempt to disguise the selfishness of his motives.

"You have been looking for that lady as long as I've known you," said Caroline. "Why don't you settle for rather less—Hilary's cousin Henrietta, for instance? She has a nice little dowry, even if it's not thirty thousand."

"Miss Tollington is a very cool customer," said Ridgway, "and I doubt if she would succumb to the famous Caynnes charm. But if I see her in town, I will bear your suggestion in mind. She is fond of dancing—not a country girl."

"Oh lord, who is?" said Caroline, impatiently. "But as it happens she is not in town, but has come down to Woodford with Hilary and an old aunt for chaperone—I have had his note this morning."

"What, has he abandoned politics so early in the summer?" asked Ridgway, surprised.

"He says his physician ordered him off, but I fancy he can't face the laughter after Miss Julia's public jilt," said Caroline. "He seems perfectly well, for he plans to come over and see my steward and asks to bring Henrietta to visit. So you see you must stay, Caynnes."

"When do they come?" he asked, not uninterested.

"Tomorrow or the next day," said Caroline, with a smile. "Come tomorrow and stay overnight, if you like."

So that when the Tollingtons arrived, Caynnes Ridgway was at Rosewell, and turned out in his best, lazy and elegant.

The Tollingtons came in a chaise, driven by a coachman. They might have been brother and sister, there was such a likeness between them. Henrietta was nearly twenty but did not seem to Louie to have grown much since the Rosewell wedding, when she had been twelve. She was a slim neat creature, with clear-cut features and dark gold hair done up in a classical knot; her soft mouth, with its slightly prominent upper teeth, small and pearly, was smiling, her large hazel eyes, with sweeping lashes, bright and alert.

"What an age since I saw Rosewell," she exclaimed, looking round. "And how beautiful it is! Why, Caroline, can these be your children? I thought they were babies."

Caroline laughed, saying it was dreadful the rate at which children grew. "At least I have had no more, after that miscarriage," she said, referring thus casually to an event Louie had not heard of before. "And what has brought you down to this remote place, Henrietta, at the height of the season?"

"Hilary!" said Henrietta, laughing. "He declared he must have company, and so I came. But Woodford still seems like home to me."

"I'll tell you why she came," said Hilary Tollington. "It is to escape a persistent suitor whom our dear tyrant Tinna approves."

"If Lady Hayford approves him he must be a good match," observed Caynnes Ridgway. "My trouble has always been that Lady Hayford does *not* approve of me—or so I suspect, from never receiving invitations."

"Do you not? What a shame! Well, I do not agree with my dear sister upon everything," said Henrietta gaily. "Least of all upon husbands, since Hayford, though he is very distinguished to be sure, already has a grown up family by his first marriage. My suitor, as Hilary calls him, is an *old* friend of Hayford's!" And she gave Caynnes Ridgway a mischievous glance, encouraging him.

He at once took her up, with remarks upon the unfairness of old gentlemen's snapping up the young beauties, and they went into the house, all laughing, to take refreshments in the morning-room. Mary Anne and Adrian came too, eyeing the loaded table with eager looks. It seemed to Louie like a town party, so many young people chattering together.

Hilary Tollington she remembered as a mere youth at the wedding; even now he looked younger than his twenty-six years, for he had a smooth face and his thick fairish hair fell forward in a curly lock over his forehead; the family teeth were more noticeable in him and spoilt his looks, she thought. A slender figure, he wore clothes as fashionable as Ridgway's, but in a casual way that was almost untidy, as if, having spent a long time choosing them, he forgot them once he had put them on. But that might be part of a pose, for he gave an impression of carelessness, even of foolishness, and appeared to enjoy exaggerating it.

"Hilary, I am sorry to hear you lost your bride," Caroline presently observed.

"Oh, yes, wasn't it remiss of me?" he replied, and Louie noticed that the teeth gave him a slight lisp. He had a soft husky voice and spoke with a sort of suppressed chuckle. "But perhaps it is just as well, for now I can still get partners at the balls and be merry, as

I could not have done, once I was tied down."

"You would have had to spend your time keeping Miss Julia tied down," remarked Caynnes Ridgway, not without a spice of malice.

"Quite—I comfort myself with that thought daily," said Hilary cheerfully, taking up his wine glass. "Here's a health to bachelordom!"

Presently he went off to visit the old steward Pendry and the others went to walk in the garden. Louie was puzzled why Caroline's cousin should have business with her steward, but she did not like to make enquiries. Henrietta was coming out with the latest stories from town; she had a lively manner and kept the others laughing, but her tales were not scurrilous as Caynnes Ridgway's had been.

He paid a good deal of attention to the little lady but though at times she seemed to Louie to be flirting with him, she remained perfectly self-possessed and cool.

After about half an hour Hilary rejoined the party, walking towards them with his hands in his pockets and his hat on the back of his head. He sat down on a bench next to Louie.

"Everything satisfactory, Hilary?" Caroline asked.

"Everything," he replied. "I must allow that Dynham leaves nothing for me to do. He still manages it all, in effect, and most efficiently."

"Oh, he makes an idol of efficiency," replied Caroline. "And besides, he must manage everything that comes his way. Dynham must be in command, in control. You know he manages Brentland for that sickly boy, his nephew. I daresay the child will die, just to oblige him, so that he may be Sir Rowland!"

"Rowland? Is that his name? I had forgot," said Henrietta. "Well, if one is given so Gothic a name, it must be next to impossible not to wish to be called Sir!"

"As to Gothic romance, no one could despise it so much as Dynham," said Caroline. "But surely, you knew him before I did, being a neighbour in this county?"

Caroline had not been brought up at Rosewell but in Lady Caynnes's great houses, in London and in Wiltshire.

Henrietta laughed. "No, indeed! My father considered them far too rough and wild to know his daughters!" she said. "Their cousin Cary Vyner fell in love with Tinna, later, but my father thought him the wildest of the lot and sent him off. And he used to quarrel with this particular cousin, I believe. Cary Vyner was full of revolutionary opinions, whereas Colonel Dynham, I understand, has always been traditional in his."

"He has not the imagination to be anything else," said Caroline scornfully. "He certainly has no conception of freedom. But let us not speak of Dynham, since we have the good luck to enjoy his absence just now."

And she began to ask Henrietta about the Vyners, and who was to inherit the place, now that Sir Brandon had cast off his wild young grandson.

Hilary Tollington turned to Louie and asked her if Devon did not seem uncivilised after Bath.

"I have been but rarely in Bath," said Louie shyly. "We lived in Bristol you know."

Then he praised the Avon gorge as fine romantic scenery and remarked that he had once heard a wonderful singer at the theatre in Bristol.

"Why, Hilary, I have not shown you the pianoforte you sent down for me," Caroline suddenly interrupted him, and Louie had an uncomfortable feeling that she did not like any man, even a cousin younger than herself, to be attentive to another woman in her presence. "I should never have got Dynham to buy it for me—you would never believe how mean he is about what he calls unnecessary expense. Come and see it." And she rose.

"I obliged Tinna as well as you, Caroline," said Hilary, obediently rising too. "For I bought it from a protégé of hers, an emigrant count from Luxembourg who keeps his family by playing at her musical evenings and selling pianofortes by day. Imagine it! I declare, there is nothing I could do for my living if I were to get thrown out of my country by revolutionaries."

They went into the house and to the long gallery that ran almost the length of one wing. Caroline sat down at her new instrument and struck some dramatic chords. She was not a very good player for she did not practise enough, but she could accompany her own singing, which had a certain vibrant quality, and she looked superb in action.

Hilary ransacked the music stand to find favourite airs; he did not sing himself but Caynnes Ridgway had a pleasant tenor voice though Caroline did not allow him to exercise it much alone. He might only sing duets with her.

Henrietta walked to the window and stood looking out towards the sea. Louie had a feeling she did not much care for Caroline's style.

"What a room for dancing!" she said presently. "Do you use it for balls, Caroline?"

"As if I could have a ball here!" Caroline exclaimed. "Why, I am avoided as if I had the plague. That is the result of Dynham's banishing me from town—everyone thinks I have done something very wicked. They don't imagine a man can be so mean as to shut up his wife for losing money at the races!"

Her tone was bitter, and Louie was relieved that soon afterwards dinner was served. The conversation again became light and amusing. After the meal they went into the drawing-room and Henrietta Tollington sat down near Louie and reminded her of their meeting at the wedding, two little girls, one fair and one dark.

"You must come and see us at Woodford, Caroline must bring you," she said. "Colonel Dynham could not object to her visiting us, stern moral man though he may be."

Louie had not thought of Rowland as such. "I suppose he is moral," she said. "He is certainly extremely correct in his conduct."

"Virtue must be its own reward," said Henrietta, with a smile. "For it is unattractive to others, don't you think? None of us likes a man to be a model of virtue."

Hilary overheard this and laughed. "It is pride, not virtue that makes Dynham so hard," he said. "I'll never forget when he came to us about the loan, two years ago. He was like ice; it was a terrible humiliation to him to have to beg for help from Warstowe and myself, both of whom he had always disliked, for different reasons."

"Oh!" cried Caroline, jumping up. "Must we ever be talking of Dynham? Hilary, let me show you my phaeton—Caynnes has advised me upon it and I think you will grant it is elegant."

They strolled outside again and as Caynnes Ridgway was drawn into the conversation about the phaeton, Louie, walking with Henrietta, asked her what was the loan to which Mr. Tollington had referred.

"Oh, don't you know?" Henrietta said, arching her fine brows in surprise. "Well, it is no secret—I imagine that is just what riles

109

Colonel Dynham. Poor Caroline got into the hands of moneylenders while he was at the war and to set things right he had to raise a loan on the property. It was arranged then that Hilary, as next Caynnes heir after Adrian, and Frederick Warstowe the banker, should be trustees of the Rosewell estate. Colonel Dynham had to give up control of it, as a condition of their helping him. That's why Hilary came to see the steward here."

Louie was amazed. "But Cousin Rowland seemed to be doing so much about the estate," she said.

"No doubt, but all the accounts have to be seen, and he does not control it any more," said Henrietta. "It must be particularly galling to him, since they say he married Caroline for her property—though she is beautiful enough to have taken any man's fancy, if she had not a penny." As they crossed the gravel sweep she asked, "Is he not an unpleasant man to know? People say so, in town."

Louie did not know how to answer; when everyone criticised Rowland she found herself remembering the day at Brentland, or the time when he played soldiers with Adrian, joking at the limbless state of his scratch army.

110

But Henrietta had not stayed for an answer. Caroline called her to admire the phaeton and she tripped off across the cobbles, ready to exclaim at the neatness of the vehicle and its smart lines.

The Tollingtons presently went home in their chaise and Caroline immediately began to take Henrietta's character to pieces.

"She is frivolous and shallow," she pronounced. "I do not think she has any real feeling in her."

"I told you she was a cool customer," said Caynnes Ridgway. "And to tell you the truth, Caroline, I don't fancy her as a wife. She is much too sharp, and incapable of loving one as one wishes to be loved."

"You expect too much, Caynnes, if your wife is to be both rich and doting," said Caroline, with a laugh.

"Maybe—but I won't settle for a critic on the hearth," said he. "No, I shall set forth for London tomorrow."

Caroline protested in vain. He kissed her cheek when he said goodbye, adding as a farewell shot, "If you want to amuse youself, my dear, why not console Cousin Hilary? He's more civilised than George Godfrey."

"Hilary? Such a fool as dear Hilary? You

must be mad!" said Caroline, laughing. "No! Louie and I will entertain ourselves very well without any of you vain fellows to worry us—shall we not, Louie?"

Caynnes Ridgway went away laughing.

6

THE weather was warm now, as May was ending; the roses were coming out and the old place began to look as Louie remembered it. Henrietta Tollington wrote to invite them over to Woodford St. Petrock but to Louie's disappointment Caroline found some excuse to refuse. She had taken a dislike to Henrietta and said she did not love her cousin Hilary so well that she would endure the visit for his sake.

One morning when they were both in the library hearing the children recite poetry, a little maid came in with a printed card.

"Madam, there's a man at the door wants to paint your picture," she said.

Caroline laid the card on the table and they all looked at it.

Peter Paul Raine, Portrait Painter of Bath. The son of the late Mr. Thomas Raine R.A. will execute portraits, especially of children, expeditiously at home. Mr. Raine undertakes both water colours and oils and has exhibited drawings of gentlemen's houses and land-scape paintings.

Caroline laughed. "A travelling painter, like a pedlar!" she said. "Let us see this novelty! Betsey, show him in." And she added to Louie, "Imagine being called Peter Paul—after Rubens, I suppose!"

Betsey had left the library door open and they could see the painter standing on the threshold of the house, with a wide-brimmed hat on the back of his head. When he took it off to come inside his copper red curly hair shone like a flame in the sun, and even after he had stepped into the cool dim hall showed up with a gleam in the shade.

He was quite a young man, several years under thirty, Louie guessed, with a pleasant sunburnt face. His coat was patched at the elbows and his boots were worn. He had a big satchel hanging from his shoulder and took a portfolio from a back pocket of it to display some of his work. Smiling at the children who were staring up at him with fascination he said, "I have two little children of my own, ma'am. Here is a water colour of my daughter."

A charming small face looked out at them,

with a halo of copper curls and bright blue eyes. Peter Raine also had blue eyes.

Caroline said suddenly, "Raine! Why, Louie, was not that the name of the painter who did my portrait for my mother, in Bath, before I was married?"

Before Louie could answer Raine said, "Yes, ma'am, I think it was my father, for I was looking up his accounts to see if I could get in touch with any of his clients, and that is how I found your name. It was a full length portrait, was it not?"

"Yes, and you shall see it, for it is in the gallery here," said Caroline and they all walked to the long room together.

In the picture Caroline, young and graceful, was posed as in a garden, one hand resting on the base of an urn and the other holding a basket, from which flowers were elegantly falling. They stood and looked at it.

Suddenly Mary Anne said, "Papa says he always wants to put the basket straight."

Caroline laughed. "He would!" she said.

"My father was a good painter," said Peter Paul Raine. "I doubt if I shall ever be as good. I do it because he trained me up to the trade and people say I can take a good likeness. But if I hadn't got married young, I think I might have done something different—gone to sea perhaps, to see the world."

Caroline glanced at him, amused at his free and easy manner. "You don't advertise yourself very well, Mr. Raine."

"Well, let me show you a small picture I have taken away to finish, for the Rector of Monkhampton," he said. "I am quite pleased with it, though little Miss has not a very pretty face."

"I should think not! A pudding, with boot button eyes," said Caroline. "Mary Anne has more feature than the Rector's child, even if her face is as round as a plate."

They went back to look at more of the painter's samples and Caroline soon decided she would like to have her children painted. "It is some time since their miniatures were taken, and my husband has them in London." And then she asked the painter where he was staying.

"I have been at the inn in Monkhampton the last three days."

"Monkhampton! You'll waste half your time walking to and fro," said Caroline. "We can give you a room here."

It appeared that Mr. Raine had actually

paid his score at the inn and had all his luggage in his satchel; if she had not wanted him to execute a painting he would have gone on, northwards, for he was working his way back to Bath, having made a circuit through Somerset and Devon. He was quite ready to stay in the house but not in the least obsequious in his thanks; he had an independent manner without being at all insolent. In fact, he was full of good humour. He made the children laugh while he drew them and the sketches, though not inspired, were sufficiently characteristic to please Caroline. She decided that she wanted oil portraits of their heads, so there was work for several days. Peter Raine settled in at Rosewell and proved quite an addition to the party.

For one thing, he was talkative and not shy of expressing his opinions. When the newspaper was brought in Caroline glanced at the gossip column to see if her friends were mentioned but Peter Raine, as soon as he could get hold of it, read the news of politics and the war with attention. His comments struck Caroline as radical, and one morning she said so.

Peter Raine smiled. "I expect you will be

shocked to hear I am a republican by conviction," he said.

"What! So you would cut off my head, Citizen Raine, cut off all of our heads at the guillotine?" she cried.

"I did not say I was a revolutionary," said Raine. "The Parisians have given republicanism a bad name, but still I think it is the fairest form of government. However, in England I do not mind that we have a king, since he does not have the power the French king had. The principal object is that we should have more share in the government."

"We? Who is we?" Caroline enquired, still smiling.

"The people of England," answered Raine. "The people who make up that England, ma'am, which men like your husband assume to be theirs to rule."

"But the people are represented in Parliament," said Caroline.

"Represented! By whom? By gentlemen—like Mr. Tollington of Woodford," said Peter Raine. "And who has the right to vote him in? Men of property. These are not true representatives of the real people."

"What, do you think our stablemen should have a voice in governing the country?" said

Caroline. "What could they know about it?"

"Well, perhaps not yet, not till they have more education," admitted Peter Raine. "But there are more of us who know their letters than you think."

"You for instance," said Caroline, with a teasing look. "Do you want to be an M.P. Mr. Raine? What fun if you would fight an election against Hilary Tollington! I declare, I will canvass for you, rather than for him, though he is my cousin."

"It is a joke, of course," said Raine cheerfully. "You have to have money for these things, as well as to be born a gentleman, like your husband."

"Oh heavens, do not continually make my husband your example," cried Caroline. "I have quite enough of his ruling powers when he is at home, let me tell you. What would you say, Citizen Raine, if I joined your revolution?"

"You would be another Madame Roland!" said Peter Raine mischievously. He knew Rowland Dynham's name.

"I would be myself!" Caroline said, vexed, but laughing.

"But allow me to say, ma'am, that you know nothing at all of the people you so generously wish to join," said Raine, good-humoured as ever, and looking at her with a mixture of admiration and amusement.

Later, Caroline said to Louie, "Do you know what I will do, Louie? I shall make Citizen Raine fall in love with me."

She was in high spirits, delighted at the idea of capturing the heart of a declared republican.

The first thing she did was to get out her old drawings and declare she would take up art again, and Mr. Raine must give her lessons. Louie was drawn in and the children's portraits remained unfinished, put aside while the painter instructed them in his craft. They soon discovered that on his way through the country he had been making sketches of the landscape.

"People will buy a romantic scene," he said. "I shall work them up, during the winter, put in a few blasted oaks, full moons sailing through wracks of cloud and the Bath ladies will delight in them—I hope!"

So then there were sketching parties out of doors. And one day Caroline remarked that their beach was dull in comparison with Honycombe, further up the coast.

"That is romantic indeed, a very deserted

place with a great rock jutting out into the sea," she said.

"Oh Mamma, let us go to Honycombe and see the Henna Rock," pleaded Mary Anne. "I've heard Papa speak of it. Let us have a picnic there, Mamma, please."

But Caroline said she could not take the children, for it was impossible to get a carriage down to the sea. "I should ride there with Mr. Raine," she said, "Can you ride, Citizen?"

He laughed. "I fancy I can ride as well as you, my lady," he said. He called her that in retort for "Citizen". And he added, "For when I was a lad I worked as a courier, riding post between Bristol and London. That's why I never saw you in my father's studio. It was only after he'd had a stroke that I went back, to help him."

"A courier! What strange things you have done," she said.

"I didn't like sitting still," said Peter Raine. "And I did not choose to go into the army or navy to be ordered about by gentlemen, and flogged for insolence, as like as not. No, thank you!"

"Let us go too on our ponies," said Adrian

eagerly and began to shout and cry when his mother said it was too far.

Then Caroline yielded, decided that Louie and the children could be driven in the gig as far as Honycombe Mill and walk out to the sea from there. But she herself was determined to ride over the cliffs with Peter Raine.

Tom Prust drove the gig; a dark-browed Cornishman, silent but not unfriendly. They went north by the coast road, through the village of Holstowe where the church had a tall square tower—"sailor's landmark" Mary Anne said, repeating what she had been told. The sea glittered, away on their left, a wrinkled grey plain, silvered by the high bright light of summer. Then they turned down a steep winding lane, where a drag had to be put on the back wheels. On each side rose up tall spindly oak trees, their lichened stems bent in serpentine forms as they stretched towards the sun. Thick above, the green fretted leaves swayed and midges danced in the slanting sunbeams.

At the bottom they came to a mill with a waterwheel dripping above a dark leat, and a tumbledown cob cottage with children playing outside and a tethered pig lying on its side in the sun. Dogs barked as they came to a halt and a woman appeared at the door, staring silently.

She knew Tom Prust and accepted the whim of the lady of Rosewell without comment. The miller came out and the horse was unharnessed, and one of the bigger boys told to carry the picnic basket and show them the way. Tom Prust seemed to think it his duty to stay with horse and gig.

The path to the shore ran alongside the stream, through thickets of alder and hazel at first, but later emerging in the rough land at the bottom of the narrow valley. It was much steeper and wilder than the coombe where Rosewell stood. Great headlands reared up each side, with the sea between, peacock blue and green now under a sky cleared of cloud, the long waves breaking in puffs of white spray on the distant rocks.

"Sea! Sea!" cried Adrian, running and jumping about on the short turf in his delight.

Over uneven ground near the stream's mouth they climbed on to a grassy lip overlooking the shore, a mass of grey boulders, with blocks of black and reddish stone heaped at the foot of the headlands.

"Oh, look! There's a dead sailor down

123

there!" cried Adrian clutching at Louie.

There was certainly a man stretched out on the grey shingle of the tide ridge, and he was wearing a pair of old bleached trousers such as sailors wore, but he was lying on his back and as they looked, moved a large sunburnt hand to brush away a fly or wasp.

"He's not dead," said Mary Anne, with relief.

"Perhaps he's been washed up from a wreck," said Adrian hopefully and off he went, careering down the path before Louie could stop him. He went jumping and leaping over the stones shouting, "Hallo, Sailorman!"

The boy from the mill, struggling along with the picnic basket, grinned.

"That bean't a sailorman," he said scornfully. " 'Tes Mester Dynham of Brentland—Mester Josce, the silly one. Slept in our barn last night, 'e did, too."

"Joscelin Dynham?" said Louie, and though she was surprised she remembered that Rowland had said his brother turned up from time to time at their old home.

As they came down on to the shore they saw him sit up and look round and then hastily pick up a faded blue shirt and pull it on.

Adrian stopped just short of him, staring, somewhat in awe of his size and even stepped backwards when he got up, gaping with his head tilted back.

Mary Anne went stumbling clumsily over the stones.

"Adrian, it's Uncle Josce."

"M-Mary Anne? So it is! Adrian, why, you're n-not in—*petticoats* any more."

When he spoke Louie remembered that slight stammer, more a hesitation than a stutter, so that some words came out suddenly with a disproportionate emphasis.

Because he seemed so shy and awkward, Louie for once did not feel so, and found herself saying that he would not remember her as she had been only a little girl at her cousin Caroline's wedding.

"I d-*do*, though. You were the dark one."

He was standing lower than they were, at the bottom of the steep bank the tide had thrown up across the beach, and so Louie did not feel dwarfed, even though he was quite the biggest man she had ever seen. He must be as tall as his brother and he was considerably broader, though not fat, merely brawny. His head was massive, with thick tufty dark hair sticking up, his eyebrows were as bushy as the Dynhams' in the portraits and his features even more rugged than theirs; they did not seem to fit together very well, so that he was almost ugly, though not unpleasantly so. Louie noticed his very big mouth, perhaps because of his difficulty in speaking.

When they had got through their greetings they sat down again and told Joscelin that Caroline and the painter were riding over the cliffs.

"I hope they won't break their—*n-necks*," he said, glancing up at the southern cliff. "It's full of rabbit holes up there." And then he asked, "Is he a—*g-good* painter?"

Surprised at this question Louie said, "Not very, but he is a pleasant sort of person."

Adrian, annoyed at being thought still an infant in petticoats, had already run off to play in the stream with the mill boy, and presently Mary Anne wandered away, searching for treasures at the high-tide line.

"I didn't know C-Caroline was down here," said Joscelin, in a worried tone. "Is Rowland?"

When Louie said he had gone back to

London, Joscelin seemed relieved. "Rowland gets so irritated with m-me," he said. "For n-never d-doing anything useful." He told her he had landed at Bristol and was making his way to Brentland. "Truscott still there? *G-good*." Then, after a pause, he asked, hesitantly, why Caroline was in the country.

"I'm afraid it's because Cousin Rowland thinks it's the only way to keep her from getting into debt," said Louie. "She is very angry with him about it."

Joscelin said nothing for some time, staring at the waves as they curled and crashed below the shingle bank. Then he sighed. "They bring out the w-worst in each other, those *t-two*," he said.

It was true, but Louie was surprised that he should be aware of it. Joscelin seemed to her an unusual person, unpredictable. He was quite unlike Rowland.

Presently they heard a shout from Adrian and saw him pointing up the cliff and waving. Two tiny figures had appeared on top of the headland, two figures on horseback, and one was in scarlet.

"There they are!"

It was some time before they got down the diagonal track on the steep hillside, and appeared at the head of the path to the beach, having left their horses by the stream.

Caroline was surprised to see Joscelin but welcomed him gaily, demanding where he had sprung from—"You gipsy!" she teased him. "But I shall be a gipsy today too!" She pulled off her shoes and stockings and jumped about on the smooth stones, carefree and light-footed. The boy from the mill gaped at her, fascinated.

They opened the picnic basket, Caroline crying out that all their supplies would disappear inside Joscelin, and though it was a joke, it made him afraid to accept anything. He was shy and more tongue-tied than ever in Caroline's presence.

After eating they sat for some time, Peter Raine sketching Caroline, and the children went back to the stream, playing in the pools among the rocks. Presently Caroline jumped up and went down to the water's edge. The tide was falling and she climbed over to the big rocks, daring the waves to deluge her. Peter Raine had soon followed her, barefoot too, agile and quick as he jumped from one rock to another. Their laughter floated back to the beach, between the bursting of the waves. They went on, climbing further over the pile of rocks northward, which divided this bay from the next, and presently disappeared from view.

Joscelin lay on the stones, propped against a smooth rock, gazing out to sea. He did not volunteer any conversation, but in answer to Louie's questions he brought out some interesting information, in his slow, halting way, about the German states west of the Rhine, where he had been lately. He had worked his way home on fishing vessels, transferring from a Dutch to an English one at sea.

Presently the children, tired out, came over to them and dropped down. Adrian fell asleep, like a puppy in the sun, but Mary Anne's eyes roamed northwards.

"Where's Mamma?" she asked. "You don't think she's fallen into the sea?"

"No," said Joscelin. "What's that piece of wood you h-have there?"

"I picked it up," said the child. "I thought it looked like a funny man."

"Shall I give him a proper f-face?" said Joscelin. He picked up his old jacket, took a knife from its pocket, and to Mary Anne's delight carved a smiling face on her piece of twisted wreckwood.

Caroline had not fallen in the sea, but it was long before she came back, and when she first appeared on the rocks again Peter Raine was helping her over them, holding her by the hand as he had not done when they went the other way. And when they came over the beach to join the others, both of them were laughing like old friends—or like lovers.

The tide was now far out, across the weeded rocks now exposed the waves were breaking, much smaller, on a bank of sand beyond. The sun had come round above the sea, the water glittered, the wind had dropped.

"We must go home," said Caroline, and Adrian woke up, yawning.

They all climbed up to the grassy plat together, but then Caroline and Peter Raine went up the hill again; as the others walked inland by the path alongside the stream they could see the pair of them riding slowly out along the headland to the cliff, the downsliding sun catching Peter Raine's mop of coppery hair as he turned towards Caroline.

7

AFTER that day at Honycombe Louie could not believe that Caroline was merely amusing herself, making the painter fall in love with her; surely she herself was not untouched. Now it was June and in those long summer days Caroline seemed always to be out with Peter Raine, ostensibly sketching—and they did bring back some sketches.

Caroline at no time cared much about the proprieties. Just as she had ridden over the countryside with Caynnes Ridgway and George Godfrey, so now she roamed it with Peter Raine. Even on wet days she did not leave him long to himself. He had now started a full-scale conversation piece of Caroline with her children and two of the dogs. Louie privately thought that he was not up to his subject, for the painting was conventional, stiff and dull. Indeed Raine himself often expressed dissatisfaction, especially with his efforts at Caroline's face, painting out mouth and eyes so often that she said he would wear out the canvas.

Joscelin Dynham's view of the picture agreed with Louie's, as she discovered when she came upon him standing before it and saying aloud, with a shake of his big head, "N-no, it won't—*do*."

Joscelin had gone to Brentland and was staying there with the Hickmans, but he often walked the ten miles across the moor to the sea and sometimes called at Rosewell. He was soon a favourite with the children, for he was very good-natured and seemed content to spend hours listening to them, carrying them on his back up hills, or making things to amuse them. He was a good wood-carver and had worked with Austrian craftsmen as well as, earlier, with an old Devonian in Exeter. In his pack he had a leather case of tools and the children loved watching him at work, especially Mary Anne, who had more patience than the volatile Adrian.

In that pack Joscelin also had a set of wooden recorders and when the children heard him playing, they wanted to learn too, and in this case Adrian was the quicker; Mary Anne was painstaking but not so able in co-ordinating fingers and ears.

Joscelin saw little of Caroline, for he only came over on fine days and by the time he reached Rosewell she had usually gone out with Raine. When she did see him she treated him as a walking joke; Joscelin became tongue-tied in her presence and as clumsy as a bear. Once, after she had gone away laughing, because he had cracked a chair, he said to Louie ruefully that he would bring his tools next time and try to mend it.

"You never do things like that when Caroline is not here," she observed, for generally he moved with deliberation.

"She d-does frighten me," Joscelin admitted. "My m-mother did too. She used to call me a c-clown, and so I was, in her presence. Rowland was her favourite—he was like her in being sarcastic and c-cool, though if he once let go—" Joscelin broke off and whistled, to express the startling result.

"Caroline says he has a fierce temper but it does not appear," said Louie. "She loses hers, but he never loses his."

Joscelin said, "Rowland cannot b-bear to be overmastered by passion. He m-must feel himself in command of his circumstances. That's why Caroline's wildness hits him so—*h-hard*."

Louie brooded on this comment; Joscelin's understanding of people's motives surprised her; he seemed able to divine the causes of contradiction in them.

"When Rowland came b-back from the Low Countries, two years ago, after that disastrous retreat, when M-Mark was killed, he found everything he had worked for in ruins," said Joscelin. "C-Caroline in the hands of m-moneylenders, the estate heavily in debt, the children alternately spoilt and n-neglected. And he found he could not rule C-Caroline. He knows people in London l-laugh at him because she had gone her own way. Now, n-no one would like that, but to Rowland it is an intolerable humiliation. And I mean intolerable—I d-don't think he knows how to bear it. And that's dangerous, Louie." He stood by the window, and gazed for some moments towards the sea. Then he ended suddenly, "I think Peter Raine ought to l-leave, before Rowland comes home."

Rowland was coming back in July though they were not quite sure when, for he had some Militia exercises first.

Louie felt she ought to defend Caroline. "She only meant to tease Peter Raine, by making him fall in love with her."

Joscelin was frowning unhappily. "But I think she c-cares more than he does," he said.

"He is simply drawn in by the flame—like a *m-moth*."

Louie had not imagined that a man could be less active than a woman in an affair of love; she looked at Joscelin uncertainly. It was so difficult to believe that this large and slow-moving young man was not slow and stupid in mind, too. Yet he could play deftly on those wooden pipes of his and he had found an old lute in the house and restrung it, humming and singing over songs and ballads in his deep bass as he plucked it; Louie had noticed that he did not stammer when he sang. He was not the clownish giant he looked, and that Caroline too plainly thought him.

"Do you think Cousin Rowland would be—very angry," she said doubtfully, "if he knew how much they were together?"

Joscelin turned his dark grey meditative eyes on her.

"Louie, playing with l-love is playing with f-fire."

He said no more, but she often remembered it, afterwards.

Things went on much the same, though Joscelin went off to visit friends, walking away with his pack on his back. June ended,

July began and a letter came from Rowland giving the date of his arrival. The news came on a rainy day when the painting of the picture was in progress; the children had been sent off for their walk with Lizzie Jewell, in hooded cloaks against the drizzle, and Peter Raine was now painting Caroline's beautiful arms, while she sat like a queen on her chair.

The letter lost her the pose. "Oh, confound it, Dynham is returning already," she said impatiently. "I had hoped the Militia would keep him busy into August."

There was a pause and then Raine said, "I ought to be getting on my way, back to Bath."

"It is for me to dismiss you," said Caroline sharply.

He flushed and put down his paintbrush. "If that is how you think of me, the sooner I go the better," he said.

"You are afraid of Dynham!" she accused him, scornfully. "So much for Liberty and Equality, Citizen!" She flung the nickname at him like an insult.

"I am not afraid of him, but he is your husband," said Peter Raine, still flushed and speaking with a quick edge of anger in his voice.

"Husband! Who leaves me here alone against my will!" said Caroline. She jumped up and began to pace restlessly about. "He cares nothing for me—never has. It was Rosewell he wanted, my property. Yes, and I am to be his property—but I will not have it so. I must be free, I must have my own life. Dynham is nothing to me, now that I have discovered what loving can be."

Raine glanced at Louie; Caroline saw it and said quickly, "I do not care if Louie knows—you have guessed it already, have you not, Louie? For you have never seen me so happy as in these last weeks."

It seemed to be a declaration of love for the painter, and Louie felt acutely embarrassed.

"Caroline," said Peter Raine, and Louie had not heard him use her Christian name before, "you had much better not go on like this. You know that I must go home, and it is better I should go before your husband returns."

"No!" she cried, wildly. "How can you be so cruel? No, Peter! Why, the picture is not even finished, Dynham may not stay long—I will let him suspect nothing. What can he do? I tell you, he cannot do anything."

She had gone up to him and stood face to

face, putting her hands on his arms. "Don't go yet, I beg you."

"I might move into the village," said Peter Raine at last.

Caroline appeared delighted at this solution and began to decide the details at once. He was to lodge in a cottage beyond the church; there was a path through the churchyard to the garden by which he could easily reach Rosewell. She arranged it all gaily, happy to have gained her point and kept her lover.

Peter Raine moved his things to the cottage next day and Louie happened to meet him as he came back. He looked at her self-consciously and then said awkwardly, "I ought to have gone." And as she did not answer he went on defensively, "What can I do? It is hard to refuse her. She has been so unhappy with this cold-hearted Dynham—cold but jealous, he seems to be."

"Is that what she said of him?" Louie asked.

"Yes, of course she told me how unhappy he has made her," said Raine. "If it had not been so, she would hardly have made a friend of me . . ." He made a helpless gesture. "She is so beautiful, so vital! It has been like a kind of wild dream—and so it will seem, when I

138

have gone, I suppose." He sighed. "I should have gone now. But how can I, when she begs me to stay?"

Louie saw that, as Joscelin had perceived, he was as fascinated as the moth by the candle flame.

"I shan't be able to bear it, if he treats her ill, in my presence," Raine said suddenly.

"What do you think he is?" said Louie, indignantly. "It is she who behaves ill to him."

They looked at each other for a moment in silence and then Raine said uncertainly, "You won't give us away to him?"

"Of course not," said Louie, irritated, and somehow feeling some contempt for the harassed young man, so much out of his depth in the situation he had walked into unawares.

She left him, walking back fast across the lawn, her shoes squeaking on the wet grass.

Caroline did not speak further to Louie about her love; nor did her manner to Raine change from what it had been before the news of Rowland's imminent return had startled her real feelings out of her. But now when Louie saw them go out on the cliffs together she guessed they were escaping into a private world in which there were only Caroline and

139

Peter—no wife at home in Bath for him, no husband coming down from London for her.

But when Rowland Dynham did come back to Rosewell, at the end of July, Louie was surprised to see how differently Caroline behaved to him this time. From the first evening, when she was waiting to receive him in one of her most charming gowns, with her beautiful hair combed up at the back and falling in long side curls on her warm ivory neck, she seemed like a wife whose one thought was to please her husband. Louie noticed Rowland glancing often at her that first evening, as if he could not believe in this unexpected kindness. Perhaps he put it down to the fact that he had written recently to tell her he had taken a house in London for Michaelmas.

Louie remembered how Caroline had tossed that letter aside with an impatient sigh and said, "Oh, what do I care *now*? I don't want to go to London, now."

But she did not say that to her husband; she expressed gratitude as if she felt it.

"I am afraid you will not like the situation," he said. "It is in Westminister, but that is convenient for me, and it is relatively cheap, so I hope you will not find it too much out of the fashionable world. I am sure you can make it look very pleasant. It has a pretty room upstairs which would do for your drawing-room."

"I am sure it will do very well," said Caroline.

Louie thought Rowland looked puzzled; he could not make this unusual meekness out. He made no comment on it but remarked how well she looked. "That style of doing your hair is very charming," he said, standing near her chair, looking down at her.

He went out a moment later to go and see the children, who were in bed, and Caroline gave an uneasy laugh.

"Oh! It will not do to make Dynham fall in love with me again!"

"Why not, Caroline?" Louie burst out, impulsively. "Would not that be the very best thing?"

"My poor Louie, what a good girl you are!" said Caroline. "The only reason why I find it easy to be pleasant to Dynham is because I am in love—but not with him!"

"You can't be in love with Peter Raine," said Louie, with a sort of distaste which she could not quite conceal.

"Why can't I?" Caroline rose and walked

to the window, gazing out at the cool evening garden. "As a matter of fact, Louie, I never have been in love till now. I never cared about anyone the way I care for Peter—not Dynham, certainly, nor those others he was so jealous of, when he came back from the war. I liked to have them love me—that is something different."

"But how can you?" Louie reiterated, bewildered. "Raine is—so very ordinary."

Caroline laughed. "That's just what I like!" she said. "He's not trying to be anything but himself. He says what he thinks, what he feels, straight out. When I'm with him I feel I am myself too. I feel free."

Louie thought it seemed all feeling but she did not say so. She said, "But what is the use of loving him? You are married and so is he."

"That has not mattered till now—why should it matter?" said Caroline, impatiently. "But I hope Dynham will not think, because he finds me happy, that I am reconciled to *him*. I wonder now that I have lived with him so long. It is like being married to a suit of armour—with no one inside."

She laughed, amused at her own comparison.

But when Rowland came back into the

142

room she continued to listen to what he said and to answer with apparent interest. Louie was suddenly able to imagine what their marriage had been like at the beginning, after that wedding she remembered with such clarity.

The next day, at breakfast, Caroline said casually, "Mr. Raine is coming from the village to paint the children's portraits—did I mention it?"

"Yes, I think you did," said Rowland. "Is he good?"

"Competent, not very imaginative," said Caroline. "Louie and I have been taking lessons. He's the son of that man who painted me in Bath, before we were married."

"Then I hope he doesn't tip all the flowers out of the garden basket too," said Rowland at once. "I can't think why you let the fellow paint it like that."

Caroline laughed and could hardly stop laughing. She had to run away to get her painting things, her laughter still floating through the house behind her.

Later, Rowland came to see them at work. Peter Raine had actually got Caroline and the children into the correct pose all together and was trying to pull his composite portrait into shape. Rowland inspected it in silence for some time and then hazarded the opinion that Mary Anne looked too short in it. "She is quite tall for her age," he said.

"Yes, I think you are right, sir," said Raine.

"What have you done, Dynham? Now he will rub out Mary Anne and begin again!" said Caroline, laughing. "Look what has happened to my poor face! Mr. Raine is too painstaking."

Louie felt that she was amused by the situation, whereas Peter Raine was painfully embarrassed, though Rowland probably took it for mere social shyness. He made some vague commendation and then took up some of Caroline's sketches and said, with more enthusiasm, that she had made a lot of progress. "These are quite professional, don't you think, Mr. Raine? I am sure they are no worse than many I have seen hanging in gilt frames in other people's houses."

"Mrs. Dynham has a good eye for landscape," said Raine.

Caroline gave him a gay smile, which Rowland did not see, because he was leaning over the table looking at her pictures.

"This is nowhere but Honycombe—the Henna Rock," he said. "You have caught the legendary feeling of it, the Scylla and Charybdis look."

Caroline glanced at him in surprise. "I didn't know you felt like that about Henna Rock," she said, "or knew it so well."

"Climbed it, when I was a boy," said Rowland briefly.

"But there's always water surging round it," said Caroline.

"Swam that," said Rowland, and somehow, in spite of the dry brevity of his comment, Louie felt an echo of youthful adventure, a first daring of danger, which reminded her that he had been a soldier before he had gone into staid civil life. "Let's have this one framed," he said, turning to the artist. "Can you do it, Raine, or shall I ask the carpenter?"

"I'll do it, sir," said Peter Raine.

Louie felt that he had given up his resentful view of Rowland Dynham very quickly and she saw that his respectful manner amused Caroline.

Rowland, always said by Caroline to be so suspicious of her, certainly did not notice anything between her and the painter, Louie was sure of it. He accepted Caroline's good temper as an improvement of character and responded to it with the easier manner he had before shown only to Louie and the children. He occupied himself with estate business, riding to visit the farms, and old Mr. Ridgway in Monkhampton. On one of these expeditions he met his brother Joscelin on his way back to Brentland, and was evidently not unfriendly, for Josce turned up at Rosewell from time to time, and though Rowland was inclined to tease him, he seemed in a very good humour with all the world.

One day in August he remarked to Louie, "It seems to have done Caroline a great deal of good having you here, Cousin Louie. She has pulled herself together in an amazing way since May."

"I am sure it is not due to me," said Louie, inwardly trembling. It seemed dreadful to her that he should so mistake the real situation. She wondered what he would think of her if he knew that Caroline often took her out when she started to walk for the cliffs where she was to meet Peter Raine. At a certain point she always sent Louie home.

"Say you left me sketching," she said, "since Dynham so much admires my landscapes!" And she would go, laughing, up the path between the heather and the furze.

146

She was going to her lover, Louie knew it; she hated to think of it but could not keep her mind from it. Caroline was deceiving her husband; her pleasant manner to him was put on, so that she could meet her lover more easily. What would Rowland do, if he found out? All kinds of dramatic pictures presented themselves to Louie's imagination—Rowland locking Caroline in her room, horsewhipping Peter Raine or, as she could not imagine Raine taking that, a fight between them. If only the painter would go, was always her most fervent wish, and sometimes she thought he wanted to bring the affair to an end. It was Caroline who would not see that there must be an end. She was deliberately prolonging the present, refusing to look ahead.

Then came a spell of grey wet weather when there was no possibility of Caroline's meeting Peter Raine except when he came to work on the paintings. She became moody and irritable once more, and when he spoke again of leaving, flashed out at him, accusing him of being "afraid of Dynham".

"I notice your republican principles wilt before him," she said. "And you say 'sir' like any servant."

Raine flushed. "If it were not for my

147

children, I would take nothing from your husband," he said.

"It is my money, not his," she retorted.

"Do you think that makes it any easier for me to take it?" he replied, with bitterness. "It is you, not he, that puts me in dependence."

Louie felt so uncomfortable at witnessing this quarrel that she went out of the room, but then, recollecting that she had left the children's lesson book behind, she went back to fetch it.

Caroline had run across the room to Peter Raine. She had her arms round him and was kissing him passionately on the lips.

Louie stopped dead, acutely embarrassed, not only by the sight of such an embrace, but because it was so clearly Caroline who was taking the initiative. Raine had been hurt and angry but Louie saw that he could not resist Caroline when she so frankly made love to him and yet could hardly bear to be thrust into this inferior passive role, which Caroline seemed not to realize as such.

Turning her head, she saw it was Louie who had come in and laughed. "I thought it might have been Dynham!" she said. "But if it had been, I should not care. I should be glad he knew the truth."

Louie said nothing at all. She seized her book and retreated, her feelings in a tumult between disgust and pity.

"How can she? It is like madness," she thought.

The next day it rained hard in the morning and after dinner, which they ate at two, the light was not good enough for painting and Peter Raine went back to the village. About four it cleared up and Rowland Dynham, who had been reading the newspaper, went out to see Pendry; because he was an old man, Rowland generally went to his house, instead of summoning him to Rosewell.

Caroline turned to Louie with a mischievous smile. "And I'm going to see Peter."

"Oh Caroline, don't go into the village after him—everyone will know it."

"Nonsense, the cottage is near the church and I shall go up our path. I don't have to go near the village. Besides, I must see him; he's still angry for what I said yesterday."

"I'm not surprised," said Louie. "It was humiliating for him."

"A devil gets inside me when I can't get what I want," said Caroline, but she did not sound deeply concerned.

Louie watched her walk across the lawn to the church path, her long cloak swinging. She was sitting at the end of the drawing-room which looked that way and also took in a view of the gate to the lane. Louie had nothing to do till it was time to change for the evening, as the children were upstairs with the nursery maid. She sat with her embroidery, thinking about Caroline and occasionally looking out, watching for her return. Now that the sun had come out, the light glittered on the wet grass, the dripping leaves; the taller flowers seemed hung with crystals, brilliant and sparkling.

It must have been nearly six when she heard the gravel crunch and looked up to see Rowland Dynham walk in from the lane, in his outdoor coat and round hat. He did not see her at the window for he left the gravel almost at once and walked across the grass to where the sundial stood; watching, she saw he had noticed a snail on it, which he flicked off with his fingers. It was a typical gesture, she thought; he did not want the dial messed up by snails.

The church clock struck the hour and he looked up towards the tower. And then he stood there, suddenly stiff and motionless, staring at something she could not see. He always carried himself very upright but there was something unnatural in this rigidity, this absolute concentration.

Louie had a sudden intense conviction that he had caught sight of Caroline and Peter Raine together, probably in the churchyard, which she could not see from where she sat but which must be in view from where he was standing. Perhaps they were embracing, as she had seen them yesterday in the library.

It seemed minutes that Rowland stood there, stiff and still. Then he took a step forward, but stopped. It was the first time Louie had ever seen him hesitate. The next moment he turned round, with deliberation, his back to the church, and stared down at the dial, though she did not believe he was consulting it.

Louie's heart was beating fast. She did not know why she felt so agitated, for Rowland Dynham's face was impassive, but somehow the whole way he was standing, gripping the sundial and staring down at it, suggested to Louie that he was in a passion of anger far stronger than any of Caroline's she had witnessed. Louie sensed the force of it and it frightened her. How could people call him cold? She would not have liked to be Caroline, meeting him at that moment.

Then he suddenly left the sundial and without looking back walked straight across the lawn to the house and in at the door, which was never locked in the daytime. She heard him going upstairs.

A few minutes later Caroline, looking particularly happy and beautiful, came walking across the grass with some wild flowers in her hand. It was quite plain that she did not know she had been observed.

Louie wondered if she ought to warn her, but after all she had nothing to say except that she thought it had been a shock to Rowland Dynham to see what he had seen—and Louie did not know, she had only guessed, what he had seen, and what he had felt. So she made no attempt to speak to Caroline, though she waited nervously for Rowland's reappearance.

But when he came into the drawing-room later, having changed out of his morning clothes, as he invariably did even when no visitors were expected, he showed no signs of disturbed feelings, though he was more silent than he had been lately, especially after the children had been sent up to bed.

Caroline amused herself at the pianoforte, playing and singing. Rowland sat with a book in his hand, but Louie did not see many pages turned. Nothing was said.

8

AFTER that day, Rowland seemed different to Louie. Perhaps it was just that he had retired into the dry reserve of his first visit and that she noticed it only in contrast to the easier manner he had showed this time. Yet that one moment of silent rage had revealed to Louie what Caroline and Joscelin in their different ways had already suggested: that his reserve, so often called cold by those who saw only the hard purposeful face which gave nothing away, was in fact powered by a temper which was not cold at all.

Louie wondered what he was going to do, now that he knew his wife had a lover, and a mere red-headed painter at that. If Rowland had been humiliated and enraged when he suspected Caroline of entertaining lovers such as Lord Walter Chervill, what would he not do now, when his supplanter was someone of inferior social standing?

The next time Peter Raine came to the house Louie was expecting some dramatic scene, she hardly knew what. But Rowland talked to him rather more than before, asking whether he got many commissions, whether painting were not a precarious profession, how many children he had, and their ages, apparently with all the friendly interest of a patron. If he looked keenly at the young artist as he answered, this was not unusual. Louie herself had often been disconcerted by his direct and penetrating gaze.

Peter Raine was uneasy at this interest but he was still under Caroline's spell; while she demanded his presence he could not tear himself away.

Adrian's birthday came in August; it turned out a warm day. Joscelin was sitting outside on a low wall with the children each side of him, teaching them to play recorders, while Caroline and Louie were inside, at the open windows of the drawing-room. Suddenly Caynnes Ridgway came riding through the gate.

Caroline waved to him, and giving his horse to a groom, he came straight into the house, glancing round the room as he entered it.

"It is all right—Dynham is out," said Caroline, with a smile. "I did not expect you

155

here at the height of summer, Caynnes."

"I fell out with mine host, and failed to get the further invitation I expected," said Ridgway, sitting down. "Not surprising, perhaps, since his wife was conducting a rather warm flirtation with me!" He laughed, but then leant forward and regarded Caroline thoughtfully. "I came down here for free board with the old man while I laid new plans, and I find Monkhampton ringing with the news that the Honourable Mrs. Dynham has taken up with a rapscallion painter and roams the cliffs in his company."

Caroline frowned. "I've no wish to discuss my affairs with anyone," she said, rising and walking down the room away from him.

Ridgway raised his eyebrows. "What, not even with brother Jack? That's new! Come, you must be hard up for company, Caroline, if you're driven to patronise the lower orders."

Caroline flushed angrily. "That's enough, Jack! It's nothing to do with you."

"It's true, then," was all he said, looking at her speculatively.

"What is it to you?" she demanded scornfully, but with some curiosity.

Louie felt that she was uneasy; she guessed

156

that till now Caroline had discussed everything with this rakish bastard brother of hers
and that the reason she did not wish to do so
now was because she feared his caustic
tongue and the cynical comments which
usually amused her.

"Only that I happen to be quite fond of
you, my dear, and don't like to see you make
a fool of yourself," said Ridgway, leaning
back in his chair and gazing up at her as she
came, tall and graceful, down the room
towards him and then stopped, hesitating.

"Besides," he added, "be careful how you
give Dynham grounds against you."

"What more can he do?" said Caroline,
proud and uncaring again. She walked away
from him.

"If he suspects this affair it will bring out
all the Dynham temper and pride that is there,
under that civilised mask," said Caynnes
Ridgway. "I daresay he'll beat your lover and
you too. It would not surprise me."

"He would not dare," said Caroline, but
her tone was not as confident as her words.

"I'm just warning you," said Ridgway,
crossing one leg over the other. "Down here
things could happen which would hardly be
possible in town. Don't forget I knew these

157

Dynhams long before you did, my girl. He could be pushed too far and then you would find out what I mean."

"But he does not care two pins for me," said Caroline. "He despises me. It's impossible he could be so violently jealous."

"It's not his jealousy I'm talking about, it's his pride," said Ridgway. "Don't you think he'll be glad to vent his spleen for earlier humiliations on someone who is his inferior? And on you, my poor girl, for stooping so low?"

Caroline turned away, flushing again. "How can you? And before Louie!"

"I rely on Miss Louisa to reinforce my warning," said Caynnes Ridgway. "She agrees with me—I see it in her fine dark eye."

Louie was too much surprised at Mr. Ridgway's acting the part of mentor to answer, or even to feel confused at his compliment.

Just at that moment Rowland Dynham walked into the room, in his riding clothes. He stopped dead.

"What are you doing here, Ridgway?" he demanded. "I thought I told you not to come here again."

"I do not propose to give up my sister to

158

please a husband I consider unworthy of her," retorted Caynnes Ridgway, remaining in his chair and staring at Rowland with insolent dislike. "But I admit I hoped to avoid you. I thought you were out visiting Caroline's farms."

"I do not choose to account for my movements to you," said Rowland coldly. "Caroline, I was told at Venn that you had instructed Pendry to sell the place to George Godfrey."

"Why not? He wants it, and the rent is nothing."

"Venn was one of our farms," Rowland said. "If it was to be sold, Warstowe might have been persuaded to buy it for Brentland, with Miles's funds. I have told Pendry to go no further."

"How dare you contradict my orders!" cried Caroline, furious. "You care for nothing but Brentland. I shall write to Hilary."

"Do so, for I've no doubt I can carry my point with him," said Rowland.

Caroline stood still, staring at him with angry, thwarted eyes.

Caynnes Ridgway rose to his feet. "Well, my dear," he said to Caroline, "I cannot endure to hear Dynham bully you and I cannot prevent him from doing it, so I will take myself off, forthwith." He went up to her and patted her arm. "Goodbye."

"Caynnes—" she said, turning to him. "Wait, I'll come with you."

"My dear, to Monkhampton?" he said, raising his eyebrows.

"Just to dinner," she said. "I'll drive myself, in my phaeton. All I need is a hat."

"Caroline, will you drive out in this heat?" said Rowland. "And besides, you cannot go out to dinner—it is Adrian's birthday, have you forgotten?"

Caroline gave an impatient exclamation and ran out of the room. They heard her calling to a servant to have the phaeton fetched round to the door.

Rowland stared at Caynnes Ridgway with intense resentment, but he said nothing.

Ridgway picked up his hat and bowed to Louie. "Good day, Miss Louisa," he said and walked out without looking at Rowland at all.

Rowland stood a moment, hesitating. Then seeing that Ridgway had gone round to the stables, he too went out of the house and towards the place where the children were still playing recorders with Joscelin. Louie, after a few minutes of uncertainty, went after him.

When the phaeton was brought round, Adrian immediately jumped up. "Oh! Where's Mamma going?"

"Only to Monkhampton," said Rowland.

"Now?" said Mary Anne in surprise. "How will she get back to dinner?"

Caroline, wearing a big flat hat tied on with a flowing scarf, came out of the house, pulling on her long gloves. The nervous mare was dancing, while the stableman tried to quiet her.

"Mamma!" cried Adrian, running across the gravel. "Why are you going away? Don't go! It's my birfday. I want you here."

Caroline caught him up in her arms. "My darling boy! You shall come with me."

Adrian laughed with excitement. Rowland started forward.

"Caroline, you are not to take Adrian in that vehicle," he said. "I wish you would not go in it yourself. Give up this silly plan of going with Jack and stay here for the child's birthday."

"I am not taking orders from you, Dynham," Caroline retorted and she lifted Adrian on to the seat.

Rowland went up to the side of the vehicle. "Adrian, come down," he said, reaching up to his son.

Adrian wriggled as far away as possible. "I'm going out with Mamma!" he announced gleefully. "It's my birfday."

Caroline climbed up into the driving seat, laughing.

"You see, he is more my son than yours!" she taunted her husband. "He likes to come with me."

It was childish, but it stung Rowland, as Louie, anxiously watching could see.

He jumped on to the step of the phaeton, caught hold of Adrian and swung him out of it, leaping back with him as the restless horses jerked the spindly carriage.

Adrian yelled and kicked. He felt his father's anger and was frightened. He was also furious at being so ignominiously removed from his place of honour and adventure.

"Want to go with Mamma!" he screamed, red in the face, tears starting from his eyes.

"Be quiet!" said Rowland sternly.

Caroline, busy getting control of the horses, looked down, saw that she could hardly regain Adrian from Rowland by force and decided she would prefer to leave without him rather than yield to her husband and give up her own plan.

Caynnes Ridgway had mounted his horse and was watching from the gate.

"Go on, Caynnes! I'm coming!" she called out, and a moment later off went the high-wheeled phaeton at a rattling speed.

Adrian screamed with frustration. "Let me go! I hate you! I hate you!" he shouted, fighting and struggling with his father.

Joscelin who had jumped up from the wall at the beginning of this domestic conflict, came uncertainly nearer.

"Adrian!" said Rowland, with a note of exasperation in his voice. "Stop this nonsense."

But Adrian had gone into a wild tantrum, almost unconscious with fury.

Rowland shook him, and as that had no effect, he held him by the arms and bent down, glaring into his face. "Stop it!" he said, with unmistakable anger.

The result was that fear overpowered fury in the little boy's feelings. His scream took on a note of pure terror.

Joscelin said, "Rowland, I think you had better l-let him go."

Rowland was so astonished at this intervention that he straightened up. Adrian immediately wrested himself free and ran to Joscelin, hiding behind his massive form and clinging to his legs. "No! No!" he shouted hysterically, as if he thought his father was about to do something terrible to him.

Joscelin put his hand round and patted the child's back. "All right, Adrian, no one's going to h-hurt you."

"What the hell do you mean by that, Josce?" demanded Rowland, standing face to face with his brother. Joscelin was one of the few men to equal him in height; indeed, he seemed even a little taller because he was so big.

"I know you're n-not going to hurt Adrian, but he thinks so," said Joscelin. "Just l-leave him alone for a m-minute, Rowland, for God's sake."

It seemed to Louie as if all the frustrated rage pent up in Rowland Dynham was now turned against his brother. Not that he stormed and shouted. But there was intense bitterness in his voice as he said, "So you think you know better than I do what's good for my son? My God, Josce, I'm not going to stand this interference from you. What have you ever done but idle about the world like a tramp? What right have you to criticise me?"

"I'm not c-criticising you, Rowland," said Joscelin, moving a little sideways, but still keeping Adrian behind him. "It's just that Adrian's frightened, and if you glare at him, you only m-make it worse."

"You know nothing about it," said Rowland. "He's my son, not yours. Get out of the way and let me talk to him."

But Joscelin did not move. Nor did he speak.

"Josce," said Rowland, with a white face and quiet anger which Louie thought far more terrifying than a storm of words would have been "will you move?"

For answer Joscelin turned round and picked up Adrian, whose terror had now somewhat subsided, holding him in his arms. The little boy shrank away from the sight of his father's face, burying his own on Josce's shoulder.

There was a moment of silence which Louie felt was one of agony for Rowland Dynham; it was almost more than he could stand to see his child turn away from him to another. But still his voice was under control as he said at last, in freezing tones, "Since he is not afraid of you, it seems, will you take

165

him indoors to Lizzie Jewell and tell her to wash his face? I suppose you want your dinner, Adrian, so I advise you to behave yourself. As for you, Josce, I'd be glad if you would take yourself off after dinner. I don't recollect asking you here and I don't see why I should put up with your presence any longer."

"I'm sorry, Rowland," said Joscelin, who seemed now upset and anxious, as he had not been when he was defending Adrian.

Rowland said nothing but turned on his heel and walked quickly away.

Mary Anne, who had been staring wide-eyed at the scene, suddenly ran to Louie.

"Cousin Louisa! Why was Papa so angry with Uncle Josce?" she said in bewilderment. "Why has he sent him away?"

Louie only said, "Come and wash your hands, Mary Anne."

But as they went upstairs she felt she knew why it was Joscelin who had finally drawn on his head all the resentment roused in Rowland by others. All his love was concentrated on his two children and failure with them was for him an unbearable defeat.

Somehow he had recovered his usual coolness by dinner time and Adrian, swollen-eyed and subdued, was not made to feel he had disgraced himself, or required to apologise. By the end of the meal when he was allowed to drink toasts in wine and water, the little boy was happy again, the storm blown over. His temperament was resilient and open; he was quite unlike his father.

But Rowland remained extremely chilly towards his brother and did not recall anything he had said, so that Joscelin, in the afternoon, took his tools and his recorders and walked slowly away from Rosewell, going inland up to the moor and across it to Brentland. But he only stayed there one night, they heard, and then went on.

"Where will Uncle Josce go, Papa?" Mary Anne wondered.

"What does it matter?" said Rowland coldly. "He doesn't choose to have work or a home. He prefers to be a tramp. So let him go on his way."

Nobody liked to say anything more on that subject.

Caroline came back before the children's bedtime, her arms full of presents for Adrian. But she seemed subdued and moody and went upstairs soon afterwards, pleading fatigue.

It was only a few days after Joscelin had gone that Caroline came into the library one afternoon, when the children were out for their walk, and said, "Has not Mr. Raine been in today? He will never get the picture done at this rate."

Louie was correcting the children's sums at the table; Rowland was sitting by the window reading the newspaper. He folded it with deliberation, put it down and rose to his feet.

"Mr. Raine will not be coming any more," he said.

Caroline stood and stared at him. "What do you mean?" she said, in a strained voice.

"He has gone," said Rowland. "I sent him away."

Caroline was silent from the shock.

"It seemed the best thing to do," Rowland said. He spoke quite quietly, but he was watching Caroline intently.

"You—sent—him—away?" she repeated slowly, gazing at him. "And he's gone—without a word to me? What did you do to make him go?" Suddenly indignation nerved her to defiance. "Dynham, if you threatened him—if you touched him—"

"Calm yourself, Caroline. He perfectly understood the necessity, even if you do not.

168

He has a duty to his wife and children and he has gone back to them."

Caroline walked across the room and back, with quick nervous movements. "How could you do such a thing, Dynham?" she broke out. "Without speaking to me? You act as though I had no feelings in the matter at all."

"It was to spare your feelings that he left without seeing you," said Rowland. "But I have a note for you from him." He took it from his pocket and held it out.

"Dictated by you, I've no doubt!" said Caroline, a wave of anger flushing her face. She took the note and held it, but did not open it.

Rowland was silent.

Caroline suddenly burst out, "Oh, how can I bear this? I will not be treated like a slave! Just because Peter is not a gentleman by birth you send him away as if he were a servant. You did not dare take such a line with my friends in town. I did not notice that any words, let alone deeds, passed between you and Lord Walter, for instance."

"Lord Walter Chervill is able to live as he pleases," said Rowland coolly, "nor does it incommode Lady Walter that he indulges in affairs with other men's wives. Your other friends were of the same kind. But Peter Raine's life could be ruined by his association with you and his wife made utterly miserable."

"What!" cried Caroline. "Do you dare to pretend you are acting on his behalf?"

"And on yours," said Rowland. "For if you consider it, Caroline, I am sure you must realise that to prolong such a connexion could not bring you happiness."

"What do you know about it?" Caroline said scornfully. "You know nothing about me, nothing about love either—you are quite incapable of love, Dynham."

"I hope I am incapable of a passion which brings unhappiness to so many people—I do not call it love," he replied, with a sharp edge to his voice.

"You know nothing about it," Caroline repeated. "When did Peter go?"

"Very early this morning," said Rowland. "I sent him in the chaise to Bideford. He should be on his way to Bath by now. But you had better read his letter to you."

Caroline stood there, staring at him, hardly yet believing what had happened, holding Peter Raine's letter in her hand.

"You have no heart," she said at last in a

low voice. "You don't even know what you have done to me."

"Come, Caroline," said Rowland, moving towards her, "soon we shall be in London and you will be glad that this affair is no more than a summer memory."

"I don't want to go to London—not with you," Caroline said bitterly. "Don't you understand that I hate you, Dynham? Oh God, how I hate you!" She clenched her hands crumpling Raine's note.

"But you don't hate the children," he said. "For their sake, Caroline, consent at least to live under the same roof."

"I see! You want the children, so you must have me too," said Caroline passionately. "Well, here's Louie—mum as a mouse in her corner—she can look after the children and you too, Dynham. I am sure she would be delighted, for she was astonished that I could prefer Peter to you."

She gave a wild laugh and flung out of the room, leaving Louie petrified with embarrassment, not daring to look at Rowland.

He walked away to the window and after a moment he said, in the gentle tone he used to Mary Anne, "Take no notice of that, Cousin

Louisa. Caroline is not herself. She does not mean it."

Louie was suffering from the painful shock that Caroline could turn against her so spitefully. She looked up, and then away again.

"I take it you knew about her love for this painter fellow," Rowland said. "I am very sorry you should have been mixed up with such an affair—it is most unsuitable for a young girl like yourself. I hope it will not prevent your coming to town with us, for I think you do Caroline good, and the children are so fond of you."

"Certainly, I will come, Cousin Rowland," Louie found herself saying and in fact she could not imagine life now with anyone else. Uncomfortable it might be, but she was under a spell, fascinated by Caroline still and not less, she was vaguely aware, by Rowland himself.

He seemed to take it for granted that they would all go to London at Michaelmas and as September was now beginning, he gave orders for the children's winter clothes to be got ready.

Caroline, after that first encounter, became unusually silent; to Rowland she scarcely spoke at all. She wandered alone on the cliffs at all hours, she left meals forgotten, she refused to see her cousin Hilary Tollington when he called. Rowland said she was unwell and Hilary tactfully made no further enquiries. He had been away most of August and Henrietta had rejoined her sister, Lady Hayford. Hilary, who did not get on with Caroline's husband, did not stay long.

Caroline said once to Louie, "What will become of Peter now, with that humdrum wife of his, and children to slave for? He'll never *live* . . . And how shall I live, mewed up with Dynham in his deadly routine in London? I cannot stand it! It will kill me, Louie."

"But you could not have stayed here with Raine for ever," said Louie, irritated by Caroline's impractical imagination.

"Why not?" Caroline said, impatiently. "If Dynham had been content to leave me here . . . " But she would not think practically of anything. She could only feel, and feel desperately, the parting from her lover. Her anguish was genuine, her loss of appetite, her restlessness, her sleepless nights. Sometimes she shut herself in her room and cried for hours together.

One night, lying awake and listening to this desolate sobbing, and moaning, Louie could bear it no longer and got up, with some idea of taking Caroline a hot drink. The moonlight shone across the floor in white blanks from the windows, for she had drawn back the curtains so as not to have to light a candle. She went to her door and then stopped dead.

Someone else was on the landing—Rowland Dynham, standing near Caroline's door. His back was towards Louie, so that he did not see her. He was wearing a dressing gown over most of his clothes, so he had not yet gone to bed. Evidently, like herself, he had been listening to Caroline's crying.

He stood irresolute some time and then reached out his hand and pressed the handle. The door was locked.

He said, hesitantly, "Caroline?"

There was no answer, but a kind of impatient groan.

"Caroline, you will make yourself ill, crying like this. Do let me bring you a glass of wine."

Silence; she was not crying now.

"Tell me what you would like, Caroline."

"You to go away!" shouted Caroline, in a

voice like a child's, high and sharp. And she gave an hysterical laugh.

Louie felt her spine tingle; it was frightening somehow, that voice.

Rowland was standing by the door; he did not move away for some time. Louie felt that he did not know what to do. When he did begin to turn she suddenly felt she did not want him to know she had been watching and stepped back into her room, holding the door as close shut as it would go without the latch clicking.

She listened, hearing his steps go across the landing. When she heard his door shut, she shut hers. There was silence from Caroline's room now. Shivering, Louie crept back across the moonlit squares and got into bed. The house was still.

9

ROWLAND DYNHAM said nothing to Caroline about her weeping, or what he knew to be the cause of it, but he talked about London, the new house, and about people they both were acquainted with, evidently with the intention of taking her mind off Peter Raine. Louie did not think he had succeeded. Once, when she was upstairs with Caroline in her own room, she noticed her cousin standing by the window, looking across the lawn to the church tower, pale and square against the dark climbing woods. She was smiling slightly.

"What do you think, Louie? Is a woman her husband's possession? To be moved here and there at his choice?"

"Aren't you distorting the position, Caroline?" said Louie. "After all, the man as much as the woman promises faithfulness; both expect to live together. And," she added boldly, "you would not want Cousin Rowland to go where you chose to live."

"No I would not!" said Caroline, and she

laughed. But she gave Louie a keen glance and turned the subject; nor did she speak any further about it in the days that followed. But she seemed suddenly more cheerful. There was no more crying at night.

One grey windy morning in the middle of September Rowland appeared at breakfast in his riding clothes.

"Where are you going?" Caroline asked. "To Monkhampton?"

"No, the other way, to East Marsh Farm to see Jem Prust. But do you want something at Monkhampton?"

But Caroline said she did not. All the same, when he had gone it was not long before she came downstairs in her travelling pelisse with big sleeves and the hat she wore to drive in, tied down with ribbons. Hannah Colwill came down after her, carrying a valise.

"I'm taking some things to the alms-houses," said Caroline, standing in the hall and pulling on her driving gloves. A row of cottages had been built after her marriage, to house the old and poor. "I may go on to the town."

"Oh, Mamma! Take me too!" cried Adrian, jumping about excitedly.

"No, my love—Papa says I am not to take you in the phaeton."

"Oh, damnation!" said Adrian grandly.

Caroline laughed and caught him up in her arms, kissing him repeatedly. She gave Mary Anne a kiss too and they went out to watch the phaeton brought round, with its lively pair of horses.

Caroline climbed up to her high perch, waved her whip, and drove out through the gateway.

Louie and the children went into the library to do lessons. In the middle of the morning glasses of milk were always put in the hall for them and when they went out they saw that the letters had been fetched and were laid on the table.

"This one's come from Bath," said Mary Anne, examining the mark on a letter that looked like two sheets folded together and sealed.

Louie immediately thought Peter Raine must have been writing to Caroline; to send two sheets cost double the money. But Mary Anne added, "For Papa, he always gets all the letters."

But not from Bath, thought Louie. The suspicion entered her mind that Peter Raine's wife had discovered the affair and was writing to Rowland Dynham, probably not realising that he was already aware of it. So, although curious, she did not think much about it.

They were still drinking their milk when Rowland came in, saying that he was soon back because Jem Prust had gone to Monkhampton. He took up his letters, putting some aside, and then opened the one from Bath. There were certainly two sheets.

He stood there reading while the children climbed on the bench by the table, fingering the other letters and chattering.

Louie saw him put the first sheet under the second, and concentrate on that. He seemed to have forgotten anyone else was present.

"Papa, who's writing to you from Bath?" Mary Anne asked.

"What? Oh, it is business, child." But he folded the two sheets carefully and walked through the drawing-room to the study, where they heard him open his desk. He came back without the letter and asked, "Louie, where is Caroline?"

"She has gone out," said Louie.

"In the phaeton," said Adrian. "With a case full of clothes for the poor old people in the almshouses."

"Surely she could have got one of the men to carry it that far?" said Rowland.

"She said she might go on to Monkhampton," said Mary Anne.

Rowland took out his watch, looked at it, and asked when she had started. Then he ran upstairs, calling for Hannah Colwill.

"What does he want Hannah for?" Mary Anne wondered.

They all stayed in the hall, curious as to what was happening. In a few moments Rowland came down again. Hannah Colwill, behind him, stopped, looking down over the bannisters.

"Papa, where are you going?" asked Mary Anne, running after him as he walked quickly across to the door.

"I want to catch up Mamma," he said. "Now go and get on with your lessons like good children."

But they lingered in the doorway, watching grooms hurry about.

"He's taking another horse," said Louie.

"That's Caesar—his best hunter," said Mary Anne.

On that fine animal Rowland too looked fine; a commanding figure. Louie was not surprised that Adrian shouted "Hurrah!" as his father passed the door.

Rowland took off his hat and waved it to them, but his smile was fleeting. As he went out of the gate his face looked set and hard.

"Why is he angry?" Mary Anne wondered.

"Reckon he thinks madam has run away," said Hannah Colwill, who had come downstairs and was standing behind them. "He was asking me what was in that valise. Pound weights, I'd say, it was so heavy. Then off he goes to her dressing table and opens her jewel cases and would you believe it, they were all empty. I thought he was going to accuse me of taking them, but all he says is, 'She's gone' and out he goes. Reckon he thinks she's run away, and maybe he's not far wrong."

"Run away? Why should she run away?" said Mary Anne, puzzled. "This is her home."

"That will do, Hannah," said Louie hastily, for the woman looked ready to come out with anything.

She shepherded the children back to the library but found it difficult to concentrate on their lessons. She felt certain that Caroline had indeed run away, and intended to meet Peter Raine. That must be the explanation of the letter. Mrs. Raine had discovered it and written to warn Rowland Dynham. But the letter had come too late—or had it?

Dinner time came; there was no sign of Rowland or Caroline. Afterwards, while the children were resting, Louie sought out Hannah Colwill, who was tidying her mistress's room.

"She's gone all right, miss—taken everything that's valuable," said the maid, with a kind of relish.

"But she can't drive far in that phaeton," said Louie.

"She could get to Bideford all right, and then take a public coach, if she's going where I think she's going."

"Then Colonel Dynham will never catch her up," said Louie. "She was gone an hour or more before him."

"Ah, but he'll have cut across the moor," said Hannah. "She will have to go by the carriage road, round by Monkhampton and Ashworthy, but he'll cut across, save miles like that. He's a very good rider, is the Colonel, and knows this country like the back of his hand."

She straightened her back and looked at Louie with her dark oblique eyes. "I wouldn't care to be madam, when he catches up with her."

Louie went downstairs, feeling apprehensive. She sent Lizzie Jewell to take the children for a walk when they got up from their rest. It was still a cold windy day with grey cloud racing overhead; summer seemed far away, although the trees were still full of leaves and green. Louie could see them, on the north side of the valley, swept in waves and swirls by the strong south-west gale. She sat staring out of the window, yet only half seeing what she stared at. She was thinking of Caroline driving away in the phaeton, running away from Rosewell, from the whole of her life—from her inherited lands, the home of her family, from husband and children.

And what did she mean to do? Take Peter Raine away from his home and his wife and children and roam the world with him? What sort of life would that be, in the end?

And then Louie thought of Rowland Dynham, riding across the moor this cold wild day, to do what? Stop Caroline, and bring her home? But how would he do that? Caroline had quite as much determination as he; it was only in physical strength that he had the advantage of her, and Louie could not imagine him dragging her back by force.

She saw Lizzie and the children, in their warm coats, walking along the path by the stream, going inland, Mary Anne holding the nursemaid's hand, Adrian, as usual, cantering ahead, waving a stick.

Louie felt that she ought to be doing something, but she could concentrate on nothing, not even sewing.

And then she heard a noise in the lane; it sounded like a lot of people coming, horses, carts and country voices, burring and soft. Louie went out into the hall and as she reached the front door she saw Rowland ride through the gate on Caesar.

He saw her, dismounted and came towards her.

"Louie, where are the children?"

"Out with Lizzie Jewell."

"I'm glad. There's been an accident." He turned and called out to Noah Beer, who had come out from the back of the house. "Tell them it's all right to come in, but to be quick about it."

Then he took Louie's arm and guided her into the library. From there the front of the house was invisible. Rowland shut the door. "Louie, you must prepare for a shock."

184

"Caroline?" Louie faltered. "What happened? Is she hurt?"

"She is dead," he replied.

He was still holding her arm and made her sit down. "I am sorry to tell you so suddenly, Louie, but they are bringing in her body now, and I must meet the children if I can, so as to prevent them hearing it from anyone else."

"But—dead!" she said, staring up at him. "How did it happen?"

"She fell out of that cursed phaeton and struck her head on the road—never came round."

"Never came round? Were you there? Where was it?"

"Yes, at Moor Cross, near Top Leys on the way to Woodford—you would not know the place; it is above Brentland."

There was a sound of shuffling feet in the hall, and low voices.

"Stay here, don't come out," Rowland said and went out, shutting the door behind him.

Louie sat there, her mind in confusion, hearing the sound of men in farm boots carrying something across the hall—Caroline's body. Caroline! Could she, so vital, have been so suddenly reduced to nothing, a lifeless corpse? Louie tried to think of the soul, translated to another life, but what she believed would not become real to her imagination. Instead fantasies of the accident kept springing up. Fallen out of the phaeton . . . but why, if she had already met Rowland?

Presently he came back. "I am sorry to leave you, Louie. Are you all right?"

She now had time to wonder at this extraordinary composure; his manner was more businesslike than anything. He took her into the dining-room and poured a glass of wine for her, and another for himself, but he had hardly drunk a mouthful when the children's voices were heard in the hall. He set down the glass and walked out quickly to them.

"Oh Papa, what are all these people doing here? There's a cart from Top Leys outside, all the way from Top Leys." That was Mary Anne, already knowing the countryside.

"Come in here," said Rowland, and taking her hand and Adrian's he led them back into the dining-room, sending Lizzie away.

"Why is Cousin Louie drinking your health, Papa?" Adrian demanded. "Can I?"

Rowland sat down on the big polished chest and pulled the children up, one on each knee. "You must be brave children, for something very unfortunate has happened," he said. "Something that will make you sad. Mamma has had an accident."

"Oh, did the phaeton overturn?" Mary Anne said, turning pale. "Oh Papa, has she hurt herself?"

"My poor child . . . I don't think she can have felt the hurt, or not for more than an instant," he said. "She hit her head so hard that it could not get better."

"Never? Not get better for years?" Adrian asked, wonderingly.

"Papa," said Mary Anne nervously, "you don't mean she's—she's dead, do you?"

"Yes, that is it," he answered.

The two children appeared hardly to realise the fact. They both looked solemn and gazed at him, saying nothing.

At last Adrian said, "Won't she ever come back?"

"Not here, to us," said Rowland. "You must remember that when people die they go to live with God. We can't see them any more."

There was another pause and then Mary Anne said, "Well, Hannah said Mamma was running away but I didn't think that meant she was going to die."

Rowland frowned. "Why should Hannah

say that?" He looked at Louie and then said, "Oh, of course, the jewels. Yes, I must see what they have done with the valise."

He put the children down. "Stay with Cousin Louie and be good."

"Oh Papa, how muddy you are," said Mary Anne.

There was dried mud on the knees of his breeches as well as on his boots, and muddy splashes on his coat.

He kissed the little girl without saying anything more and went away quickly. For some time he was busy directing everyone what to do, sending this person and that on errands, to the surgeon in Monkhampton, to the undertaker, to the clergyman at Holstowe, the larger village from which Rosewell was served. He also wrote a hurried note to Caroline's cousin, Hilary Tollington, and sent it off by messenger to Woodford St. Petrock.

Louie took the children upstairs and gave them their supper and saw them into bed. She realised that they could not really take in what had happened, could not believe that Mamma would not appear next day as usual. She felt it was a good thing they were so young; a few years later the shock would have been worse.

Louie herself was in a daze, bewildered by the half-told tale she had heard. She changed her dress and went downstairs. The farmers had all gone, the servants had swept up; all was quiet and clean again. Yet in one of the rooms Caroline's body must be lying.

Rowland had changed his clothes too and looked just as he did on any evening, in his dark coat and with his cravat crisply arranged. As they sat down he apologised for the fact that he was hungry, having missed dinner altogether. "It seems unfeeling, but I can't help it," he said, and settled down to make a good meal.

It seemed to Louie extraordinary that he could; she herself felt as if the food was tasteless and choking her. They sat in silence, Rowland too much occupied in eating to talk.

They had not finished when Caynnes Ridgway suddenly walked in. He was very much agitated, quite unlike his usual careless self.

"I can scarcely believe this frightful news, Dynham," he said. "Such a very sudden disaster!"

"Driving accidents generally are sudden,"

said Rowland, dryly. He had risen to greet Ridgway but now sat down again and once more addressed himself to his plate.

Caynnes Ridgway stood on the other side of the table, staring across it at him, incredulous of such heartless behaviour.

"But I don't understand what happened," he said, after a moment.

Rowland buttered a piece of bread. "She fell out of her phaeton and hit her head on the road," he said mechanically.

Louie realised that he must have had to say this already a hundred times, but it did sound as if he were merely reporting the death of a pet dog, and somebody else's dog at that.

Caynnes continued to stare at him; at last he said, "I heard that the accident was at Moor Cross and that Caroline was driving on the Bideford road. But what were you doing there?,"

"I rode across the moor to try to intercept her at the cross," and Rowland. "I got there before her."

"But if you met her, how did the accident happen?" Caynnes Ridgway's voice expressed genuine puzzlement, but also suspicion.

Louie realised then that she too had felt

uneasy at Rowland's explanation, though she had not known why.

"I did not meet her, in fact," said Rowland. "When she saw me there she slewed round into that lane which goes down to the cottages where the Top Leys men live. The wheel went up the bank and she was thrown out. I did not see it happen because of the high bank between us. When I got round the corner she was lying lifeless in the road. I carried her to the grass by the cross post, but I think she was already dead." He stopped and then added, "It was better that she never came round—there was a terrible headwound."

Caynnes Ridgway stood there, frowning.

"She swerved aside to avoid meeting you, Dynham," he said. "Why did you go to cut her off like that?"

"I thought it better she should return home," said Rowland. He had finished eating and now drank some wine.

After a moment's silence, heavily charged with feeling, Caynnes broke out, "There's more in this than you are telling, Dynham. Where was Caroline going? Why did you want to prevent her?"

"What does it matter?" said Rowland.

"She's dead now, poor girl, and that's the end of it."

"I very much doubt if it is the end of it," said Ridgway. "Do you know what people are saying, that she was running away?"

Rowland got up and moved away from the table. "Look here, Ridgway, if she was, what difference does it make? Let us try to get through this without defaming her."

Caynnes gave a sudden angry laugh. "Hush it up for *her* sake?" he said. "Don't you mean for your own?"

Rowland turned and looked straight at him. "Are you accusing me of killing Caroline?" he demanded. His voice was dead level and emotionless.

Until he said that, a suspicion that had hovered at the back of Louie's mind all the evening had not taken recognisable shape. Now it did. She saw in imagination Rowland jumping up on to the phaeton, as he had when he caught Adrian out of it, Caroline resisting him and being thrown out—accidentally, Louie hoped—as a result. She could easily believe that Caroline had refused to return, had defied Rowland, defied him once too often.

Caynnes Ridgway did not answer Rowland

directly. He said, "You believed she was running away to her lover in Bath. You must have found out what everyone else in the district has known for weeks, that she had taken up with that painter fellow. I warned her that you would never stand for that, but she would not listen—poor Caroline."

"Keep your over-heated imaginations to yourself, Ridgway," said Rowland, sharply. "You are entirely mistaken if you suppose I am the sort of man who thinks infidelity deserves death. Caroline was very impulsive; I hoped to bring her to her senses. That is all."

"I very much doubt if the Coroner will think it is all," said Caynnes Ridgway.

"Coroner?" said Rowland slowly. It was evident that he had not thought of that official before.

"Of course there will be an inquest," said Caynnes Ridgway.

The silence that suddenly fell seemed frightening to Louie. She was relieved when one of the servants came to say that the Vicar of Holstowe had arrived. Rowland went out into the hall, shook hands with the clergyman and took him into the library, closing the door behind them.

Caynnes Ridgway looked at Louie. "Poor Miss Louisa, what a shock this must have been for you," he said. "I am truly sorry if I have upset you still more by what has just been said. But still, it is what I feel, and I think I owe it to Caroline's memory to discover the truth of this affair. Shall we go into the drawing-room?"

A fire was lit in the grate there and they sat down, somewhat awkwardly, one each side of it.

"Tell me honestly, Miss Louisa, don't you think Dynham's manner very strange?" Caynnes said. "Unnaturally calm?"

"He is always more cool than most people," said Louie.

"But after such a catastrophe! And on the day when he found out she was running away from him to a red-headed dauber of paint? I heard from the servants there was a letter from Bath—a love letter from Raine, I suppose, and he read it."

"Oh no, it was addressed to Cousin Rowland," said Louie. "I suppose it must have been from Mr. Raine's wife, warning him about what Caroline planned. It came after she left."

Vividly she remembered Rowland's grim absorption in the letter.

"Ah," said Caynnes Ridgway thoughtfully. "I wish we could get hold of that letter, but I suppose he destroyed it."

As he spoke, Louie remembered that Rowland had gone to the little study that opened out of this very room, with the letter in his hand, to put it away in his bureau, she had presumed. But somehow she felt reluctant to tell this to Mr. Ridgway. If Rowland was unnaturally calm about Caroline's sudden death, Ridgway seemed to her unnaturally determined to treat it as murder. Perhaps his feeling for his half-sister, which she knew was genuine, led him thus to concentrate on retribution for the man he believed had killed her, but it frightened Louie.

He was still talking about the letter and its effect.

"It must have been that letter which sent Dynham off in a rage across the moor. I don't say he went intending to kill her but I am nearly certain that is what happened. The letter would be convincing evidence for the motive."

The butler came in and asked Mr. Ridgway to step across to the library: Colonel Dynham wished to consult him on the funeral arrangements.

As soon as Caynnes Ridgway had gone Louie jumped up and, as if drawn by a magnet, went through into the study room. There stood the bureau and she tried the top, but it was locked, as usual. That was a relief. But then she noticed a newspaper lying folded on the top, below the mirror which was screwed to the wall, and Louie saw a double edge of paper sticking out from underneath. She lifted the newspaper and saw the two sheets of the letter from Bath, still folded one inside the other. Rowland must have left them there; perhaps he could not find the key to his desk, though it was unlike him not to have his keys about him.

"Oh, suppose Mr. Ridgway had found it?" Louie whispered to herself. And then it occurred to her that the letter might not be as incriminating as he had imagined. With a feeling of guilt she opened the sheets and found herself staring at Caroline's rapid scrawling writing.

Peter, dearest love, I cannot stand this life without you. Life! I cannot call it life, it is death to me—a living death. They say a woman loves her children more than anything on earth but it is not so with me. I must have a life of my own. I cannot live with Dynham. He despises me and I detest him. With you, Peter, life will begin again, I shall live, I shall be happy. I will come to Bath and put up at the White Hart. Come there to enquire for me, but you must be ready to leave at once. I hope we may get a ship for America—that is the land of freedom. I shall bring my jewels so that we shall have money to start with and you will win fame with your painting, I am sure of it. We shall have a new life in the new world, Peter, our dream will come true.

That was not all there was in the letter but Louie heard steps in the hall and imagined it to be Ridgway returning. Panic stricken, horrified at what she had read, which seemed to incriminate both Caroline and Rowland in different ways, Louie looked wildly for somewhere to hide the letter and then pushed it behind the wall mirror, shoving with trembling fingers and giving a last hasty poke with a paper knife.

Then, her heart beating hard, she went back into the drawing-room, just as the further door opened. But it was only the butler who entered, to ask if she had any more orders that evening.

Now that Caroline was dead, she was regarded as the mistress of the household.

After she had sent the man away Louie sank down on a chair by the fire, unable to think coherently. But Mrs. Raine must have discovered that wild letter of Caroline's and sent it to Rowland Dynham. And so he had gone off to that lonely place on the moor to meet the wife who had deserted him and their children for the sake of this man she had known only for a few summer weeks. And when they met, what had happened? Her mind shied away from the pictures that kept forming against her will.

"It must have been an accident," she whispered, nervously tense. "He would never intend to kill her."

That was why she had hidden the letter, which seemed to contain such damning evidence, the motive for the crime. Rowland could not be guilty in the way Caynnes Ridgway imagined; no, that was impossible. But she could not forget the sight of his silent anger by the sundial when he had seen Caroline and Raine embracing up by the churchyard, nor the tales she had heard of his rare outbursts of rage. And he was strong, he was active.

"He could have done it," Louie thought, in an agony.

Then she began to wonder what would happen when Rowland went to look for the letter and could not find it. She went back to the study and tried to recover it from behind the wall mirror, with the paper knife, but could not. The paper slipped still further out of reach.

In a misery of fears and suspicions Louie returned to the drawing-room and sat there. Presently Caynnes Ridgway and the clergyman having both left, Rowland came back. Louie gazed at him, paralysed by the knowledge she had gained in a way she felt she could never confess to him.

Rowland, however, had not come to talk about Caroline, or the inquest. He asked Louie to excuse him if he now retired to bed. "I confess I am dead tired," he said. "And you must be too. My poor little Cousin Louie, this has been a shocking day for you. Do you think you should take a sleeping draught? Mrs. Heard makes up a very good one."

But somehow Louie shrank from the idea of a draught, and spent a restless night in consequence. She had hardly as yet fully realised the death of her cousin and now she was possessed with the fear that Rowland was somehow responsible for it and that the inquest would end with his arrest on a charge of murder.

Perhaps fortunately the children took up most of her attention the next day and she saw little of Rowland, who was seeing medical men, undertakers and lawyers. In the evening, however, he remarked suddenly, "It is a curious thing but I thought I had put that letter from Bath away in my desk. I cannot find it. I intended to destroy it, but as long as Ridgway does not get his hands on it, loss is as good as destruction."

Inwardly trembling Louie asked, "Would it tell against you, if it were produced at the inquest?"

"Against me? No, why should it?" he answered. "But I do not want Caroline's intimate affairs broadcast to the world. As it is, the inquest will make talk enough."

Louie thought she need not confess what she had done; no one would find the letter behind the wall mirror. She was afraid to tell Rowland she had read Caroline's letter to her lover and afraid to suggest that to many it would give the obvious motive for any violent action taken up there on the moor. Perhaps people might even think that Rowland had not known that Raine was his wife's lover before he received the letter. Although Louie knew he had been aware of it, she also knew that it was Caroline's proposed desertion of the children which would have enraged him, and not jealousy. It was for their sake that he had appealed to her to come and live under the same roof in London. She knew now why he had looked so grim, as he set off to meet Caroline.

The inquest was held on the second day and because old Mr. Ridgway, the chief lawyer in Monkhampton, was the family adviser, the Coroner was another member of the legal profession from the nearest Cornish town. He held his court in the hall of Rosewell Abbey, which was packed with local people, the poorer sort hanging about outside the house and in the lane. Tongues had been busy and many people besides Caynnes Ridgway were saying that Caroline Dynham's death had been no accident.

The jury of seven men viewed the body of Caroline Caynnes Dynham, laid out in a locked room on the ground floor. Louie had been into that room the day before and had gazed dumbly at the wax-like mask that had once been Caroline's face. The wound on her head was hidden in a cap. Rowland had taken his children in for a few moments and they had left bunches of flowers there.

Today the children were kept upstairs with Lizzie Jewell, but Louie came down. She knew that anyone might be questioned and anyone ask questions. She sat beside Rowland, who seemed quite collected and calm. His black mourning coat made him look even more stern, more formidable than usual. He appeared to be unaware that everyone was staring at him.

It was impossible to hide the fact that Mrs. Dynham had been running away; Hannah Colwill knew she had taken her jewels and that fact was easily elicited from her. Soon established, too, was the letter from Bath, from which Rowland had learned of his wife's intentions; he admitted this himself.

"I was advised that my wife was leaving for Bath and I went across the moor expressly to persuade her to return, as I have no doubt she would have done," he said firmly. "She always acted very much upon impulse."

"Where is this letter?" the Coroner asked.

"I have mislaid it," said Rowland.

"You mean you have destroyed it?"

"No, but it is of no consequence."

It was thought of sufficient consequence for a clerk to be sent to search his desk, but of course no letter was found. Most people assumed that whatever he said, Rowland had burnt it. Louie sat in guilty silence, yet relieved that its contents would not be made public.

As to the accident itself, the chief difficulty was the lack of witnesses. There was no one to check the truth of Rowland's own account; only a little girl who had later appeared on the scene, whom he had sent to Top Leys for help. She was a farm apprentice, not a child of the house. She was brought along by her mistress, Mrs. Cornish, a large determined woman. The child, a sturdy ten year old, looked scared to death.

"Now, Nancy Cottle, do you know what truth is?" the Coroner asked her.

"I should hope she does," said Mrs. Cornish. "For I teach all my boys and girls their catechism of a Sunday. I take care they know their duty."

"Nancy, what is truth?" the Coroner asked the child.

"Telling right," she answered nervously.

"Good. Now you tell me what happened the day before yesterday, up at Moor Cross."

"I was a-minding the sheep up to the moor and I looked over the hedge and I saw a poor lady with a hole in her head."

"And what did you do then?"

"The gentleman said, 'Coom yurr, my little maid.' " Nancy had a broad accent. "And 'e did send me to the farm, where I work, to bring the men."

"What was the gentleman doing?"

"A-standing in the road."

"And the lady, where was she?"

"A-laying on the grass."

"And was she dead or alive then?"

"I can't tell, sir. She laid still."

The Coroner indicated Rowland. "Do you know this gentleman?"

"Oh 'ess, 'tes Colonel Dynham of Brentland," said Nancy.

"Of Rosewell Abbey," corrected the Coroner.

"Top Leys is a Brentland farm," said Rowland. "She thinks of me in connexion with my old home, which I run for my nephew."

He seemed perfectly cool during the whole of the proceedings, too cool for most of the spectators, who thought such composure unnatural and even sinister.

Caroline had certainly been dead when the labourers arrived from the farm; according to the surgeon she had died from a severe blow on the head, probably but not certainly caused by falling. Rowland said that she had struck her head on a sharp ridge of rock sticking up in the lane, but it was possible that she had been hit with some unidentified instrument.

The jury decided, not unanimously but by a majority, that the death had been accidental. Rowland Dynham was not accused of murder or manslaughter, but many people thought him guilty of it. In that district his disagreement with his wife was well known and the episode when he had injured his cousin in a fight years ago was not forgotten. But, since there was no evidence, his story was officially accepted as the truth.

Lady Caynnes, in heavy mourning but otherwise not much changed from the formidable dame Louie remembered seeing at the wedding eight years ago, arrived on the day of the funeral with Hilary Tollington, with whom she had stayed the night at Woodford St. Petrock. While Hilary and Rowland, an ill-assorted pair, followed Caroline's coffin to the graveyard, she sat with Louie and the children in the drawing-room, reading the prayers of the burial service aloud. Mary Anne and Adrian were solemn but tearless, still unable to understand that Mamma would never wake up again, never come back.

Presently Lady Caynnes sent them upstairs to Lizzie and turned to Louie. "My poor child, I intend to take you home with me, as I am sure dear Caroline would have wished."

Her intention was quite a shock to Louie, still dazed by the complex events and motions of the last few days.

"Leave the children?" she said.

"For the time being I am afraid you must," said Lady Caynnes. "It would be improper for you to stay here with Colonel Dynham. I am not sure it would not even be dangerous for I am convinced that man is responsible for poor Caroline's death. I am determined to do something for her children, but that can only be settled in London. So, Louisa, will you pack your necessaries immediately and be ready to accompany me back to Woodford at once."

"I must ask Cousin Rowland," said Louie,

bewildered, still used to considering him as the head of the household.

"What must you ask Cousin Rowland?" he said, coming in from the hall at that moment.

When he heard Lady Caynnes's proposal he seemed disappointed. "I had thought Louie might stay with the children, when we go to London," he said. "I shall engage a respectable governess."

"Quite impossible, sir," pronounced Lady Caynnes. "Louisa must come with me."

So Louie found her life determined for her once more and went upstairs. Suddenly she was packing again, packing away this half year in the far corner of the west country, packing up in her mind the vivid experience of other people's loves and quarrels, putting away the memory of her cousin, so beautiful, so wild, whose body now lay in the green churchyard where not so long ago she had gone to meet her lover, careless and laughing.

Caroline was dead and Louie was still not quite eighteen.

II

THE CAYNNES HEIR

1

"HENRIETTA, I want you to come with me to call on Lady Caynnes," said Lady Hayford to her sister, one morning in October.

"Oh, must I?" replied Henrietta, who was lying on the sofa of her own sitting-room upstairs reading a French novel. "Lady Caynnes's conversation is so predictable, Tinna."

Lady Hayford had been christened Thomasina, but was always known as Tinna, which seemed to suit her lively, worldly-wise character. She was now within a year or two of thirty, but looked even more charming than when she had been the age which Henrietta was now. Tinna too was small and trim but whereas Henrietta's hair was dusky gold, hers was dark and smooth.

She laughed at Henrietta's naughtiness and said, "I want you to make friends with that poor little cousin of Caroline's, Louisa Pierce. Lady Caynnes has brought her up from Cornwall to live with her—a somewhat crushing charity!"

Henrietta, who had liked Louie, though finding her rather shy and serious, tossed her book aside and got up to accompany her sister. As they walked through the few streets which separated Lord Hayford's big London house from that of Lady Caynnes, she remarked, "I suppose, having rated Caroline heartily while she lived, Lady Caynnes has now translated her to perfection."

It was a shrewd guess, though even Lady Caynnes was not able to claim perfect virtue for her husband's niece.

"Poor Caroline was certainly imprudent," she said, when they were sitting in the large formal drawing-room. "And she was careless of idle tongues in a way that was unwise, but I am sure all this scandal about her running away to a lover must be untrue."

She could talk freely to Hilary Tollington's cousins, almost like his sisters, whom she had known for years. Not only was the scandal in everyone's mouth, hints of it had even appeared in the papers, in small paragraphs reporting the inquest; hints too that the gentleman most concerned was fortunate in that the accident to his wife had happened in so remote a place.

"But if she was not running away to a

lover, why should Colonel Dynham have killed her?" said Henrietta innocently, pretending to be unaware of Tinna's threatening glance.

Lady Caynnes, who had always considered Henrietta a forward young lady, stared at her with suspicion, uncertain of the drift of her question. Although she herself believed Rowland Dynham guilty, she was shocked to have his misdeed spoken of in what seemed to her a casual manner.

"Henrietta has taken it into her head to discount the reports," Tinna hastened to explain.

"Well, I always understood from Caroline that Colonel Dynham despised her," said Henrietta. "Quite without feeling, she said; cold-tempered and self-controlled, others say. He does not appear the type to commit a violent act in a fit of jealousy."

Lady Caynnes continued to observe her with disapproval, but could not resist further discussion of Colonel Dynham and his activities. He had come up to town at Michaelmas, as he had planned, established his children in the house he had leased in Westminster, under the care of Lizzie Jewell, and had engaged a governess to superintend their education.

"But I do not intend to allow poor Caroline's children to be brought up by that monster," said Lady Caynnes, with decision.

Henrietta had some difficulty in suppressing laughter at this epithet; her sister said doubtfully, "But will he hand them over to anyone else?"

"Of course he wishes to keep control of Adrian," said Lady Caynnes, "even though the property is now all held in trust. But I cannot tolerate the notion of that dear little boy, who has such a look of the family, left in the hands of a man who, at the least, is under such very grave suspicion."

"I suppose Hilary is their nearest Caynnes relation, besides yourself, Lady Caynnes," said Tinna. "But I do not see Colonel Dynham accepting Hilary as a guardian for his children."

"I intend them to live with me," said Lady Caynnes. "Dear Louisa will assist me with them."

Louie, who had been sitting dumbly listening, looked up in surprise. "But Lady Hayford is right," she said. "He will never give up his children."

"A way must be found," said Lady Caynnes, with emphasis, "to make him do what must be done, for their advantage."

The conversation began to repeat itself and presently Henrietta became bored and suggested that Louie might like to take a walk in the park with her.

"An excellent plan," said Lady Caynnes, "and you could take my poor pug dog—tell James to accompany you."

Louie had already taken a dislike to the fat snuffling pug, to whose comfort she was forced to minister daily, but at least if James came, she would not have to lead it. James was a footman of mature years and stately gait, suited to the dog's, and the two girls walked quickly ahead.

It was a fine autumn day and they walked towards the water in St. James's Park where, though the ground was rather uneven, people were stopping on the paths to look at the ducks and other birds, especially at the places where there were railings, first put up years ago when some sedan-chair men had walked into the water in the mist and been drowned.

Among the frieze of strollers by the Ornamental Water, Louie suddenly saw two small familiar figures: Adrian bowling a hoop and Mary Anne solemnly feeding ducks.

"Why, there are the children—the Dynham children," she said. She had not seen them since they had arrived in town. "I suppose that is the governess. She looks somewhat severe."

A tall upright lady was watching attentively over her charges. They had not seen the two girls making their way down from the Mall, among the crowd of strollers.

A few moments later they both saw Rowland Dynham below them on the slope, walking with long strides across the grass and looking towards the children.

"Why, it's the monster himself!" exclaimed Henrietta, in her light clear voice.

"Oh, he will hear you," murmured Louie.

It was quite plain that he had heard, for he instantly turned his head; when he saw who had spoken he changed direction and came up to them.

"Cousin Louie, how pleasant to see you again," he said. "Good morning, Miss Tollington. You have come to observe the fauna, I take it? Animal or human?"

Not at all abashed Henrietta replied, "Both" and smiled sweetly.

Then the children came running up to greet Louie.

"Why didn't you come and see us?" Mary Anne demanded. "Nobody comes to see us. Even Polly Taylor wasn't allowed to come to tea."

Rowland frowned. "Who would not allow her?"

"Her mamma," said Mary Anne sadly. "The lady who did not answer you on Sunday, when we came out of church."

It was clear enough that the scandal about Colonel Dynham was even affecting his children; respectable people refused acquaintance with a man reputed to have killed his wife in a violent quarrel.

The governess came up and he introduced her as Miss Curtis. "She is trying to knock some learning into these scatterbrains—you will sympathise with her difficulties, Louie."

"Oh, Papa, I am not a scatterbrain," said Mary Anne, hanging on to his hand.

"No, it is Adrian who scatters his brains," said Rowland, ruffling up the boy's curls with his other hand. "You are my little pudding-head, Mary Anne, aren't you?"

Miss Curtis gave a discreet smile. Elderly, upright and plain, it was evident, Henrietta thought, that Colonel Dynham was determined not to employ a marriageable governess. She was inclined to think that he intended to marry Louisa; he spoke to her as gently as he did to Mary Anne, and enquired after her experiences in Caynnes House with kindness.

"I hope that Lady Caynnes will allow you to visit us," he said. "The children miss you very much."

"See me bowl my hoop, Papa!" Adrian shouted. "Look, Louie!"

Off he went, a flying graceful figure.

"Adrian fancies himself the hoop champion of England," said his father, with a smile. "Are you staying with your sister, Miss Tollington? I am to see Lord Hayford at the office before dinner, so I knew they were in town."

"Before dinner, Papa?" said Mary Anne dolefully. "Then you are not coming back with us now?"

"Not today," he answered. "But I shall see you at bedtime, so mind and make sure La Belle has her curlpapers in."

"Oh Papa, but you are much better at putting them in than I am," said Mary Anne anxiously.

Rowland looked down at her round puzzled

face with a smile tucking in the corners of his mouth.

"Heavens, Colonel Dynham, who would have imagined you in the role of hair-dresser?" said Henrietta. "I take it that La Belle is Marianne's doll."

"Yes—but we call her Mary Anne; I don't care for the French form," he said. He took out his watch. "I must go. I just came to tell you not to wait for me today, Miss Curtis."

"Oh Papa, but I want to show you my special duck," pleaded Mary Anne.

Rowland glanced at the crowd of ducks quacking on the water.

"How can you possibly tell one from another in this mélange, *my* special duck?" he asked.

"Because it swims *boppity*," said Mary Anne earnestly.

Rowland glanced up, smiling, and then took his leave of the two girls with a bow, and walked down to the water's edge with Mary Anne holding his hand and pointing out her lame duck with a plump pink finger.

When they went back into the drawing-room at Caynnes House Henrietta immediately announced, "Well, Tinna, we have just met the monster and I am sorry to tell you that I think him perfectly charming."

"Perverse girl!" cried her sister, laughing. "I knew she would affect to like Colonel Dynham if she met him, Lady Caynnes, just because she knows I distrust his character."

"I do not pronounce on his character," said Henrietta serenely. "His *looks* are enough for me."

"Wicked girl," said Tinna cheerfully. But she thought it wise to remove Henrietta before Lady Caynnes's evident disapproval found voice.

As it was, she could be heard pronouncing her verdict on Miss Tollington's character before the sisters were out of earshot. "A bold little flirt! The impudence of her praising Colonel Dynham's looks to *me*!"

Henrietta glanced, smiling, at her sister, amused that Lady Caynnes should take this as a personal insult. But Tinna shook her head at her and lectured her for pertness, on the way home.

Henrietta did not tell her sister that she had walked to St. James's Park because her cousin Hilary had told her that Dynham often went to meet his children there, while he was working at the Foreign Office.

Hilary Tollington had come to town with

Lady Caynnes and was staying with her, but as soon as his cousins arrived he spent a good deal of time in their house and it was Henrietta he took with him when he went to call on the banker Frederick Warstowe, his co-trustee for the Caynnes estate.

"I don't want dear Tinna, she is too managing," he said. "But use your intelligence, Miss Hen, and tell me what you think of the Warstowes afterwards."

"I don't think I've met Mrs. Warstowe since she was Judith Vyner and our tiresome neighbour at Hartleigh Court," said Henrietta. "She is far more managing than Tinna, Hilary, and never can forget that her grandfather was an Earl. Dear me, the nobility have a lot to answer for."

Hilary drove his cousin in his curricle, which he managed very well. Although he was lightly built, he was agile and cool-headed, a good driver and a good rider.

Judith Vyner's persistent attachment to her noble blood was no doubt increased by her having married, at the age of thirty, a mere banker of the middle class, though one of the wealthiest in London. She was now a few years over forty, a thin flat-chested woman with a piercing eye, who dressed in great

221

style. She was sitting in her drawing-room surrounded by her children, who were repeating their lessons to her. The eldest was a fine looking girl, her younger sister a snub-nosed romp and the boy, a handsome dark-haired eight year old, stood at her elbow.

A second boy leant against a chair opposite, rubbing one foot nervously against the other, so that his shoe suddenly came off. He had a mop of fairish tow-like hair flopping almost into his eyes, which peered out, a cloudy, puzzled blue, as he stared with his mouth open at pretty Henrietta.

Greetings had scarcely been exchanged before Mrs. Warstowe said to him in severe tones, "Miles! How many times must I tell you not to gape at people? It is very bad manners. You never see Edmund doing it."

"Sorry," mumbled the boy, ducking awkwardly. He was thin and bony so that his head, with its thick hair, seemed too big for his body.

"You should say 'I beg your pardon, ma'am,'" said Mrs. Warstowe sharply. "You do not recognise him, Miss Tollington, I expect. It is Miles Dynham, my husband's nephew."

"And the monster's nephew!" said

Henrietta and then laughed. "I really must not call him so, but it is Lady Caynnes's epithet and amused me because Colonel Dynham is such a conventional man, not at all monstrous."

"This is very shocking news we hear about him," said Mrs. Warstowe. "Though it does not altogether surprise me, since I know him, perhaps, better than you do, Miss Tollington."

"What is shocking news, Mamma?" immediately asked snub-nosed Charlotte.

"Never mind," said her mother and she sent the children out of the room. Her daughters curtsied and Edmund bowed very properly but Miles Dynham's attempt was awkward and he blundered clumsily against a small table as he turned to go.

"Miles! Dear me, that child is almost an idiot," said Mrs. Warstowe, with irritation.

Henrietta watched the little fellow's back as he walked to the door; she felt that he was used to hearing such criticisms of himself. He shuffled along, trying to get his heel into his shoe again without being noticed. At the door he turned back to look at her once more and she smiled at him. At once he smiled back. He had a big mouth with a wide full lip, like

Joscelin Dynham's; half-open it certainly made him look stupid but when he smiled it put meaning into his face. But how unlike his cousin Adrian, she thought, how unlike Rowland Dynham, his uncle.

Mrs. Warstowe said, when he had gone, "It is a pity Miles is such a sickly child for I should much dislike Colonel Dynham to have Brentland and the title. He is always trying to get hold of Miles, but we could not allow it when there was all that talk about your unfortunate cousin Caroline, Mr. Tollington. Now, of course, it is out of the question. Frederick tells me that Lady Caynnes even wishes to take charge of Colonel Dynham's own children. It would be quite the proper thing, considering that the boy is the Caynnes heir."

Hilary was indeed coming to consult Frederick Warstowe on this very subject, pushed into it by Lady Caynnes, for he had no desire to interfere in Rowland Dynham's affairs. Warstowe returned from the bank soon afterwards; he was a big red-faced man who looked more like a choleric country squire than a London man of business. It was his father who had built up the bank and, as Hilary had told Henrietta, his partners did most of the work. But Frederick Warstowe had, all the same, a shrewd understanding of the power of money and a great liking to control other people's. His delicate nephew Sir Miles Dynham had far more coming to him from his mother's side than his father's, and Frederick Warstowe controlled this as well as the Caynnes estate for Adrian's future benefit.

"Bad business this about poor Caroline," he said perfunctorily, for he had never liked her. "But Dynham's behaviour puts him into our hands at last."

"There's nothing to prove he caused Caroline's death," said Hilary. "And as far as I can see, there never will be."

"No, but the suspicion is strong enough to put him under a cloud, perhaps for life," said Frederick Warstowe, with evident satisfaction. "Caynnes Ridgway is not a fellow one can altogether respect but he's no fool and it's his tale that has gone round the clubs. I'm told a great many people are cutting Dynham and he does not attempt to go out into society."

"In that case, he may be glad enough to get away from the country," said Hilary, and outlined a plan which his cousin Tinna and

Lady Caynnes had laid, between them. Lord Hayford was to get Rowland Dynham sent abroad on some mission, and Lady Caynnes was to take charge of his children. "Dynham's an excellent French-speaker—did his military training in France," said Hilary. "I daresay a trip to Vienna would suit him."

"It won't suit him to leave his children with Lady Caynnes," Henrietta observed, with conviction.

"They will have a good time with Aunt Caynnes," protested Hilary. "Especially as that nice little Louie is there—good for her, too, to have them. Otherwise she's in danger of being crushed into mere companionship."

Although Hilary did not see how the children could be permanently removed from their father's care, that was what Lady Caynnes wanted, and Mr. Warstowe agreed with her that it was desirable. "I have an idea how to manage it," he said. "Leave it to me, Tollington."

When they left, Henrietta remarked that she did not see how such a thing could be done, and added that she disliked what appeared to be a conspiracy against Colonel Dynham.

But Hilary maintained that the arrangement was all to the good for everyone concerned, until the scandal had blown over at any rate. He accepted the charge of guardianship himself, though the children were to live with Lady Caynnes. And somewhat to Henrietta's surprise Rowland Dynham agreed, though after some hesitation. Lord Hayford had promoted his wife's plan and got him the special mission to Vienna, which was of indefinite duration. Although Austria was no longer at war with France, England was still in arms, and as his journey necessarily exposed him to some danger, Rowland decided to accept Lady Caynnes's offer, and sign the document giving temporary guardianship to her and to Hilary Tollington. As to their living at Caynnes House, he was materially swayed by Louie's presence there, as he told her when he arrived to sign the documents.

Henrietta was in the drawing-room and watched as Rowland, standing in the window with Louie, told her warmly that he was happy his children should be under her care.

"The excellent Miss Curtis is a little old, and Lizzie Jewell not old enough, or sensible enough, to have sole charge," he said. "Both will be here but you, Louie, you will care for them, love them for me, will you not?"

"Of course I will, Cousin Rowland."

Louie had a soft voice but Henrietta heard the slight tremble in it. "She's in love with him, poor thing," she thought.

Then Colonel Dynham was called into the library to sign the legal documents, which he did without fuss, remarking that his brother Joscelin would hardly make a suitable guardian, though he glanced at Hilary Tollington with some contempt as if he did not think much of him either. But he signed.

He did not stay long in Caynnes House but left shortly afterwards, on foot, walking briskly away, holding down his hat against the wind.

Hilary watched from the window, hands in pockets.

"He doesn't care as much about the children as you thought, Henrietta," he remarked. "He hasn't an ounce of feeling in him."

Henrietta saw Louie look round, a denial in her eyes, though she was too shy to speak it.

Not long afterwards the children were removed to Caynnes House. Rowland found a tenant for his own house and prepared to

228

leave England. He came for a final farewell the evening he was to sail, when the children were in bed—or at least Mary Anne was in bed, while Adrian was scampering about in his nightshirt, evading Lizzie Jewell's attempts to brush his hair.

"Coom yurr, Master Adrian, you pesky little toad!" cried Lizzie, waving the brush, while Adrian laughed and hopped about and made faces at her.

Louie had just come in to read to them when Rowland appeared at the nursery door in his outdoor coat and carrying his hat. He had evaded the drawing-room and Lady Caynnes, coming straight up the stairs to the top of the house. He threw his hat on a chair, caught Adrian by the tail of his nightshirt and tossed him up in the air.

The little boy shrieked in joyful excitement. "Again, Papa!" he demanded. "Right up to the ceiling!"

Rowland, laughing, threw him up again and caught him, and then put him in his crib, rosy and bright-eyed, and sat down next to him, on a wooden chair.

"Well, Master Adrian, you seem happy enough here," he said.

"Papa, this is the biggest house I ever did

see," cried Adrian. "And do you know what? It's *mine!*"

"Not unless Lady Caynnes gives it to you, when you are grown up," said his father.

"But she's going to, she said so. And I shall be Lord Caynnes one day. Aunt told me."

Adrian bounced excitedly on his bed. He was already a favourite with his great-aunt Caynnes.

"You are Adrian Dynham," said his father. "There's no lordship in question."

"Adrian *Caynnes* Dynham," said the child, not in the least overawed.

"Goodnight, Lord Caynnes," said Rowland with a smile, and he went over to Mary Anne.

The little girl was inclined to turn tearful. "Oh Papa, must you go and talk to the Emperor in Vienna? And why can't we stay in our own house? I don't want to be here."

"But think what an enlightening experience it must be for La Belle," he said, patting the doll's woolly head where it lay on the pillow. "She will be a *grande dame* by the time I come back."

"But Papa, La Belle is a *grande dame*

230

already," said Mary Anne seriously. "She's a princess, you know, and she can't be grander than that."

"Dear me, so she is," said Rowland. "Profound apologies to Her Highness! And now, both of you get ready for Cousin Louie's story book, for I must go. The boat sails tonight from London Bridge."

Mary Anne clung to him. "Oh, Papa, you're always going away!" she cried piteously.

"My darling, I will come back as soon as I can," he said, kissing her again and settling her down in bed.

Louie went out on to the landing with him and he stood there for a moment in the half dark, looking back into the warm candle-lit nursery. She had a strong impression of his reluctance to leave his children, his intense affection for them.

But he only said, at last, "You will write, Louie? Your letters can go in the bag—the diplomatic bag."

"Of course I will," said Louie.

"Bless you for a good cousin," he said, pressing her hand, and then hurried away down the shadowy stairs.

Standing there, Louie presently heard the street door close. He had not attempted to say

231

farewell to Lady Caynnes, or to anyone but her, besides the children. After a moment she went back to read to them.

2

HENRIETTA certainly tried to make a friend of Louie, but they were too unlike to become intimate. Henrietta indeed had never been one for confidences; she was a self-contained person who liked a wide circle of friends. Louie was shy, youthful even for her age, and was inclined to give her heart only to a few near people. She now became very fond of Caroline's two children and took a great interest in their doings and sayings. Henrietta called Adrian a charming little rascal but was more interested in Miles Dynham, imprisoned, as she felt, in the uncongenial Warstowe household. She exerted herself to bring him into contact with his Dynham cousins, which was not difficult, since Mrs. Warstowe had no objection to his going often to Caynnes House, only lecturing him so sternly on his manners beforehand as to fill him with apprehension, so that he blundered more clumsily than ever.

On being presented to Lady Caynnes he contrived to send an elegant bowl flying with a jerk of his elbow; it broke in half as it hit the floor and he was never allowed to forget it.

"That boy is a perfect booby," pronounced Lady Caynnes.

However, once upstairs with the two young ladies and his cousins, Miles became happier. Mary Anne, shy herself, got on well with him, and Adrian, though he was inclined to show off and laugh at a boy he could beat at everything although he was over a year younger, was sunny tempered by nature and liked almost anyone not actively unpleasant towards him.

Miles adored Henrietta, not merely for her kindness but because, as he once solemnly told her, she was the prettiest lady he knew.

"Oh Miles, my dear, you flatter me!" cried Henrietta, amused, but pleased nevertheless at the odd little boy's admiration. She knew she was no beauty, but was quite content with her own kind of prettiness; content too with her many admirers older than Miles, so long as they did not become so infatuated as to propose marriage, which several had done in the last few years. She always refused them.

"It is all very well dancing and amusing oneself with people," she said to Louie once, "but to choose to spend the rest of one's life with one man—that is something quite different."

Louie was amazed at Henrietta's self-possession. She could not imagine what it would be like to have a man in love with her, still less to refuse him. But she approved Henrietta's seriousness about marriage, contrasting it in her mind with Caroline's frequent hymns to the all-importance of love. She often thought about Caroline, but of the manner of her death she tried not to think, though in Lady Caynnes's house she could not escape the continual talk of Rowland Dynham's probable guilt and his unsuitability to bring up his own children. And all the time she was receiving his letters, for herself and the children, and replying to them, enclosing Mary Anne's laborious epistles and the occasional scribbly picture by Adrian.

Once, in the winter months at the beginning of the year 1798, Louie was confined to bed with a severe cold and Henrietta undertook to write the covering letter.

My dear Sir,

You will no doubt be surprised to receive this from a comparative stranger, but I assure

235

you Louisa is not in a decline, but simply laid up with a cold, and we must catch the bag, or you will miss hearing from Mary Anne the important news that she has been given a kitten and that La Belle went for a ride on it, much to kitty's mystification.

You need not reply to me, since Louie will certainly be better by the time your letter comes.

Some weeks later she found Louie laughing over Rowland's reply.

My dear Louie (he wrote in his regular clear hand),

Miss Tollington orders me not to reply to her, so I hope you will be kind enough to thank her for her goodness, not to say her fearlessness, in addressing a letter to a Monster, even though it is lurking so many miles away.

Louie with her sudden wide smile, glanced at Henrietta and said, "So you see he *did* hear you call him a monster, that day in the park."

"Does he say any more to me?" Henrietta asked and Louie showed her the letter, which was indeed written as much to her as to Louie. They read it together.

The news of Mademoiselle La Belle's audacious ride (wrote Rowland), has not been well received by an Austrian cat which has chosen my room as the one most suited to its comfort. It considers that feline rights have been infringed by the *émigrée Princesse du Bois Dormant*, since it is well known that the race of Cats has never been subject to any, and are not only born equal, but unlike the inferior race of Men, have nowhere been in chains.

Henrietta was amused and composed a diplomatic reply from the doll. Mary Anne was most interested in the Austrian cat.

"Cats always do like Papa," she said. "We had one when we lived in London which always jumped on his knee when he sat down, and it annoyed him if he was wearing his best breeches."

She spoke of "when we lived in London" as if it were a different place; she was referring to the time when Caroline was alive, before Rowland had given up their house and sent her down to Rosewell with the children.

237

Henrietta recalled the gossip she had heard then. "He was very much laughed at and Caroline was pitied," she said to Louie, when the children were not there. "Yet Caroline certainly behaved very carelessly. Not that I blame her as much as Caynnes Ridgway, for it was he who introduced her to that fashionable fast set, who live for pleasure and take no account of the reckoning."

Louie was willing enough to blame Caynnes Ridgway, for since Caroline's death he had made himself acceptable to Lady Caynnes, managing various small pieces of business expeditiously for her, flattering her and pleasing her by praising Adrian to the skies. He brought presents for Adrian too, applauded his sallies and frequently said he did not see why the King should not revive the barony for the boy when he grew up. And he lost no opportunity to increase Lady Caynnes's suspicion of Rowland Dynham.

In spite of Louie's lurking fear that Rowland might have been responsible for Caroline's violent death, she did not waver in her conviction that he loved his children. The image of him was strong in her mind, formidable, perhaps, but also fascinating. In London she saw no man she thought his equal.

And now she saw many, for Henrietta was determined to bring her more into society. She was invited to evening parties at Lady Hayford's, and went with Henrietta and Hilary Tollington to exhibitions and to the theatre. Hilary enjoyed escorting them.

"I like to have *two* young ladies the right size," he once said, taking an arm of each, "the dark and the fair beauties!"

Not tall himself, he liked girls to be small.

He was so like Henrietta that Louie thought of him at first as her brother and found him the easier to converse with—or to listen to, for he certainly liked talking himself. She thought he had more feeling than Henrietta, especially when she discovered that he was still unhappy on account of the broken engagement which he had treated so lightly last year at Rosewell.

She found it out at a ball in the spring, when she saw him bow to a pretty girl who gave him a laughing reply and turned away on the arm of a handsome officer. Hilary came over to Louie with an unusually melancholy face.

"What is the matter, Mr. Tollington? You look sad," she said with sympathy.

"That is Julia Whichcote—Mrs. Grant,

now," said Hilary, sitting down by Louie. "That is Captain Grant, with her. She was laughing at me."

"Oh no, it would be too ill-mannered," said Louie. "Too unkind."

"She *is* unkind," said Hilary, turning his hazel eyes, usually so bright and teasing but now overclouded, towards her. "And I know now that she never did care twopence for me; she thought she might as well have me as any, till Grant stepped in. You see the sort he is—women like that kind of fellow—looks masterful and commanding but actually can't do anything if it isn't laid down in the book of rules. A bit like Rowland Dynham."

Louie did not think Captain Grant at all like Rowland Dynham, though he too was tall and good looking, in contrast to Hilary Tollington. She realised that the physical presence of such men made him feel inferior and that he resented it, since in other ways he felt himself quite their equal. His pride as well as his heart had been hurt when his betrothed left him for Grant.

Louie watched Julia Grant dancing with another officer and she presently observed, "I don't think you should grieve too much, Mr. Tollington. I think she is going to cause Captain Grant as many heartaches as she would have caused you, had she been your wife."

The fact that Hilary was obviously cheered by this judgment suggested to Louie that he would not prove inconsolable, even though he had once been quite in love with the heartless Julia. Discussing it later with Henrietta, she found her of the same opinion.

"Julia Whichcote was a minx—there's no other word for it," said Henrietta. "But Hilary would never believe it—people are besotted when they are in love. I never mean to be, myself."

"Never in love?" said Louie, feeling the prospect of life without love was uninviting.

"No," said Henrietta firmly. "I shall love my husband, of course, if I marry. Anything further is more trouble than it is worth. Almost any other amusement is more enjoyable, to judge by other people's experiences."

It was this sort of conversation which made Louie feel she understood Hilary better than Henrietta. He was more vulnerable than his gay little cousin.

"How can someone make a *pretence* of love?" he said, at another ball where he was again forced to see Julia dancing and carefree.

241

"She *seemed* content, till the last moment. But she was just acting a part."

At the reference to acting, Louie's mind immediately reverted to Caroline. Yet Caroline's dramatising was the reverse of Julia's, it was not at all a pretence, and yet there was something unreal about it. What could be more unreal than to cast Peter Raine in the rôle of genius, which he had never imagined himself to be, and to propose to roam the world with him, as if youth and love were immortal and immune to the necessities of human life? In this London ballroom, surrounded by the people among whom Caroline had moved before she had been banished to Cornwall, the full incongruity of her intentions came home to Louie. These people, who were for ever gossiping of each other's love affairs, would have laughed at Caroline's stepping outside the bounds of convention. Julia might get away with elopement because she had married her lover and he was one of her set; but for Caroline to abandon husband and children for a red-headed painter would have provoked mockery more cruel than the jilted Hilary had to endure, and total ostracism.

She became aware that Hilary was watching

242

her. "What are you thinking of, Miss Louie?" he asked, with quiet interest.

"Of Caroline," said Louie with a sigh.

"She haunts you, Louie," said Hilary. "But did you really like her?"

"Like—I don't know," said Louie. It seemed the wrong word. "Do you think she ever loved Cousin Rowland? When she married him, I mean."

"I am not the right person to ask, for I don't think him very lovable," said Hilary with a smile. "I think he married for position and property and she—well, she may have been taken with his looks, as Julia with Grant."

"I am sure she wanted him to love her but that is not the same thing," said Louie, surprising Hilary, so that he did not answer.

"I can't help feeling that Caroline wanted everyone to adore her," Louie went on. "Perhaps she did not realise it. She made Peter Raine do what she wanted but she could not make Rowland—that's why she fought him so, I am sure of it."

"You may well be right," said Hilary, still astonished that little Louie should show so much perception. "But she met her match in Dynham. *He* was going to make everyone do what *he* wanted—he's always been like that. Cary Vyner used to chant at him: 'Rowland is always right!' when they were boys—daring Olympus, I thought it, for Rowland was a couple of years older. I believe he did go for Cary once and knocked him about so badly they had to get the surgeon."

And then both of them recalled another time when Rowland might have given way to violent passion, and fell silent.

"Forget the past and come and dance with me," said Hilary, rising and offering her his hand, with a smile.

Louie liked dancing with Hilary; she had done it often, ever since he had once come upon Henrietta teaching her steps and figures and had insisted on joining in. Miss Curtis had played the tunes for them, sitting upright at the pianoforte but plainly enjoying the scene.

Louie had soon discovered that Miss Curtis, though the model of propriety, was a well-read woman who had travelled widely; her attainments put her above teaching such small children as Adrian and Mary Anne, but she had taken the job so as to be near a married sister who was in poor health.

"Colonel Dynham was most kind about my

taking time to see her," she had told Louie. Although she had only lived about a month in his household, Miss Curtis had a firm respect for her employer, and that in spite of the gossip, with which she was soon conversant. It led to some skirmishes with Lady Caynnes, who was not at all pleased to be informed of some proposed treat for Adrian, that "The Colonel would not have wished it."

Louie thought Miss Curtis's judgment better than Lady Caynnes's and her conversation far more interesting. So she was quite content to be sent off for the summer into the country with the governess and the children, while Lady Caynnes visited friends. The Hayfords went visiting too and so did Henrietta; Hilary Tollington went down to Woodford St. Petrock.

Lady Caynnes did not send the children to Rosewell but to her own country house in Wiltshire, which she proposed to leave to Adrian, as well as the house in Mayfair. Judith Warstowe considered this unfair; her husband was Lady Caynnes's own nephew, whereas Adrian was simply a relation by marriage.

"I do think she might remember Edmund," she had once said in Louie's hearing. "But Adrian is the child of good fortune. he is to have everything."

Adrian was in a fair way to getting spoilt in London but his country holiday, when he was kept in order by Miss Curtis, did him good. Erlington Hall was a fine Palladian mansion, bought years ago with Lady Caynnes's dowry; the great rooms were shut and the children and their attendants lived comfortably in one corner of the building, with the gardens and park to roam in, ponies to ride and everything they could want. Louie was still amazed at this rich life and often compared the fate of these two children with her friends in Bristol or with the children of Miss Curtis's sister, mewed up in a narrow London house.

"As these would be, if they depended only on their father," observed Miss Curtis one summer day, as they sat outside on the lawn, supervising a dolls' tea party and trying to prevent Adrian from drinking up all the tiny cups of sugared milk before Mary Anne had served her silent guests with slices of currant bun.

It reminded Louie of Lady Caynnes's view of Rowland's marriage, made out of ambition, carrying off an heiress and her fortune when he was a penniless Captain of twenty-two; and her mind went back to the memory of the pair of them, handsome and proud, in the garden at Rosewell, before the wedding. And she sighed, thinking of Caroline, who seemed to have been given all the gifts of the gods, and yet had never found contentment.

"I hope it will not be so for Adrian," she thought, watching the charming lively child as he played on the green grass, laughing in his delight.

The time in Wiltshire was a healing time, when Louie began to recover from the shattering events of last summer. Rowland's letters continued to arrive; the date of his return was uncertain, so that Mary Anne could happily anticipate the day "when we go back to live with Papa," and hope it would be soon. Adrian, Louie felt, was happy enough without his father, enjoying his position as heir to all he surveyed.

3

WHEN they returned to London in the autumn Lady Caynnes was at Tunbridge Wells, accompanying an old friend who was taking the cure. As Lord Hayford was back in town early on account of his work, Tinna invited the children to stay with them and so Caynnes House was not opened and Louie settled into yet another big household. This one she already knew and though Lady Caynnes had remarked that Henrietta Tollington seemed determined to make a fine lady out of Louisa, hinting that she was wanted only as a foil to Miss Tollington's liveliness, Louie felt more like a member of the family at the Hayfords' house than she did in Lady Caynnes's, where she was always made to feel her dependence. It turned out a gay October for Louie.

Lord Hayford, a grey-haired courtly man, had a grown-up family by his first wife and liked a house full of people—his last daughter had married very young the year before. Tinna, who had no children of her own, enjoyed entertaining, loved political gossip and party manoeuvres and found London, even when most of society was out of it, much more to her taste than the country.

"I think Tinna married Hayford just to be in the midst of things," Henrietta told Louie one afternoon, chatting by the fire in her sitting-room upstairs. "He is a nice old fellow, though he will say his say, however many times one has heard it before." She sewed in the eye of a daisy on her embroidery and then remarked, "Colonel Dynham's cousin Cary Vyner was in love with Tinna but Papa disapproved his revolutionary opinions and so she refused him. And yet she is always being annoyed at me for refusing young men who profess themselves in love with me. How inconsistent people are!"

Her mind was preoccupied with the problem for in the summer she had collected another admirer; he was Harry Chervill, Lord Stanbourne, son and heir of the Duke of Wiltshire. He had not yet celebrated his twenty-first birthday and Henrietta was his senior by a few months. She felt his senior by more than days, for Lord Stanbourne was youthful by nature as well as in looks, a cheeful young man with no pretensions to cleverness, no ambition, a great love of hunting and shooting and a fund of simple good humour. His devotion to Henrietta was such that he had actually left the country in October so as to see her in town, where he was like a fish out of water.

"Poor Stanbourne, I do wish he would go back to his horses," Henrietta said more than once, calling down remonstrance from her sister.

"Henrietta, I beg you will not behave ill to Lord Stanbourne. He is a very good-hearted young man, such as one would hardly expect in Lord Walter's nephew."

"All the Chervills are good *except* Lord Walter," observed Henrietta. "You know how terribly good and dull Stanbourne's sisters are, Tinna. I thought I should die of boredom, staying at the castle."

Louie, who had been in Wiltshire all the summer, was puzzled because the Duke of Wiltshire's seat was in quite a different county. The Hayfords had taken Henrietta there and Tinna was congratulating herself already upon having made the ideal match for her sister. Henrietta to be Duchess of Wiltshire one day, very well off and married to such a nice young man as Stanbourne: it seemed to her perfection. And here was Henrietta complaining of Stanbourne's lover-like following of her to London, and sighing that he and his family bored her sadly.

"You don't have to marry his sisters," said Tinna briskly.

"I'm sure I should, for I can't conceive their marrying for years," Henrietta replied, naughtily.

She relied on her belief that the Duke would not consider her a suitable match for his heir, though she was well-endowed and the Tollingtons an old and respectable family. But Tinna had noticed that the Duke had been much taken himself by little Miss Henrietta and she did not anticipate insuperable difficulties.

Stanbourne, though he had no understanding of music, was one of the guests at a musical evening Tinna gave to entertain some foreign diplomatists—music was always a help when French conversation gave out. At dinner Henrietta chattered in French, laughing at her own mistakes, while Lord Stanbourne blushed and could hardly bring out a word. Louie, sitting equally dumb, sympathised with him. He was a sturdy, fair young man with innocent blue eyes.

After dinner more guests assembled for the evening, but at the first group of songs, Henrietta took Louie's arm and they slipped out into the hall. They had promised to take the children some of the sweets made of almond paste and coloured to resemble fruits, which had greatly taken Mary Anne's fancy when she had seen them on the dish; she coveted them for her dolls' house dinner table.

Henrietta ran down the passage to the pantries and was soon making Whitbread, the butler, laugh with her childish demands.

"I declare, Miss Henrietta, you want them yourself!" he teased her, but gave her the plate, which she carried up the stairs.

The girls found the children on the landing, peering over the bannisters. Mary Anne was in her nightgown, rosy-faced and smelling softly of soap. Adrian, as usual, had escaped from Lizzie Jewell half undressed; he was still in his trousers and shirt but barefoot, with his hair in a tousle and eyes bright with mischief.

As they were given their promised delicacies the front door bell rang and they all looked down, watching Whitbread cross the hall with stately tread.

"Too late for a guest, surely?" said Louie, as the strains of a flute quartet by Mozart sounded from the drawing-room.

It was windy and wet outside and when Whitbread opened the door a gust blew dead leaves in from the dark night, rasping over the polished floor. They all saw a tall figure in a long black travelling coat step over the threshold, taking off his hat.

Mary Anne gave a shriek. "Papa! It's Papa!"

She ran down the stairs and across the hall into his arms before the others had quite realised that it was indeed Rowland Dynham. Adrian, staring, said slowly, "Is that really my father?"

"Yes, of course; come down and greet him," said Henrietta.

Rowland set Mary Anne on her feet and came towards them, seeing Henrietta on the stairs in her bright evening gown, holding Adrian by the hand, and Louie, surprised and smiling, behind them.

He explained that he had got a boat sooner than he expected, had gone to Caynnes House, heard his children were at the Hayfords' and came on at once.

"My letter probably travelled on the same

boat and will arrive tomorrow," he said.

Louie stood on the stairs looking down at him, feeling a difference but uncertain what it was. That sharp cut profile was the same, that upright arrogant carriage. Perhaps he was less taut and tense; he was certainly smiling as he spoke to Henrietta. Then it occurred to Louie that perhaps it was not Rowland who had changed in the intervening year, but herself. She was nineteen, and no longer quite the simple girl she had been at Rosewell.

Adrian was staring at his father, standing about three steps from the bottom of the flight, and standing very straight, with an expression that was more watchful than welcoming.

"Well, Adrian?" said Rowland, looking down at him.

"How do you do, father?" said Adrian in a reserved tone, and held out his hand.

Rowland shook it solemnly. "You are more grown than Mary Anne," he said. "You are not a baby any more."

"I wasn't a baby when you went away," said Adrian, offended. "And now I'm seven—I'm seven and nearly a quarter."

"I seem to remember writing on the occasion of your birthday," said Rowland, with his tucked-in smile.

But Louie felt he missed the child's simple demand to be tossed up to the ceiling by his tall father. Adrian was perhaps too old for that now, but not to have run to him like Mary Anne. Louie saw that his son's cool reception took some of the pleasure out of Rowland's homecoming, in spite of his ever-loving little girl hanging on his arm, smiling with happiness, so that her round cheeks looked like two pink peaches.

Whitbread had informed Lady Hayford of Colonel Dynham's arrival and presently she came into the hall and invited him to stay the night. But he refused, saying he had already left his luggage at an hotel.

"I would not put you to such inconvenience," he said. "But I have a letter which I should like to deliver straight away to Lord Hayford."

Hayford came out of the drawing-room and shook him by the hand, while Tinna chased the children upstairs. "Barefoot in the hall! You naughty things," she said.

Lord Hayford took Rowland into the library, Tinna marshalled Henrietta back to the side of Lord Stanbourne, and Louie ran upstairs to see that Lizzie Jewell had the children under control. On the upper landing she met a smiling Miss Curtis.

"Is it true that the Colonel is returned?" she asked, evidently finding it good news.

His return was not so welcome to others. Lady Hayford issued a standing invitation to dinner, but there was a slight reserve in her manner to him which was noticeable to those who knew her well. The fatal accident, forgotten while Rowland Dynham was abroad, was remembered when he was seen again in London, though he was not cut so generally as he had been before. Lady Caynnes was written to and replied that she did not at all like Colonel Dynham's returning in this inconsiderate, sudden, not to say secret way, but that nothing was to be done until she returned to London, which was not possible until her friend's health improved.

As she did not come at once life went on in its usual busy entertaining way at the Hayfords' and Rowland, as November began, was so often there as to seem almost part of the household. Tinna could not but admit that he was an asset to her evenings, for in spite of his stiff look he was not silent and was useful in making conversation with diplomatic barons and counts and their wives, in excellent French. Lord Hayford, although it was he who had sent him to Vienna to be out of the way, was so pleased with his work there that he had decided to forget the past, dismissing the suspicions as unproven.

One evening when the party was mostly a family one, the younger people made up a set for dancing with much laughter and moving of chairs. Louie was sitting near Lord Hayford when Rowland noticed that she was alone and came across to ask her to dance with him.

"It is very kind of you, Cousin Rowland," she said, "but Mr. Tollington has already asked me."

She saw Hilary coming towards her and stood up to meet him. He smiled toothily, with some satisfaction, as he led her away. Louie found she did not feel disappointed, but relieved. As they took their places she saw Henrietta looking at her with an expression she could not make out. Henrietta, of course, was dancing with Lord Stanbourne.

Rowland did not ask anyone else but stood by Lord Hayford's chair, watching.

There was applause at the end of the dance and cries of "Another! Let us have another!"

"Everyone change partners!" commanded Tinna, who had not been dancing, but was now seized by Hilary, who declared that she must.

"And Stanbourne cannot have Henrietta all the evening, he must dance with Miss Louisa," he said, firmly setting them opposite each other.

Louie could not help thinking how it would annoy Lady Caynnes to see her dancing with a future Duke. It did not alarm her to have Lord Stanbourne for a partner, for he was as shy as herself and a much worse dancer, having to be directed all the time by Hilary who was standing next to him.

In the reshuffle, when the Hayford daughters and their husbands had changed over, Henrietta was left without a partner, a most unusual situation for her. She turned with a sudden smile to Rowland Dynham.

"Will you only dance with Louie, Colonel Dynham?"

He stepped towards her at once, saying, "It would give me the greatest pleasure if you would dance with me, Miss Tollington."

Tinna was not at all pleased by this little manoeuvre.

Henrietta, who enjoyed dancing and had

found poor Stanbourne a drag on her amusement, had picked a partner who was better able to execute the movements than she had guessed from his rather formal manner. Rowland might look stiff on occasion but it was because he stood so straight and because, in company, his face tended to take on an impassive reserve; when dancing he moved with precision but quite elegantly, so that his balance and muscular control were more evident than any stiffness.

Conversation when dancing in a set had to be held in snatches but Henrietta seemed at no loss for gay talk, Louie thought, glancing that way several times and thinking she had never seen Rowland smile so often. Henrietta was teasing him; well, she always teased and no one seemed to mind it. Louie heard one exchange only.

"I see what you have been doing in Vienna all this year, Colonel Dynham," Henrietta said. "You have been dancing every night with all those charming countesses. I do believe that Austrian cat saw more of your rooms than you did."

"You are quite mistaken, Miss Tollington," he replied. "I went to very few

259

balls and danced only with heavyweight German princesses."

"Princesses! I wonder you can condescend now to a mere miss."

"One might almost say princesses are mere, in that part of the world," said Rowland, with a smile. "Mary Anne's La Belle would easily pass as a distinguished personage."

Henrietta laughed. "Oh, but I've no doubt you told *them* that all Englishwomen have prominent teeth!" She made a tiny grimace, showing her own, laughing at herself, but in fact looking quite charming.

"That is what *they* told *me*," said Rowland. "Of course, as an Englishman I maintained that I preferred our island teeth to any, in whatever array they were set. And now my patriotism is justified."

It seemed harmless enough to Louie but later that night, when she and Henrietta, having sent away the maid, were brushing their hair in the same room, Tinna came in, holding an elegant wrap round herself with one small white hand and carrying a candlestick in the other.

"Henrietta, I declare, you were positively flirting with Colonel Dynham this evening!"

Henrietta, sitting at her dressing table,

twiddled a curl round her fingers and replied casually, "Oh my dear Tinna, but you know I flirt with everybody! It would really distinguish Colonel Dynham if I did *not*."

This was perfectly true but Tinna was not to be put off.

"But I think he is just the man, and in just the position, to take advantage of any liking you may show," she said. "Would it not suit his book very well to marry again now, especially as he must know you have quite a respectable little fortune of your own?"

"Poor Colonel Dynham, is he not allowed to talk nonsense for an evening without being supposed to have designs of marriage?" said Henrietta, taking up her hairbrush again. "I should imagine, after his recent experiences, the state would have few attractions for him."

"I know you are sympathetic to him," said Tinna, grumbling at her. "It is very thoughtless of you, when you have Lord Stanbourne so very attentive that I am sure he must mean to propose soon."

"I do not want him to propose," said Henrietta impatiently. "I shall be delighted if he perceives my real character in time to prevent his doing any such thing."

Tinna sighed. "It is hopeless talking to

you," she said. "Well, do not stay up chattering all night."

She said goodnight and went away.

Henrietta sat silent a moment and then said, in quite a different voice, "Louie, you are not in love with Rowland Dynham, are you?"

"In love with him! No!" said Louie, startled. And yet the question unsettled her mind, so that she realised that her feelings about Rowland were extremely confused.

"Last year, I thought you were," said Henrietta. "But since he came back, I decided you were not."

Louie felt she was blushing. She brushed her hair vigorously and said, "I don't know what being in love is."

Henrietta, who had been watching her with a serious face, smiled suddenly. "Well! You know my opinion, that it is a much over-rated amusement," she said. "But with Tinna lecturing me on Colonel Dynham's matrimonial intentions, I was afraid she might have hurt you, unwittingly, of course."

Louie was astonished that Henrietta had such thoughts about her. She said, "I never imagined Cousin Rowland might consider marrying me, Henrietta, even if only to find a mother for the children. He has always treated me as if I were scarcely older than Mary Anne. Even his brother Joscelin noticed that."

Henrietta turned back to the glass, looking for a moment at the reflection of her own face between the two candles.

"I am glad Tinna's tiresome lecture has not upset you," she said.

She blew out the candles, first one and then the other, leaving only the candlestick by the bed. "Goodnight, my dear Louie."

4

ONE grey November afternoon a few days later, Louie was in Henrietta's sitting-room upstairs, unpicking a piece of Mary Anne's sewing which had gone wrong, when Henrietta herself ran in, dropped on the couch and seized up her French novel.

She had scarcely opened it when her sister came in.

"Henrietta, this is past all bearing! Do not pretend to have been reading that nonsense—I have just seen poor Lord Stanbourne."

"What, hasn't he gone yet?" said Henrietta. "I thought he would have reached his club by now and be well on the way to drowning his sorrows in the customary manner."

Louie, embarrassed, rose to go but Henrietta put out a hand and caught her dress.

"Don't leave me, my dear girl! I have committed no crime, I assure you, though Tinna looks so black at me. I have merely refused an offer of marriage from Lord Stanbourne."

"What have you got against him?" Tinna

demanded. "He is such a pleasant young fellow and plainly dotes on you."

"He'll soon get over that," said Henrietta. "I'm the first girl to make him laugh; he had no idea before that young ladies could be human. Well, his sisters scarcely are."

"I am not going to laugh with you over those tedious Chervill girls," said Tinna severely. "Come to your senses, Henrietta. You will never get such another offer. Why, you would be Duchess of Wiltshire one day!"

"When I'm as old and ugly as the present Duchess," said Henrietta. "For the Duke is a very hearty gentleman and does not look like dying to oblige a daughter-in-law within these twenty years." She caught the book, which was sliding off her lap and looked up at her sister with laughter in her bright hazel eyes. "Oh, my dear Tinna! I have nothing against becoming a Duchess, but not if it means marrying poor Stanbourne."

"There is nothing poor about Stanbourne," said Tinna sharply. "You cannot expect to marry perfection."

"I do not want perfection in a husband, imperfect as I am myself," said Henrietta. "But I will not marry a man with whom I know I should be bored inside a month."

Tinna looked down at her, so small and slim, fragile even, and yet so implacably determined.

"If I say that you will end up an old maid you will no doubt have an answer to that," she said in despair.

"Yes—I shall write novels instead of reading them," said Henrietta complacently.

Tinna gave an exclamation of impatient annoyance and then, glancing at the watch pinned on her dress, hurried away for she was going to the theatre and had to change. On the landing she met Hilary, who was staying in the house, coming upstairs in his overcoat, and passed on the news to him. He went along the passage to Henrietta's sitting-room and sat down on a chair by the fire, holding out his thin hands to the blaze.

"So you have been naughty again, Miss Hen?" he said to his cousin, glancing at her with amusement.

"Anybody would think one married merely to please one's relations," said Henrietta coolly. "A woman has only the power to refuse: why should she not exercise it at her own will?"

"I am not blaming you, Henrietta," said Hilary. "For I don't think Stanbourne will do for you. He is a nice stupid youth who will make a nice stupid Duke one day—and let us hope he will soon find a nice stupid girl to marry instead of our own Miss Hen, the unique and inimitable bird."

Henrietta laughed. "Oh dear Hilary, what a comfort you are!" she said. "We shall have to marry each other—it is the only thing to keep Tinna quiet."

Hilary leant back in his chair, smiling. "I'll bear that in mind," he said. "Certainly I would prefer you to be the first Mrs. Tollington to the second Mrs. Dynham."

Henrietta hurled the novel at him, with a cry of laughing rage. "Horrid fellow! That is quite uncalled-for!"

The book hit Hilary in the midriff and he gave a melodramatic yell which brought the children running from the nursery nearby and effectively ended the conversation.

Henrietta did not alter her manner to Rowland Dynham as a result of these family discussions but it was true that it differed little from her behaviour to other men whom she liked, and liked to tease. But Louie could not help noticing that Rowland was actively seeking Henrietta's company, going to sit or stand by her in the drawing-room, walking beside her when they went out with the children and carrying on with her a game of verbal shuttlecock and battledore. It was generally Henrietta who started it but he was always ready to pick up the challenge and quite often it was she who had to end the volley with a laughter which covered defeat. Louie noticed that she did not at all mind her defeats but possibly enjoyed them as much as her successes.

Louie was not the only one watching the pair; Tinna had her eye on her sister, but having once warned her she knew better than to nag at the same theme. But she thought it unfortunate that Lady Caynnes did not come up from Tunbridge Wells. Having gone to that establishment in perfect health she had caught cold and taken to her bed, from which she wrote letters to her nephew Frederick Warstowe every other day, demanding action in one and commanding him in the next to wait for her return.

Rowland would get his house in Westminster back from his tenants at the end of December and there he proposed to move the children in the new year, since it seemed certain that he would not now be sent back to Vienna. It looked as if a new coalition of the

Powers would soon be made against revolutionary France and war renewed.

"I am sorry you cannot come with us when we move, Louie," Rowland said. "The children will miss you and it must be very tiresome to live with Lady Caynnes. However, I hope that will not be for too long."

He did not say how Louie might be expected to escape from Caynnes House but she wondered if he hoped to be married again, so that she could once more live in his household.

And then one morning Louie, going to the drawing-room to look for a book she thought she had left there, walked into the middle of a very private interview between Lady Hayford and Rowland Dynham. Tinna was sitting, alert and upright, by a small round table. Rowland was standing a few yards away, looking at his tallest and stiffest.

As Louie came in Tinna was saying, "But you must be aware, Colonel Dynham, that even apart from Henrietta's fortune, no one who loves her could regard without foreboding her linking her fate with someone whose first marriage ended so tragically."

Then she saw Louie, who stopped on the

threshold, acutely embarrassed and murmuring words of apology.

"You had better come in, Louie," said Tinna, "since you must have heard what we were talking about. It is my fault, for beginning the conversation without premeditation, or I should have chosen a less public room."

Rowland said, "Louie must think I have been asking leave to address Miss Henrietta, but I assure you, Lady Hayford, no one is better aware than myself that I am not in a position to ask anyone to marry me, whether or not she is endowed with a fortune." His voice sounded hard and dry to Louie.

"I come back to England to find that the slander is still alive which credits me with Caroline's death," Rowland continued bitterly. "I know whom I have to thank for that; it is Caynnes Ridgway. But I cannot have it out with him, for he works underhand, by sneer and innuendo and not to my face."

He walked to the window and back; the only sign of perturbation that he showed.

"I do not think your sister believes I am guilty," he said abruptly, but with a hint of uncertainty in his voice.

"That is just why I am appealing to your sense of honour, Colonel Dynham," said

270

Tinna firmly. "I do not believe Henrietta's heart is touched but she has taken it into her head to defend you, and she is the sort of obstinate girl who could be persuaded to think she was doing something fine in marrying a man whom—I must say it—none of her relations can trust."

Rowland was silent.

From the way he had tried to defend himself Louie was inclined to think he did wish to ask Henrietta to marry him but dared not admit it, since the circumstances were so adverse.

There was an uncomfortable pause and then Rowland said stiffly, "I do not think I have given Miss Tollington any reason to believe I wished to make her an offer."

"Then will you promise not to do so?" Tinna pressed him. "Will you so command your manner as not to encourage in her any such expectation?"

"I suppose I must, if you think it necessary," he said.

Tinna looked satisfied and turned to adjure Louie not to speak of this interview to Henrietta.

"You must not suggest that Colonel Dynham's intentions have even been discussed," she said. "For that would only excite Henrietta's curiosity."

"Yes, I see," said Louie, but she wondered if Henrietta might not find out something about it all the same, shrewd and observant as she was.

Henrietta certainly noticed at once that Rowland's manner towards her had changed.

"I could almost think I had offended your Cousin Rowland," she remarked to Louie. "He is grown so distant suddenly and finds so much work to do at the Foreign Office."

Rowland came less frequently in the evenings and he no longer joined their parties for the theatre and opera. When Henrietta tossed one of her teasing remarks at him he contrived to answer in so dull a way that she could not continue the game. He visited his children every day but rarely stayed long. Otherwise he seemed the same as usual, cool and controlled, imperturbable.

Henrietta, annoyed at this withdrawal, in her turn withdrew; she avoided Rowland when they were in company and talked to others, especially to Hilary, with whom she could always get on easily. They laughed at the same things, shared the same interests.

Louie watched and wondered, but she

thought that Rowland's feeling had increased rather than otherwise; she sometimes caught him looking at Henrietta when she did not know she was observed, as if he could not prevent himself. Louie saw him once take up a paper to distract himself but a moment later it was on his knee and his eyes had gone back to their object.

Louie wondered that the others did not notice but in his face and manner Rowland maintained his usual reserve; they did not observe the minute indications to which Louie was sensitive.

An uncomfortable week or two went by and then Lady Caynnes returned from Tunbridge Wells. All attention immediately became concentrated on the fate of the Dynham children.

As Lady Caynnes intended to go back to Tunbridge Wells as soon as the business was settled, she did not open her own house but stayed with the Warstowes and came over in state, attended by Frederick Warstowe and Caynnes Ridgway, to the family meeting she had called. It was held in Lord Hayford's library but he had absented himself, rather to his wife's annoyance.

"It is nothing to do with me," he had said. "As far as I am concerned Rowland Dynham has proved himself a reliable man and I dislike Maria Caynnes's meddling ways."

Everyone else was present, even Henrietta and Louie. Louie came by right of her relationship to the children and Henrietta did not see why she should be left out.

Rowland had been asked to come at a specified time and it was only while they were waiting for him that the girls learned that Lady Caynnes intended to keep the children in her care, and was apparently confident that she had the law on her side and that their father would have to agree.

"It is in the document he signed," she said.

Hilary was walking restlessly about and occasionally stopping by the fire. He had a cough and looked pinched and pale.

"I wish you had told me about the wording, Warstowe," he said in his soft lisping voice. "It looks too like sharp practice to me, getting Dynham to sign something he was not fully aware of."

"He should have read it more carefully," said Caynnes Ridgway, lounging in his chair.

Henrietta looked at Louie and whispered, "What have they done? Colonel Dynham, is in for a shock, it seems."

A few minutes later Rowland arrived,

briskly on time, and so well-dressed that he did not look like someone who had to work for his living. He thought he had merely come to settle the legal business of the transfer of the children and it was not until Frederick Warstowe had been talking for some time that he discovered otherwise. The men were sitting at a long table as if at a business meeting; Lady Caynnes was enthroned in a huge high-backed chair to one side, Tinna sat in an armchair and the two girls on a couch.

Rowland suddenly interrupted Frederick's flow.

"Am I to understand that Lady Caynnes refuses to hand over my children?" he demanded.

"The childen are under the guardianship of Mr. Tollington and Lady Caynnes," said Frederick Warstowe. "You yourself signed the document." He put his hand on it.

"While I was abroad," said Rowland, "in case of any accident to myself."

"There is nothing stated as to the termination of the guardianship," said Caynnes Ridgway smoothly.

Rowland got up from his chair, pulled the document towards him and began to study it.

Louie could see he was reading one paragraph several times. She was suddenly reminded of that letter, the one from Bath which had warned him of Caroline's flight.

Presently Rowland put the document down on the table.

"You tricked me," he said. He was looking at Caynnes Ridgway.

Ridgway shrugged his shoulders. "I'm surprised at you, Dynham," he said. "Of course we assumed you had read what you signed."

Rowland picked up the document again to look at the signature evidently wondering whether the whole thing had been forged. But his own name stared him in the face.

"You are not going to get away with this," he said, still standing. "A father's rights are supported by the law of this country, I believe."

"I shouldn't go to law if I were you, Dynham," said Caynnes Ridgway, leaning his chair back. "If you did we should be forced to make known the reasons why we do not think you fit to be guardian of Caroline's children."

Rowland stared at him with barely concealed distaste.

"If you are referring to Caroline's death,"

he said, "I beg leave to remind you that the inquest brought it in accidental."

"There was not much evidence to prove it," said Caynnes Ridgway," and a great deal to establish the probability that it was no accident. However, Lady Caynnes does not wish to reopen the case against you because it would involve exposing poor Caroline's conduct."

Lady Caynnes nodded her head emphatically.

"Yes, indeed!" she said. "It would be a most shocking thing, and so dreadful for poor little Adrian to hear of it."

Rowland looked round at her. "Yet it is you, not I, who propose to drag all this up again," he said. "Ridgway has just used it as a threat against me, to deter me from taking the legal way to gain my rights."

"Threat? Mind your language, Dynham," said Caynnes Ridgway coolly. "I was warning you, cautioning you, if you like, against the inevitable result of legal action in this case. For I do not deny that the reason we do not think you a fit guardian for Adrian is because we are all convinced that you were responsible for the death of his mother."

There was a strained silence.

Hilary got up from his chair, coughing, and went over to the fireplace again. From there he turned and said, "I am sorry you were tricked over the document, Dynham. I did not know about that. Nevertheless, would it not be better to face the fact that the manner of Caroline's death inevitably brings suspicion on you and that it would be better for Adrian, who inherits so much from her, to be brought up by her relations?"

Rowland saw that they were all against him; he was cornered, forced into a position where he could take no action to regain his children without exposing them to all the horrors of a public case which would destroy the reputation of both their parents, however it turned out. He stood with his hands clenched at his side, the knuckles whitening. He did not answer Hilary, but turned his eyes to Caynnes Ridgway.

"You have done this," he said, resentment rasping in his voice. "I see your influence in it all. First you corrupted Caroline, and now you want to take my son from me. I will not have it. I will do anything to prevent it."

Caynnes Ridgway was smiling. "There is nothing you can do to prevent it, Dynham," he said.

278

With three strides Rowland was round the table and Caynnes barely had time to scramble to his feet before he got a hard fist full in the face. He stumbled backwards, throwing up an arm, but Rowland went at him with both fists, hitting him with such force that he fell against the wall, whereupon Rowland held him pinned there with one hand while he punched him with the other. His face was set in blind rage.

Lady Caynnes screamed, Tinna jumped up, turning white and Frederick Warstowe lumbered to his feet shouting, "Now look here Dynham—assault—can't have this! Good God, he'll kill him!"

Rowland seemed not to hear, not to be aware of any of them. For once he had totally lost control.

Then Hilary walked up to him, looking small and slight beside him, and caught his arm.

"Dynham, you must not hit him again," he said firmly.

Rowland stopped glaring at Caynnes Ridgway and looked round at Hilary. He could certainly have flung him off with one hand, but he did not. The light died out of his eyes and his expression changed. After a moment he dropped his grip on Ridgway and put up a hand to rub his face; the fingers were shaking.

Everyone in the room was staring at him. None had ever seen him other than cool, correct and controlled. Even Louie, with a shudder remembering the moment by the sundial, had then seen him mastering, not being mastered by, a surge of passionate anger.

Caynnes Ridgway, moving away along the wall, nursing his jaw, and feeling for a chair, voiced what everyone was thinking as he said, "What more convincing proof—of what he can do?"

Rowland suddenly walked away from them all and went to the window; he stood and stared out of it, without saying a word.

Hilary began to try to get everyone moving, asking Warstowe to give Lady Caynnes his arm to the drawing-room. But when she was half way across the room she turned and said, "We can't go without settling this, once and for all. Colonel Dynham, you will not fight the case at law?"

"No," he answered, without turning round.

She glanced in triumph at the others and

consented to leave the room. Hilary went up to Rowland.

"Will you have a drink, Dynham?" he suggested.

Louie thought he seemed more friendly to Rowland now than he had ever been before.

"No," said Rowland again, but in a weary dispirited tone.

He still did not look round but stood rigid, with his back to them.

Hilary turned his attention to Caynnes Ridgway and took him out of the room. Tinna signalled to the girls to follow her, waiting at the door until they did. But then she was so much taken up by Lady Caynnes's belated attack of faintness that they were able to escape into the hall.

"I am going to find Whitbread and get a glass of wine for Colonel Dynham," said Henrietta to Louie. "Whatever he says, I am sure he needs it."

But when they returned to the library, it was empty.

Hilary, coming in the next moment to collect the documents, said, "You give that wine to me, I need it. Dynham has gone."

"Gone? Out of the house?" asked Henrietta.

"Yes," said Hilary. "I could see he was

unable to face us after that extraordinary lapse. Not that I blame him for punching Ridgway's face—I've often wanted to do it myself. But he was quite beside himself; I've never seen anyone in that condition, let alone Rowland Dynham."

"At least it shows how much he loves his children," said Henrietta.

"A frightening kind of love," observed Hilary, drinking his wine. Then he added soberly, "I must say it makes it seem very unlikely that poor Caroline just fell out of that phaeton, at Moor Cross."

5

HILARY TOLLINGTON decided to take the Dynham children down to Woodford St. Petrock for Christmas. He had not bargained on having to entertain Lady Caynnes as well, but she firmly invited herself; her fear of Rowland Dynham's intentions had become obsessive since the scene in Lord Hayford's library.

"Depend upon it, a man who can make such a brutal assault on another will stop at nothing to get possession of the Caynnes heir," she said.

Hilary was not pleased to find he was expected to invite Caynnes Ridgway too, but he was higher than ever in Lady Caynnes's favour. He was to see old Ridgway on Rosewell affairs but was determined to spend his Christmas and New Year in comfort at Woodford St. Petrock, and not in Monkhampton.

"At least we shall not have the Warstowes," Hilary said to Henrietta, who was going with him instead of joining the Hayford family party; Tinna was still annoyed at her refusal of Lord Stanbourne and her only comfort was to revert to an older plan that her sister should marry their cousin.

Although they would not have the Warstowes, Henrietta was determined to take Miles Dynham.

"It is kind of you, Miss Tollington, I'm sure," said Mrs. Warstowe. "But he will be sick in the coach. He always is. We have to put him to travel with the servants and I advise you to do the same."

Henrietta instantly decided to have Miles with herself, and so she did, allowing him to look out of the window and stopping, when he felt queasy, to let him walk about in the fresh air. In consequence he was not sick and arrived in Devon even more devoted to his "prettiest lady".

"Is Uncle Rowland coming?" he had asked nervously, before starting, his small pale face looking out from the yards of woollen muffler in which his faithful servant, another of the Beer family, had swathed him. Jeremiah Beer, who had served with Mark Dynham in the army, now devoted himself to the son and Henrietta had a shrewd suspicion that Miles owed his continued existence mainly to this odd little man, with his wizened brown face and light eyes. Jeremiah insisted on coming too, travelling with the Tollington's servants.

"Aunt Warstowe says Uncle Rowland is as bad as a murderer," Miles had confided to Henrietta. "And one day it will be found out, because murder always is found out in the end. So then he will be hanged dead."

"My dear Miles!" cried Henrietta, horrified. "Be sure your uncle is not a murderer."

"But Uncle Warstowe says he tried to kill Mr. Ridgway only the other day," said Miles. "And Sally, that's our nursemaid, says she wouldn't like to be me, because if I was dead Uncle Rowland would be master of Brentland, and Sir Rowland. And Sally said, 'Suppose he was to hit you as hard as he hit Mr. Ridgway? It would kill a shrimp like you'—that's what she said."

"She had no business to say such things," said Henrietta, appalled at the extent of the gossip about Rowland Dynham.

"Of course, my uncle is really master of Brentland now," said Miles, meditatively. "He runs it because I'm a minor. But it hasn't anything to do with mines, Mr. Ridgway says."

Henrietta, while she laughed, felt uneasy.

Adrian had been subjected to the same nursery gossip, which had sent Mary Anne crying to Louie. "Lizzie says Papa must have hit Mamma very hard to make her fall down dead," she sobbed. "It isn't true, Louie, is it? He never would."

Henrietta, watching Louie comfort the child, could not help feeling that her denials were not quite whole-hearted.

Louie wanted to believe Rowland innocent but her gentle nature had recoiled from the look on his face as he had hit out with all his force at someone he despised, and she found it harder than ever to banish the images of a violent struggle up on the deserted moor.

When Mary Anne had gone, still tearful, to her dinner, Louie had looked at Henrietta. "You don't believe it, Henrietta, do you? Why not?"

"Because I do not think he is a liar," said Henrietta. Her voice was quite cool, quite even.

It had not occurred to Louie to think of it in this way; it was so long since she had heard Rowland's own account of the incident. Even now, she could not convince herself that he had told the whole truth. If he had not intended murder, could he not have convinced himself

Caroline's death was accidental? But she could not speak of it, even with Henrietta.

Adrian's reaction to the nursery gossip was quite different from his sister's. "Did he hit her with a stick, do you think? Or just give her a very big push, like I mustn't give Mary Anne?"

He did not listen to assurances that his father had done neither. "Mr. Ridgway says he did."

Not only Ridgway but Lady Caynnes now spoke openly before the boy of what they believed his father had done, and this in spite of the fact that they had made so much to Rowland of the evil a public case would do to the children. His attack on Ridgway had put him beyond consideration.

Before they left London Henrietta had not seen Rowland Dynham since the scene in the library and Louie had met him only once, briefly, in the park; he had told the children he was very busy and might not see them again before they left for Devonshire.

"I think he does not want to call here," said Louie. "He must be ashamed of what he did, that day."

Louie had seen Woodford St. Petrock on the way up from Rosewell in September the

287

year before, but she had been so overcome with the shock of Caroline's death that she had hardly taken notice of it. The Tollingtons' old home stood on an undulating hillside above the Torridge, a rambling old house, altered at every period, not imposing or architecturally interesting, but comfortable and kind. Here, far inland, the trees grew large, not bent by the winds, as at Brentland. They stood bare now at midwinter, beautiful skeleton patterns, outlined with frost.

For it had turned very cold, with the temperature dropping all the time and rumours of ice floes on the Thames. Falls of snow lay a long time because the air was so cold, by day as well as by night.

Adrian was dancing with impatience till he could get out in the snow and hurl balls of it at everyone, but mostly at Miles, an easy target who generally missed with his return fire. Mary Anne busily made little snow people. "Snow-*women*," she insisted, "because skirts are easier."

Suddenly, for Louie, the days became happier.

But just before Christmas they heard that Colonel Dynham had come to Brentland and soon after the feast he appeared at Woodford, having driven over in the old travelling carriage slowly because of the icy roads.

Mary Anne had developed a cold and was indoors but the two little boys were playing outside and came running in, Adrian shouting, "My father is coming!"

They were still in the hall, jumping about in nervous excitement, when Rowland Dynham came to the door. Hilary, who had come out of the morning room with a newspaper in his hand, immediately went up to greet him.

"Come in, Dynham. I wondered whether you would get over. I thought you might be snowbound at Brentland, on the high ground."

"Not at present," said Rowland, stepping over the threshold. "Though if we have any more snow, we shall be."

He looked down at the two boys, who were now standing still, staring up at him with fascinated fearfulness, as if an ogre out of one of their story books had walked into the house.

"You look well, Miles," he observed, with disappointing mildness. "The Devon air suits you, even at midwinter."

Mary Anne came running from the other

room, clutching La Belle, always her companion when she was not feeling well.

"Oh Papa! Have you come to stay?" she asked eagerly.

"No, but I came to ask Cousin Hilary if you might come and stay with me for the rest of the holiday," he said, and glanced at Hilary questioningly.

"I see no reason why not," Hilary was beginning, when he was interrupted by Lady Caynnes, who had heard the boys' cries from her room above and now emerged, stately and irate, at the head of the stairs.

"What can you be thinking of, Hilary?" she exclaimed. "Of course we cannot allow Colonel Dynham to take the children away. Why, how are we to know he would ever bring them back?"

"Because I say I will, ma'am," Rowland replied, with scarcely suppressed irritation.

Just then Henrietta came out from another room upstairs and looked over the bannisters. She was wearing a green dress with a long sleeved spencer over it and beside Lady Caynnes she looked like a creature of some other race, so small and so delicately made and moving with such light feet she scarcely made a sound.

Rowland had not seen her since that day in Lord Hayford's library and though he could not move away when Lady Caynnes was speaking to him, he looked down at Mary Anne rather than meet Henrietta's gaze.

"I see no reason to trust you will do as you say, Colonel Dynham," said Lady Caynnes and began to descend the stairs.

Henrietta came down after her and as soon as she could catch Rowland's eye she gave him a dazzling smile, from behind and above the menacing figure of Lady Caynnes.

It had an immediate reviving influence on Rowland, who said with something of his usual confidence, "Good morning, Miss Tollington. I did not know you were here. I thought you had gone with the Hayfords."

Lady Caynnes was annoyed at Miss Tollington's being introduced into the conversation. She reached the hall and pronounced magisterially, "Hilary, we certainly cannot receive Colonel Dynham."

"My dear aunt," he said, "considering that we have Colonel Dynham's children here, it is only to be expected that he would wish to see them."

"Wish to spirit them away," corrected a lazy voice from behind Louie. She looked round and saw Caynnes Ridgway was lounging behind her. He had come into the morning-room by another door. The bruises from Rowland's fists were still visible—another reason why he had found it convenient to retire to the country for Christmas.

"If you give in over this, Tollington, you will never recover your ground," he said. "Or, probably, the children."

"It is grossly unjust if I cannot even see my children," said Rowland. "I appeal to you, Tollington."

Hilary looked extremely uncomfortable. He was now the legal guardian of Rowland's children and still thought he had killed their mother in a moment of violent rage; but he believed Rowland loved them, or at any rate Mary Anne, who clung, snuffling from her cold, anxiously to his hand all the time.

"I don't know why we are all standing in the hall," Hilary said at last in an attempt to reduce the tension of conflicting feeling. "Let us be more comfortable. I am sure you would like some coffee or a glass of wine, Dynham, after your cold drive."

Lady Caynnes, however, announced that she would not tolerate "that man" in the house. "I wonder Colonel Dynham has the effrontery to face us after the display of violent passion we witnessed at our last meeting. Mary Anne, leave go of his hand and let Cousin Louie take you back to the nursery."

Mary Anne let out a sudden wail. "Oh! Aren't we going to Brentland with Papa? Oh . . ."

Far from letting him go she pressed against him, clinging to his coat with her other hand.

"Don't cry, my dear," he said, stroking her fair head affectionately. "I certainly mean to take you there again, even if it cannot be today."

Adrian suddenly planted himself opposite and announced in his clear ringing treble, "I shan't go. I don't want to live with you."

Rowland stared at him, frowning, but Adrian, bright-eyed with brave defiance, stared back, chin up.

"Nonsense, Adrian," said Rowland, at last. "Boys always live with their fathers."

"I'm not going to," repeated Adrian. "I wish you were not my father. Yes I do!" And with the final threat of childhood he shouted, "I hate you! You're a bad cruel man and I hate you!"

It was so unexpected that for a few moments

nobody said anything. Then Caynnes Ridgway gave one of his quiet ironical chuckles.

Rowland stiffened, though he did not look at Ridgway, but at his son. "I suppose you think that a clever thing to say, Adrian," he said coldly. "It is not a proper way for little boys to talk. Run along and play snowballs with Miles. I am not taking you to Brentland today."

Adrian, rather deflated, walked off with his head in the air, out into the garden again. "I don't care," he said loudly, as he jumped off the step on to the path, and he ran noisily away.

Hilary suddenly made up his mind. "Aunt, I will not ask you to sit down with Colonel Dynham if you do not wish it, but as he is here I propose to talk business with him while his horses are baited. Come into my study, Dynham—and Mary Anne, you may as well come too."

Dexterously he led off Rowland and his daughter, breaking up the scene and leaving Lady Caynnes only the consolation of preventing Louie and Henrietta from seeing anything more of Colonel Dynham before he presently drove away.

Louie had gone up to the old schoolroom,

294

and Hilary brought Mary Anne up there, but when she sent the little girl to Lizzie Jewell to have her face washed, he lingered, wandering restlessly about and at last, leaning on the table and looking at her, he asked, "What do you think of it all, Miss Louie?"

"I don't know what to think," said Louie, relieved to speak and yet uncertain what to say.

"The poor little girl loves him so much," said Hilary. "And I am sure he is fond of her. I am not so sure about the boy. Yet one could hardly separate the children, and indeed is a father even if he were not under suspicion, suitable to bring up a girl?"

Louie agreed that the situation was difficult and he became still more restless, looking out of the window, then going and kicking a log further into the fire, and finally saying in nervous haste, "Miss Louie, I don't know if I ought to ask you this, but has he ever suggested—given you to understand that he— that if his circumstances were otherwise, he might marry again?"

Louie wondered if he knew of the interview with Tinna; from his present uncertainty she decided it was unlikely. Hilary's obvious anxiety worried her; perhaps he had counted on marrying Henrietta and was now afraid he was to lose her to Rowland, just as last year he had lost his Julia to Grant.

"No, he hasn't," she replied. "In fact, I am sure he does not think marriage is possible under his present circumstances. But he—" she hesitated, "but I do think perhaps he wishes to. Do you think he ought not?"

With a sudden burst of irritation Hilary said, "Oh heavens, I don't know! I daresay he is not likely to kill another wife—Caroline was unique." Then he moved quickly about the room again. "I'm sorry, Louie, I shouldn't have said that."

Louie was surprised by his violent reactions, but even more sure that he suspected Rowland wanted to marry Henrietta and saw that she was not averse to him.

The bell rang for dinner and they went down together, Hilary complaining that he had to spend the whole of the next day visiting lawyers in Bideford. "I promised Dynham to get them to tell me his rights under the guardianship arrangement," he said. "I must say I feel Ridgway made a dupe of me in order to trick Dynham over the document. Yet I am not sure whether he is a fit guardian for the children. But you, Miss

Louie, you probably think I am hard upon him."

Louie turned her large brown eyes on him and said, "No, I think you are wise not to act too quickly, Mr. Tollington."

He looked at her with a curious intentness which she could not understand.

"Inscrutable girl!" he said at last, puzzling her still more.

They went into the dining-room, where the portrait of Hilary's uncle, Henrietta's father, seemed to preside with a half-smile of spry benignity full of the confidence of the age before the Revolution.

The next day, Lady Caynnes insisted on accompanying Hilary to Bideford, which did not suit him, for, as she also insisted on taking Caynnes Ridgway, it meant that as well as being hampered in his conversations with the lawyers he would have to take the carriage instead of the chaise, since that only accommodated two passengers.

When they had gone Henrietta and Louie went out to walk up through the park to the top of the hill, where there was a little folly built by old Mr. Tollington as a summer-house and observatory. But they had not reached it when they saw, below them on the drive, a carriage approaching the house. "Who can that be?" Henrietta wondered, and they turned back down the path. It ran diagonally through groves of planted evergreens and they lost sight of the carriage as they approached the house. Only as they reached the garden gate were they able to see it again—just passing out through the gates on to the road.

"Whoever it was decided very quickly not to wait," said Henrietta.

They went into the hall and Lizzie Jewell, who had been on the landing, came running down the stairs.

"Oh, Miss Louie! He's taken them away! Colonel Dynham, he came in so sudden and said, 'Pack up their night things, Lizzie, I'm taking them home.' Sir Miles too—he's taken them all."

"Colonel Dynham has been here?" Henrietta said, in a tone of disappointment.

"But Lizzie," said Louie, "do you mean to say he just walked in and took the children away?"

"Yes, just like that," said Lizzie. "Miss Mary Anne, she was on the sofa, and he picked her up, rolled her up in a blanket like and carried her downstairs. Then he tells the two boys to get inside the carriage. And Master Adrian he says, quick like, 'I'm not going with you'—well, miss, you know the way he talks. And Colonel Dynham he just says, very stern, 'Get in at once.' So they did then, and Sir Miles didn't half look scared, poor little mite."

Lizzie plainly felt a certain relish in the drama of the event.

Henrietta discovered from the butler that Colonel Dynham had first asked if he was too late to catch Mr. Tollington and on being informed that all the family were out had run upstairs to the nursery straight away, before Pillman, the butler, could stop him.

"Not that I could have stopped him, Miss Henrietta," he said, like Lizzie enjoying the excitement in retrospect. "Because Colonel Dynham is not the sort I could stop—we all know he's one of the hardiest gentlemen round here, always has been, as good with his fists as with sword and gun."

Lizzie came out of the nursery again clutching a bottle.

"Oh Miss Louie, I never thought to give the Colonel Miss Mary Anne's cough mixture," she said. "Poor little thing, she'll be coughing terrible in the night."

Henrietta took it from her. "We'll take it," she said, with sudden decision. "Louie, you and I will take the mixture and see what Colonel Dynham thinks he is doing, behaving like a kidnapper. For this seems to me a very rash act."

"Go to Brentland?" said Louie. "How can we?"

"In Hilary's chaise," said Henrietta cheerfully. "We may be back later than he is, but it can't be helped." And she began to give Pillman her orders.

Louie was carried along by her determination and in a very short time the two girls, with cloaks over their pelisses, were sitting in the chaise, driving out into the snow covered country, towards the high moorland.

6

IT began snowing again just as they got up on the moor and as there were no banks or hedges there it soon became hard to make out the edge of the road. It was not therefore surprising when one of the wheels sank into a deep rut and the chaise lurched to one side. It did not turn over as it might have done had they been going faster but it took some time to get it out and back on an even axle. Louie admired the way Henrietta ran to hold the horses so that the coachman could put his shoulder to the wheel. Small and light as she was, she managed the two horses easily and fearlessly.

The rough, sour moorland was bleak under the heavy sky, horizons blurring as the snow blew over, catching in the bent grasses. Staring round, Louie wondered if they were anywhere near Moor Cross. In fact, soon after starting again, Henrietta, looking out of the misted window glasses, said, "Here's Moor Cross. That's the lane to Top Leys."

Peering into the whiteness Louie saw the

lane, high-banked because it plunged into a dip before rising again towards the isolated farm. This was where Caroline had died on that September day, more than a year ago.

Henrietta stared into the thickening air as they slowly went past. "The bank does hide the lane from the cross post," she observed. "If he was standing by it, as he said, he could not have seen what happened down in the lane."

"Not even though the phaeton was built so high?" Louie said.

"I don't *think* so," Henrietta replied cautiously. "I could not see the top of the bank the other side, as we passed."

She sat back and for some time they were silent. Louie was thinking of the spring day when Rowland had driven them in the gig to Brentland and how Caroline's coming had upset the party. Suddenly, vividly, the thunderous atmosphere created by Caroline's wilfulness came back to her, how she had set out to provoke Rowland, encouraging Adrian to defy him, almost as if she was daring him to do what perhaps he had done at last, by that lonely cross roads.

Coming by the moor road they approached Brentland from the back and the coachman drove thankfully into the stableyard, which was also the farm yard, for Brentland had never lost its homestead buildings and the farmwork was still carried on by a bailiff whose house was just beyond the big barn.

Rowland Dynham was standing in the yard talking to two of the men, sturdy Devonians, but he was a head taller. He was wearing country clothes, as he had on the picnic day, with a loose neckerchief instead of a cravat and an old shooting coat. The snow was falling on his broad-brimmed hat, speckling the dark felt with white. As he turned to see who had come into his yard he looked unlike the well-dressed civilised man familiar to both the girls; here, suddenly, he was Dynham of Brentland, one of a hard living, hard fighting race, proudly independent of wealth and political power.

Henrietta's heart momentarily misgave her; would not her interference anger him? But for that very reason she jumped lightly down on the snow covered cobbles and picked her way across to him, holding up the bottle like a talisman.

"Colonel Dynham, you forgot Mary Anne's cough mixture!" she said, with her sweetest teasing smile.

From his answering smile it was clear that he was not at all annoyed. "My dear Miss Tollington, have you ventured into a snowstorm to save Mary Anne a cough or two? It is very good of you, though Truscott is already filling her with favourite remedies. But come inside, and tell me why I should have the pleasure of seeing you here, rather than your cousin with a battle-axe, which was what I expected when I saw the chaise."

The idea of Hilary with a battle-axe made Henrietta laugh merrily and they went into the house by the back door, out of the cold afternoon air into warmth and the smell of roasting meat.

"We're going to have dinner very shortly," said Rowland, as they went through the big kitchen, the servants looking at them with interest. "I hope you will join us, for you cannot set out on your return journey for an hour at least."

He took them into one of the old panelled rooms of the house where huge pieces of wood were burning in an open grate and Miles, kneeling in front, was pulling chestnuts with the tongs from where they were ranged on the hearth.

"Ow! It's hot! This one's burnt on one side and raw on the other."

Then he caught sight of the girls and jumped up. "Oh, Henrietta! I was just wishing you were here so that you could see our house. Isn't it an interesting place?" His odd little face was beaming with joy. Then he asked anxiously, "Have we got to go back now?"

Henrietta laughed and gave him a hug. "Well, this one seems to enjoy having been carried off by the robber baron!" she said, with a glance at Rowland.

"It is Miles's own home, after all," he said.

"Where's Adrian?" asked Louie.

"Sulking," said Rowland. "He didn't want to come."

Mary Anne, they discovered, had been put to bed in the caretaker's room on the ground floor, where Mrs. Hickman was fussing happily over her. The girls left their bonnets and cloaks there, Louie explaining that Rowland still called his old nurse "Truscott."

Finding their way back to the pannelled room, they suddenly met the enormous but not otherwise alarming figure of Joscelin Dynham, wearing a fisherman's jersey.

"I found Josce here," Rowland told them,

as they all went back to the fire. "He has been in Vienna too but somehow our paths did not cross."

"Rowland was in the p-palaces and I was in the p-pigsties," said Joscelin cheerfully.

The brothers seemed on good terms, for the time being.

Dinner was a cheerful occasion, though Adrian was unusually silent, refusing to answer when his father spoke to him. Rowland took no notice and Henrietta said nothing about the children's sudden removal but contrived to get Joscelin talking about music abroad, and the odd jobs he had taken on his travels.

Miles was still anxious lest they should be taken home again, but after dinner the Woodford coachman came in, puffing and blowing, to report that the snow was lying very thick and that he thought Bess had strained a muscle, pulling the chaise out of the rut. "I warned 'ee, Miss Henrietta, but 'ee would coom."

He had known Henrietta since she was a child.

Rowland went out to inspect the mare and the state of the road and came back stamping the snow off his shoes and saying it was quite impossible for them to leave.

"It may be better tomorrow," he said. "Truscott will make you both comfortable here for the night. I suppose Tollington will guess what has happened."

There was nothing for it but to agree and the girls went upstairs with the old house-keeper, who showed them to a wainscoted room and bustled off, saying she would get a fire lit directly.

Henrietta, tidying her hair, was full of merriment at their predicament. "Lady Caynnes will be so horrified to think of us snowed up here with two men and no married ladies to chaperone us."

She surveyed herself in the glass and announced, "Now I am going to find out why Colonel Dynham carried off his children like that—defying the law—an action that seems to me out of character for a man who is said to have been so calculating, from his youth up."

Louie said, "You take a great interest in him, Henrietta."

Henrietta gave her sudden brilliant smile.

"Is there any reason why I should not?" she said, and went quickly out of the room and down the stairs into the darkening house.

The sound of recorders echoed from the old room with the big fireplace; Joscelin was teaching the boys how to play. Rowland came out and took the girls into the morning-room, on the Georgian side of the house; it was decorated in light colours with a set of chairs made some forty years earlier, elegant in comparison with the old heavy oaken furniture. Louie did not remember it from their spring visit; Rowland apologised for not having had the drawing-room opened up.

"But this room, being smaller, is warmer," he said.

A pair of miniatures of the children were propped on the mantelpiece and the girls went to look at them, thinking them very like.

"They don't stay here," said Rowland. "I took them to Vienna with me."

Henrietta seized the opportunity to put her question, why he had taken his children away from Woodford that morning.

"It was done without premeditation," he answered. "I went with the intention of going with Tollington to the lawyers, for I distrust his ability to stand out against such rascals as Jack Ridgway." He never called Ridgway by the name of Caynnes. "Hilary Tollington has always been something of a weakling."

Louie felt hotly indignant, and then surprised at herself for feeling annoyance against Rowland on behalf of another. It was a novel sensation, and she gazed at him in silence.

Henrietta defended her cousin, but calmly. "I think you are mistaken as to Hilary's character. Even you, Colonel Dynham, must admit he is in a difficult position as Caroline's nearest relation, if we except Mr. Ridgway, and you must be aware that he is not convinced that the manner of Caroline's death was according to the account of it which you gave at the inquest."

Rowland, standing stiff and straight, said with restrained bitterness, "That is why I took my children away this morning. I saw yesterday how Adrian's mind has been turned against me. As for Mary Anne, the child was so unhappy at the thought of my going away again without her that I could not do it. Miles—well, this is his home, and Mark would not have wished him to grow up knowing nothing of it."

"You did not consider how your action might affect them, if they are taken away again?" asked Henrietta seriously.

"No," he answered. "Perhaps it was unwise." He snuffed a candle that was smoking on the table near him, with a quick pinch of finger and thumb. "But I could not see them lost to me and do nothing to regain them."

"I have every sympathy with you, please understand," said Henrietta. "But other people, unfortunately, are influenced by the grave suspicion against you."

Rowland's face tightened with nervous tension as he looked at her. "But you," he said after a moment, in a voice gone suddenly and unusually hoarse, "you do not entertain these suspicions of me?"

Henrietta, looking straight at him, answered quietly, "I believe your own account."

He did not speak at once but then said, "It is a very great relief," and sat down on a chair opposite her.

"I should not, of course," said Henrietta, in a lighter tone. "My dear father always told me never to believe anything except upon evidence. He even required evidence for the truth of the Christian Religion, though I am sure he believed it all his life. However, I claim a woman's privilege of believing a person, in spite of the evidence."

Rowland said, "In my case there is no evidence either way, unless you count the fact that Caroline and I were at odds all that year, and indeed, for longer than that, I fear."

"If every married couple at odds were suspected of murderous intent, there would hardly be enough judges to try the cases," said Henrietta. The word "murderous" seemed to cause her no embarrassment.

Louie had listened and watched in silence, sitting a little aside and less in the light, conscious of a feeling between the two speakers which was not wholly expressed in their words. She felt Henrietta had a strong desire to believe Rowland not guilty because she liked him; Louie herself remained still unconvinced, because she was sure that Rowland was overcome by a feeling for Henrietta much stronger than mere liking.

Henrietta was talking about the children again.

"Do you know, Colonel Dynham, I believe you might be able to turn the tables on Mr. Ridgway? For if you keep your children now, the burden of going to law to recover them will rest on Lady Caynnes and Hilary and so, if Caroline's conduct is to be dragged out for public scrutiny, it is they who will have to do it and not you."

Rowland gazed at her in silence; Louie had never seen him look so surprised.

"You had not thought of that?" said Henrietta.

"No, but it is an extremely clever idea," he said.

Henrietta smiled, showing her little teeth.

"Extraordinary to relate, women have minds too," she said, with the utmost sweetness.

At that Rowland's tense face relaxed and he smiled back at her. "Miss Tollington, surely you have never heard me underrate the intellect of your sex? Certainly not yours, since you have so many times caught me out in argument."

"Oh, there is no doubt but that I should have been a diplomat too," said Henrietta gaily. "Imagine Hayford's face, if I appeared in his office one morning!"

At that moment Miles came running in. "Uncle Rowland, Josce says the old man with the bells has come, and will you hear him?"

"Indeed we will—good heavens, how many years is it since I was here at Christmas?" said Rowland, getting up at once.

They all went into the kitchen where everyone was gathered round a little old man who held in his hand a long piece of wood with bells of silver metal each side, tiny at the top and at the bottom the size of large cups.

312

These he struck with a small drumstick, playing old carol tunes. The ringing silvery tone was very clear and even.

Rowland went and brought Mary Anne from her bed, wrapped up in a red quilt, and sat with her on his knee. The children were all fascinated, both by the silvery sounds and by the solemn little gnome of a man.

But at last Rowland said, "Now we must let Joe sit down to his supper. And listen, Joe, I think you had better stop the night, for it's snowing again and hardly safe to go abroad."

"Thank'ee, zurr, reckon I will stop," said the old man. "This yurr lot only coom on when I'd passed Ashworthy."

Rowland carried Mary Anne back to her bed and Joscelin told the girls that old Joe always walked round the district at Christmas time, playing his bells. "He m-must have heard we were h-home again."

Louie and Henrietta had a strong impression that the brothers, so different in temperament, both had a deep-rooted love of their old home, where so many generations of Dynhams had been born—and few had died.

The rest of the evening was spent quietly by the fire and Joscelin was persuaded to play to them on the guitar he had brought back from Vienna, and even to sing. Outside the snow went on falling softly, feather on feather.

In the morning the cold reflexion on the ceiling told the girls that last night's snow was lying. When they went to the window they saw what a heavy fall it had been. The ground was a sheet of white, even in the yard; the roofs were heavily crusted; there were steep drifts against the walls. And the sky was not yet clear; grey clouds lowered above the long high line of the moor.

"We're snowbound!" cried Miles excitedly, when they came down to breakfast. "Hickman says there are drifts four feet deep between here and Upcott Dynham."

"There won't be drifts on the moor road," said Henrietta.

"No, but there will on the way down into Torridge Vale, Hickman says so. You can't go home today!"

Adrian was so excited by the snow he forgot his sulk. "We can make a huge snow man," he said. "As big as—big as Uncle Josce."

Rowland laughed. "That will keep you busy for the morning!" he said. "Miss Tollington, no chaise can travel today, but we could send a man on foot with a message to Woodford."

Henrietta seemed to Louie careless of Hilary's possible anxieties, sure he would guess they were safe; it was Louie who persuaded her to write a note, and presently one of the farm men set off, taking his son for company.

Mary Anne was better this morning; she was allowed to get up and come into the breakfast room, where she was soon happily employed in nursing La Belle through a severe illness, which necessitated much giving of medicine and bandaging of arms and legs, and running to Mrs. Hickman for advice.

Rowland had not come back after taking the note to find a messenger and Joscelin too was out, so that the girls soon found the house dull and decided to go out and see how the boys were getting on with their snowman. The paths outside the Georgian front of the house had been swept clear, so that if they kept to these they would not damage their shoes—the only pair each had got with them. The boys were building their effigy at the corner of the lawn, industriously scooping up handfuls of snow.

"I'll show you how to make a better start than that," said Henrietta. She made a snowball and rolled it along beside the path so that it rapidly increased in size, leaving a strip of winter green grass exposed behind it, like a carpet. "Go on, you push it," she said to Miles. "Push it till it's really big and use it as the base for your man—he'll stand better then, too."

Miles was fascinated by the way the ball peeled off the snow from the grass and kept looking over his shoulder.

"Oh Miles, do look out!" cried Adrian, as the precious ball, now swollen to a good size, nearly rolled over the ha-ha at the end of the lawn. Saving it, they began to mould their snowman on top of it, where it stood.

Henrietta and Louie walked round the paths till they came to the low wall which ran along near the drive. Over it they could see Rowland talking to a man who had been shovelling snow and was leaning on his long-handled Devon spade. Rowland's back was towards them.

Henrietta gave Louie a mischievous glance. She scooped some snow off the top of the wall, pressed it quickly into a ball and threw it at Rowland.

But just then, as if he guessed he was being watched, Rowland turned round, receiving the snowball full in the chest. It burst just where his neckerchief was tucked into his shirt.

"Oh!" cried Henrietta at once. "Who could have done that? Miles, you naughty boy!"

Miles, who was carefully shaping two feet for the rotund snowman, looked up in surprise.

Rowland came towards the wall, shaking the snow out of his clothes and smiling.

"You have a very good aim, Miss Tollington!" he said.

"What can make you think it was me?" she said innocently.

"I don't suspect Louie," said Rowland.

"It is very unfair, but nobody ever suspects Louie," said Henrietta. "But whoever threw it merely intended it for your back and not to give you a cold douche. You turned too soon."

Rowland stood there, just across the wall, smiling at her.

"Ah, but you see I like to face the firing," he said.

317

"Well, since you are not slain, why not come and join us?" said Henrietta.

He looked as if he would and even made a movement towards the garden gate but then suddenly changed his mind.

"I am sorry, but I must go and see the shepherd now."

He went away, stepping through the snow with long firm strides.

"Now why does he always retire?" Henrietta exclaimed, not a little annoyed.

Louie thought of the promise Lady Hayford had extracted from Rowland and wondered if she was doing right in concealing that conversation from Henrietta. She had promised Tinna not to speak of it and she knew Hilary did not want anything to come of Rowland's attraction to Henrietta. Nor was she sure that there was any real depth in Henrietta's feelings. In the end she remained silent.

Henrietta addressed herself to assisting the two little boys to make a face for their snowman.

Later that morning Joscelin brought out a couple of old sledges and took the boys to ride down a frozen slope in the home meadow, and the girls, borrowing boots from Mrs.

Hickman, went to watch. Cottage children soon appeared to join in the fun, but Miles was at first afraid to try, though longing to do it. Adrian had already gone down several times, shrieking with excitement.

"Here, Miles, come on the biggest one with me," said Rowland suddenly, and in a few moments he was astride the sledge with Miles, looking very puny and pale, held in front of him.

They went down fast but Rowland braked with his feet so that the sledge stopped gradually and gently at the bottom.

Miles was quite as astonished to have been taken down the run by his formidable uncle as he was to have reached the bottom without falling off. He was even more surprised when Rowland, jumping up, said, "Stay where you are—I'll pull you up again."

And so Miles rode up the slope as well as down, Adrian greeting him with cries of, "You lucky dog! You lazy thing, Miles!" and, daringly, "I bet you won't pull me up, Papa."

"No, I won't," said Rowland cheerfully. "Do you good to climb."

Adrian grimaced and ran off to play with some snowballing farm children. From a safe distance he threw a snowball at his father but missed him.

"He is not such a good shot as you, Miss Tollington," said Rowland. "But then, you have had longer to practise."

"Now, how am I to take that, I wonder?" said Henrietta gaily. "As a compliment to my dexterity, or to my being a veteran campaigner, or just to my venerable age?"

Rowland smiled. "To your victorious eye!" he said.

Henrietta laughed, but Louie felt she was satisfied.

All that day was a happy one; the long evening merry.

"I have never seen Rowland so h-happy," Joscelin said to Louie, looking to the other end of the room where his brother and Henrietta were sitting, with Mary Anne between them, teasing each other over her smooth fair head.

"Not when he was young?" Louie said. To her, Rowland seemed on the verge of middle age.

Joscelin smiled. "N-No, he was too determined to get ahead to l-let go and enjoy himself. But Henrietta Tollington seems to have the power to release the spring."

Louie looked at the little group; Henrietta was making La Belle dance, flicking up her arms and legs and singing la-la, while Mary Anne giggled with delight. Only Adrian kept away, lying on the hearth rug playing draughts with Miles.

Somehow Louie still felt a deep unease. It was as if she could not believe in what was before her eyes, as if Caroline was in some way still present, preventing life from going on without her.

7

THE next day began badly; there had been more snow in the night and the clouds, low and grey, were blowing fast across the sky. Mary Anne came late to breakfast, and in tears.

"La Belle's gone!" she sobbed in despair. "I can't find her anywhere."

Louie went to make a search but had to report that she could see no sign of the favourite. Mary Anne, slumped and miserable in her chair, looked suspiciously at Adrian, who buried his nose in his mug of milk.

"You *laughed* at her, Adrian," she said.

"Well, she's a silly old thing," said Adrian defiantly. "And you're silly to care so much for her."

Rowland looked sternly at his son. "Have you hidden the doll, Adrian?" he demanded.

"No, I haven't," said Adrian, red in the face.

Rowland turned suddenly to Miles, who was watching, fearfully.

"Miles, what do you know about this?"

Miles swallowed nervously and then said, "I think she's fallen in the water butt."

Henrietta began to laugh but Mary Anne gave a wail of anguish.

"She's drowned! Oh, how could you be so beastly?"

"Surely the water butts are all frozen over?" said Henrietta.

"No, the ice is broken every morning," said Rowland. "Don't cry, Mary Anne, we'll fish your darling from her watery grave."

"She'll be spoiled," sobbed the little girl. "Soaked to pieces."

"It's very naughty of you boys to do such a thing," said Rowland sternly. "So unkind to Mary Anne."

"I didn't mean her to fall in the water butt!" shouted Adrian. "I just threw her out of the window, that's all."

Rowland rose to his feet. "Adrian! You said you knew nothing about it."

"I didn't!" said Adrian, sitting back in his chair and staring up at his tall father with all the defiance he could muster. "I said I didn't hide her, and I didn't."

"You knew the doll was lost and you knew you were responsible," said Rowland severely. "It is just an evasion to say you did not hide it. You were not telling the truth."

"I was," said Adrian.

"Not the whole truth," said Rowland. "You were afraid to own up. Get up now."

Reluctantly and awkwardly, and obviously frightened, Adrian slithered off his chair, keeping his hands behind him and his eyes on his father.

"You are to go up to your room and stay there till dinner time," said Rowland, pronouncing sentence.

"But—but I want to play with the sledges," said Adrian.

"Well, that's your punishment for being so naughty as to conceal what you had done. Go upstairs at once."

Adrian slowly turned and went to the door, dragging his feet. But when he reached it he suddenly looked round and shouted with desperate bravado, "Well! You're much worse! You never said what you did either. Nobody's punished you, have they? But you knocked my Mamma down dead—everybody says so."

There was a moment of absolute silence and then Rowland said, "Everybody likes to make a shocking tale of what they know nothing about." He spoke evenly but with a bitter undertone. "Go to your room, Adrian."

Adrian went out, banging the door behind him and stamped very loudly up the stairs.

There was an uncomfortable pause and then Josce heaved himself from his chair and announced, "Well, I'm going to get that d-doll out of the t-tub."

The tension eased and nothing was said about Adrian's final outburst.

La Belle was recovered, sodden, but Mrs. Hickman promised she would dry her out carefully and Louie said she would make some new clothes for her, so that Mary Anne was comforted, though to her sorrows for her favourite was now added apprehension for her brother, for she felt he had irretrievably disgraced himself with his father.

Although Rowland took her, well wrapped up, for a ride on the sledge, Mary Anne was not really happy all morning; nor was she much cheered when Adrian came down to dinner at two, for though Rowland said nothing further to him, he had gone back into his sulk and ate his food without a word. Nor did he say he was sorry, either to his sister or his father. Rowland simply ignored him, talking mostly to Henrietta.

After the meal was over Adrian persuaded Miles to go out with him to roll another snowball up the lane behind the farm buildings. Everyone else stayed indoors. Louie was helping Mary Anne to make a new outfit for La Belle, when she should be sufficiently dried out to wear it, and Henrietta joined in by making a very pretty little hat, cleverly contrived out of scraps.

"Poor Belle, she is hardly enough of a belle to carry off that exquisite creation," said Rowland, as he passed them. He did not stay in the same room but went into a study to write a final report on the situation in Vienna as he had observed it recently.

Joscelin, in another room, was playing Handel and Bach on an old harpsichord; there was no pianoforte at Brentland and he felt the old music was more suited to the old instrument. The wiry twangling feathery sounds appealed to Henrietta, who remarked that she liked the counterpoint and antique dances better than the new sonatas she had to listen to at her sister's musical evenings.

But after a while she became bored sitting still and said to Louie, "Let us go out and fetch those little boys home. It is time they came in, for it will be dark soon."

So, in bonnets and cloaks, they started up the lane outside the farm gates. They could see the trail of the snowball, growing wider as it had grown bigger, and followed it up the slope till they came to the ball itself, abandoned when it became too heavy to push. Small footmarks were visible in the snow at the side of the lane going up to the place where it joined the road to Woodford.

Up there it was open country and the wind was biting; grey clouds blew over, so low as to seem almost overhead, shutting the day in with gloom. Flecks of snow pecked coldly at the girls' cheeks as they stopped and looked round.

There was no sign of Miles and Adrian, but a big farm boy was coming along, whistling, with a dog bounding beside him. Henrietta asked him if he had seen the two little boys.

"What, Sir Miles?" said the boy, who evidently belonged to Brentland. "And the Colonel's son? Yes, I seen 'em!" He laughed. "That young Master Dynham, 'ee say 'ee wur running away! To Woodford, says 'ee, I'm staying there with Mr. Tollington, says 'ee, talking grand like."

"Woodford! He can't possibly walk there," said Henrietta.

"So I told en, Miss, but 'ee stuck up 'ee's chin and off 'ee marched, and poor little Sir Miles running along behind, looking as if he didn't like it at all!"

"Silly boy!" cried Henrietta. "This will make his father even more angry, if he hears of it. Well, we will fetch them back directly. They can't have gone far."

"Just over the brow, miss, I reckon," said the boy, and went on home, while the girls walked along the snowy road on top of the moor till they reached a high point from which they expected to see the boys ahead of them, or even coming back. But there was nothing on the road, which from here ran on in a wide bend, white and untrodden, skirting a shallow coombe. The wild rough land lay all round them, pale under the lowering sky.

"We had better go back and tell Cousin Rowland," said Louie, anxiously.

But Henrietta, scanning the scene, pointed to their left. "Look, isn't that them, down there?"

Two small dark figures were only just visible in the increasing gloom, going away from them and off the road, on the rough slope of the dipping ground.

"They thought they would cut off that

long bend the road makes, I expect," said Henrietta.

She cupped her hands and shouted but her voice was carried away on the wind, and the two boys scrambled on, small and far away.

"We'll have to go back and fetch someone," said Louie.

"And lose them?" said Henrietta. "It will be dark soon. No, we'll soon catch them up. They must be tired, especially Miles, who was sledging this morning and isn't used to an outdoor life. It is naughty of Adrian to drag him with him."

Adrian's naughtiness made Louie fear Rowland's anger against him; so she pulled her flapping cloak about her and followed Henrietta off the road on to the open moor.

It was rough going and the wiry grass, heavily loaded with snow, brushed wetly against their ankles. Before they had gone far the snow began coming down thickly, swaying in swirls on the wind, and Louie lost sight of the distant boys. She was frightened but dared not admit it, for Henrietta went on with such determination, only stopping once or twice to call out, "Miles!"

"I call Miles because it's easier to say and

he is more likely to listen than Adrian," she said cheerfully.

Louie marvelled at her brave spirit; she was thankful when a dip in the ground cut off the cold wind. Ahead, they saw a track winding round the slope and Henrietta made for that, not telling Louie that she too could no longer see the boys.

The lane was marked with the hoof prints of cattle and they struggled along it in the same direction, Henrietta remarking that it must lead to a farm, with more relief than she meant to show. The snow swirled thickly in the gloom, but sheltered by the steep hillside, it was silent, and presently they heard voices.

"Don't be silly, Miles, it must be the road." That was unmistakably Adrian, clear and confident.

"There weren't any hoof-marks on the road," pointed out Miles, husky and diffident. Then his voice changed. "Adrian, there's someone coming." The next moment he cried out joyfully, "It's Henrietta!" He ran stumbling towards her and she caught him and hugged him.

"You wicked boys! What are you doing so far from home?" she said. "We saw you from the top."

Adrian was hanging back, hands in pockets. "It was a short cut, but we lost the road," he said. "Miles says this can't be it."

"It certainly is not," said Henrietta. "But I think now we had better go on to the farm, for we might lose our way if we tried to get back to Brentland."

"How do you know there's a farm?" asked Adrian.

"Cows going home!" said Henrietta, laughing, and pointing at the track.

Feeling more cheerful they all went on together, Miles stumbling every other step, plainly very tired indeed, Adrian silent, head down, shoulders hunched.

Louie suddenly said, "Adrian, what possessed you to run away to Woodford?"

He wanted to know how she had discovered that and then grumbled that he supposed now everyone would hear of it.

"Father will be angry," he said. "I don't want to live with him. I'd rather live with Cousin Hilary."

"Well, we won't discuss that now," said Henrietta. "Look, isn't that the farm?"

Screwing up their eyes against the spitting snow they could see a dim shadow of buildings ahead and a few bare trees looming in the thickening twilight. There were no lights showing.

"Perhaps it's a barn," said Adrian doubtfully, as they drew nearer.

There was a black square in the wall that might be a window. But there was something strange about the roof above as if it were curiously bent. Then they saw what it was—part of the roof had fallen in. Bare rafters, smoke blackened, showed against the fading sky.

"It's a ruin," said Miles, stopping. "Burnt out."

Weary disappointment sounded in his voice and looking at his peaky face and drooping shoulders Henrietta felt anxious about him.

"Perhaps we can rest here a little while," she said.

The ruined cottage seemed to stand by itself, isolated. There was no sign of any farm. One end of the building seemed intact but the other gaped to the sky, with blackened walls. Brambles and nettles grew everywhere, weighted with snow. Evidently the fire had been a long time ago.

They stood gazing at the place, trying to overcome the feeling of eerieness a ruin always gives. Beyond, the track ran on into whiteness and the oncoming night. Snow swirled silently round them, covering their woollen cloaks and the boys' caps with feathers of cold crystals. Softly the flakes went on flicking at their faces, filling up the ruts, smoothing out the ground, burying the whole landscape.

But although Miles was so tired he could hardly stand, he said, "Don't let's go in there. It looks so—so dreary. And damp."

"Damp!" said Adrian. "What an old woman you are, Miles! It can't be as damp as it is out here."

The cottage was doorless and he walked boldly through the frame. The others followed, Henrietta taking Miles by the hand.

It was not as dark inside as they had feared, since the gaping roof let in what was left of the daylight. At the other end, where part of the roof still stood, there was a ladder leading to a loft above what must have been a separate room, for the partition wall, with its door, had survived the fire. When Adrian tried to open it the latch, rusted through, fell off, startling him. He put his hand against the door but it would not move.

"Anyway, it would be dank in there," he

said. "The loft's the place. A wooden floor—you won't get the rheumatism, Miles."

The next moment he had gone to the ladder and though Louie called out anxiously, "Wait, Adrian!" he took no notice but scrambled up it like a monkey. The rungs cracked as he trod on them but he was up before any broke, jumping off on to the floor above.

"It's all right, it's fine up here," he said, stepping away from the edge.

There was a rending sound as the rotten boards suddenly gave way and with a startled cry Adrian fell through and out of sight.

Louie screamed with terror and her own scream frightened her still more, for it had been quite involuntary. She thought Adrian must have been killed or seriously injured, but after all the height was not great and almost at once they could hear him moving about and crying. His bravado was all gone.

"Oh! Louie! Get me out! It's horrible in here." His voice sounded hollowly through the partition.

Henrietta jumped for the ladder but the bottom rung broke as she put her foot on it and she nearly fell.

"We'll get you out through the door,

Adrian," she called out, and began to push at it.

But the door resisted their combined efforts.

"The beam has sunk down on it," said Miles at last.

It was true; the big beam which ran across the width of the cottage and held the rafters of the loft floor, had sagged on to the lintel, which was pressed down on the top of the door, jamming it. The floor below was of uneven brick.

"It's no good, we can't move it," said Henrietta at last, breathless and dusty, for they had loosened plaster from the partition wall in their struggles.

"I can't stay in here," Adrian's voice came quaveringly. "There's *things* growing up from the ground."

"Come near the door," said Louie, knocking on it.

They heard him stumbling towards it and then he rapped from the other side. Louie was relieved he could move freely; he could not be much hurt.

Henrietta proposed to walk on to get help from the farm, but Louie did not want to be left alone with the children, nor to let

Henrietta set off alone into the snowbound night. Miles was far too tired to go anywhere. He was already sitting on a heap of fallen masonry. It was now almost dark, and when she looked out into the swirling snow, even Henrietta's courage failed her.

"After all, Colonel Dynham will send out men to search for us," she said. "We must just wait."

"I can't stay in here!" Adrian wailed. "It's so very dark and—and horrid. Please, Louie!"

Louie, full of sympathy for the trapped child, got him to sit down on the other side of the door, assuring him that there could not be anything dangerous. "No rats," she said, "as there have been no people here for so long."

"There might be snakes," said Miles fearfully.

"Shut up, Miles," said Henrietta crossly and then was sorry when her sharp tone drew tears from him—silent tears, for Miles rarely cried aloud.

She hugged him then, sitting down with him and wrapping her cloak round them both, while Louie sat against the door to comfort Adrian on the other side of it.

So there they were and as time went on they all became very cold and had to move and clap their arms to keep warm, however tired they felt. It seemed to get more and more difficult to talk, though if they were silent long Adrian would shout out in a panic, "Where are you? Louie! Don't go away!"

Louie was touched that he always called on her, though it emphasised how very young he was, and made her even more anxious.

None of them had much idea how long they had been in the ruined cottage when Miles, struggling once more to the doorway, announced that it had stopped snowing. Somewhere above the thinning cloud there was a moon and now a faint light illuminated the white landscape, the sweep of the moorland hillside. But it only served to show their isolation. There seemed no other building near, no other living creature. The snowstorm had covered the rutted track so that it was now hard to tell where it ran.

They sat down again but every now and then one of them would go to the door and look out, partly to keep warm. Miles found it harder and harder to move, each time, and yet it was he who was standing on the threshold when a spark of light appeared, high on the hill. For a moment he held his breath; it looked so eerie. Then he saw a shadowy moving shape and guessed it was a man carrying a lantern.

Miles began to shout and jump about, waving his arms. "Help! Help!" His voice was not strong but the girls soon added theirs, Louie producing quite a penetrating note.

The lantern stopped and then changed direction. It was coming down the slope towards them.

It was not till that lantern was quite near that Miles, who had imagined it was carried by some shepherd or farmhand, saw a tall figure looming, his hat tied on with a scarf, and suddenly feared it was a smuggler or a wrecker.

"Miles? Is that you?"

It was Rowland Dynham. He held up the lantern and saw Louie and Henrietta. "The girls too," he said in relief, and then, with sudden apprehension. "Where's Adrian?"

"He's all right," said Henrietta quickly, "but he's fallen through some rotten boards and we can't get him out."

They led Rowland to the back of the cottage. He put his lantern down on a level piece of floor and called out, "Adrian? No bones broken?"

Adrian, who had become silent as soon as

he heard his father's voice, was reassured not to be addressed angrily.

"I've bumped myself," he said dolefully.

"I should think you have, if you fell through there," said Rowland. "What a couple of little idiots! Do you know I've half the countryside out looking for you? And it's the merest chance I've found you. Josce went to Top Leys and I was cutting across to see if they had had any luck." And he added, "It is your own fault, Adrian, for running away, as I hear you did."

Silence from behind the partition; Adrian was frightened when he knew that his father was aware of his attempted flight.

"However, the first thing is to get you out of that oubliette you have so cleverly dropped into," said Rowland.

He shook the ladder, but the frame collapsed altogether, so he turned to the door.

"The beam's jammed it," said Miles watching.

Rowland examined the position of the beam and decided that he might be able to shift it up an inch or so and free the door. He put his shoulder under it and heaved. At first this merely brought down a shower of dust on his head but a second effort was more successful. The lintel, which must have been split by the sagging beam, suddenly came loose and fell out.

"Ha!" exclaimed Rowland, panting but triumphant. "Stand back, Adrian, I'm going to kick the door in."

Still with his shoulders under the beam he kicked the old door till it fell inwards, hanging on the rusty bottom hinge—the top one had fallen away.

Light from the lantern showed up the pale dirty face of his son, crouching anxiously among the elongated white stalks which had grown up through the floor.

"Come along, Adrian, you can climb over the door," said Rowland.

Adrian began to scramble out over the tilting door.

There was a sudden loud crack above and a creaking sound.

"The beam!" shrieked Louie. "The beam's coming down!"

The heavy beam was slowly sagging down in the middle above the doorway. Rowland still had his shoulder under it and now braced his arm against the wall, trying to hold it up.

"Double-quick, Adrian," he said urgently

as the boy stumbled over the tipping door and he pushed him with one foot.

Louie and Henrietta both started forward but Rowland said sharply, "Get back! Right back, both of you!"

They stopped at that tone of command, even though they could see that he was staggering under the weight of the beam, trying to hold it up until the child had got through the gap. Adrian was crawling towards them when there was a rending crash, the beam split and fell, carrying part of the partition wall and most of the rest of the ceiling with it. Clouds of dust arose.

For one moment there was nothing to be seen but a heap of rubble and then, as the dust settled, they saw a small struggling shape, Adrian's head and shoulders, with his arms grabbing about like crab's claws.

"I can't get out!" he screamed hoarsely. "Papa! I can't move my legs."

Louie caught his arms and pulled but he gave such a cry that she stopped, frightened.

Kneeling on the ground, she could see nothing of Rowland. He must have been buried under the falling ceiling, perhaps even crushed by the broken beam. Henrietta, her

341

face gone white, was staring at the heap of rubble as the dust began to clear.

"Look," said Miles, quaveringly. He pointed at something sticking out of the pile—a hand, Rowland's hand, limp and still.

"Is he dead?" Miles whispered.

It was Henrietta who crouched down to feel that horribly limp hand. And in a moment she looked up and said, "I can feel his pulse."

With more hope they moved round the heap and looking under the slanting end of the beam, which had caught on a jutting piece of masonry, they could see Rowland's head, dusty and bleeding, but not crushed. He had been knocked down on to the door, with part of the beam across his body, but because the butt had caught like that, he had been spared the full weight of it.

In a few moments, with a gurgling snort, he came round and opened his eyes.

"He's alive," said Miles, squatting on the floor, staring at his uncle's dust-coated face.

"Miles . . ." muttered Rowland, blinking and coughing. Then he remembered what had happened and demanded urgently, "Adrian! My God, where is he?"

The heap heaved as he tried to get up and the beam rocked.

"Lie still!" cried Henrietta. "You'll bring the broken end of that beam down on your head. Adrian is all right."

Rowland screwed his head round and saw how precariously he was pinned down.

"Papa, you're lying on my legs," said Adrian suddenly. "I felt you move then."

Rowland turned his head back and saw where Adrian was lying.

"Can you move your legs?" Rowland asked, anxiously. "Try."

Adrian's shoulder movements were so vigorous that they saw he could not be much hurt.

"All right, I can feel you," said Rowland. "Wait, I'll try to move so as to release you."

He freed his left arm and carefully shifted himself, but brought down a further shower of plaster.

"Don't Papa! More's coming down!" cried Adrian, frightened, and putting his arms over his head. His small dirty hands looked almost babyish suddenly.

Rowland reached out his arm and managed to pat his son on the back. "Don't be afraid, Adrian," he said gently. "You're all right—we are both all right, thank God."

"I think my legs are quite squashed flat," said Adrian, fearfully.

He could not see, but the others saw Rowland smile.

"I don't think so," he said, "from the force of your wriggling!"

Slowly and with difficulty he managed to move enough for Adrian to squirm from under him and crawl out on to the floor, where he immediately sat down to examine his trapped limbs. He was astonished to find that they looked much as usual, though scraped and bruised.

Rowland watched him. "Silly little mutton-head," he said, suddenly, with affection.

Adrian looked at him uncertainly.

"Aren't you very angry with me?" he hazarded at last.

"Yes, very," said his father, but in the mildest possible tone. "And even more with myself, for being such a fool as not to realise this beam would be as rotten as the rest of the place."

Adrian felt that things were better than he had expected. "Papa, can't you get up now?" he said. "I'll help." And he began to pick bits of wood off the pile.

Rowland did make another effort, but

the butt end of the beam rocked again, and Henrietta begged him not to try. And she had seen him screw up his mouth as he moved.

"You are more hurt than you thought," she said anxiously, kneeling on the ground near his head.

"No, but I must have damaged my knee somehow," he replied. "I don't believe anything is broken, all the same."

Henrietta got out her handkerchief and began to wipe the cut on his forehead which was oozing blood, but it was more of a bruise than a wound. "You must resign yourself to lying still," she said. "Surely someone will see the lantern and come? Why is this cottage so isolated?"

"The old beekeeper used to live here," said Rowland. "When it was burnt down the shock was too much for the old fellow and after he died, no one wanted to live out here, so it was let go. That was before I had the managing of Brentland."

Miles felt the ruinous place less frightening now that he knew it had belonged to an old beekeeper.

"Shall I put the lantern on the window sill?" he said.

Rowland assented. "A lot of use I have

been," he remarked wryly. "I wonder if you could find your way to Top Leys?"

"No, we are all too tired," said Henrietta firmly. "And we intend to stay here with you, sir, so you must endure it as best you may."

Miles put the lantern on the sill and as he turned back he thought how strange they looked, a few people huddled in a ruined house, and Rowland with the beam across him, half buried in rubble. It seemed extraordinary to Miles to see his formidable uncle for once completely helpless. The lantern light picked out faces and hands and the jagged end of the slanting beam, and cast black shadows up the crumbling walls.

And then he heard a noise like soft spitting against the glass of the lantern.

"It's snowing again," he said.

8

BECAUSE of the renewed snowstorm all thought of walking to the farm was given up and yet it was that which brought about their rescue, for Noah Beer, sent along the road with one of the Brentland sledges, became alarmed when his master did not turn up at Top Leys and went out with Joscelin to look for him. They saw the lantern in the window of the ruined cottage and soon made their way down to it. The first the others knew of it was when Josce and Noah came walking in at the doorway, snow powdering their clothes and melting like tears on their faces.

"Oh my dear life!" exclaimed Noah Beer in alarm, when he saw Rowland lying half buried under rafters and plaster. "Whatever have you done to yourself, sir?"

"Yes, that's it, I suppose," said Rowland, with a wry smile. "I have brought down the house, Noah, on my own head."

Everyone began telling how it had happened, but Josce and Noah were more interested in the problem of how to free Rowland from the beam without bringing the butt of it down on his head. Josce, crouching down, got his arm and shoulder under it and managed to lift it enough for Noah to drag Rowland out from the rubble. The little boys stared as Josce held the weight of the heavy beam on his shoulder and then rolled it off so that it fell on the door Adrian had crawled over. It seemed to them that no one else could have done that; Josce was so strong.

Even he was a bit breathless as he got to his feet and stood looking down at his brother. Noah Beer was conducting a quick but expert examination.

"I don't believe it's broke any bones," he said, in amazed relief. "It wur the butt catching that way saved 'ee, zurr."

In moments of stress Noah's accent always became broader.

"I daresay I could have got out if I hadn't been afraid of bringing it down," said Rowland. "Help me up, Beer."

In getting to his feet he discovered just how badly he had wrenched his leg and bruised his knee in falling, but that was the most serious of his injuries. He was extremely dirty and covered in dust. Adrian stood watching,

348

unusually silent. He was aware that his wilfulness had led to the accident and felt burdened with guilt.

But Rowland gave him an affectionate pat on the shoulder and said, "Well, Adrian, are those legs of yours too squashed to climb the hill?"

It seemed as if everything was going to be forgiven and forgotten, and Adrian stepped willingly into the snowbound night once more.

The two girls carried the lanterns, while Noah Beer helped Rowland, and Josce carried the two little boys, turn and turn about. Before long the snow stopped falling and the moon briefly appeared through the sliding cloud.

They had not seen Top Leys earlier because it lay round a shoulder of hill at the head of a shallow coombe in the moor, with a brush of bent trees hiding it. But it was not very far away, which was lucky, for they were all very tired and Rowland limping painfully. By the time they reached the farmhouse, he was leaning on Noah Beer, and when they got inside the big kitchen he stood there in a daze, looking quite unlike himself, his face puffy with bruises and smeared with grime and blood.

Mrs. Cornish, though she soon had them all sitting down and drinking mulled ale, said very little and looked sideways at Rowland Dynham as if she were more afraid of him than sorry for him. Louie only realised the reason for this when she overheard two little apprentices talking, and recognised one as Nancy Cottle, the child who had given evidence at the inquest. She was staring at Rowland with a sort of fascination.

The boy nudged her. "Don't 'ee be scared, Nancy, that murdering Dynham of Brentland, 'ee can't do nothing to 'ee, because you wasn't there this time. Master Ad'an, he was luckier than what missus was, last year."

"Oh don't 'ee talk so, Tom," Nancy said. "You know 'ee never killed missus."

"Didn't 'ee then? You're soft, Nancy!" the boy scoffed. "Why, 'ee's own b'y run away from 'ee because 'ee's so cruel hard, and it wur going after 'ee's b'y to beat en, that Dynham fell through the rotted floor—that's how 'twas, I tell 'ee."

Louie realised that the story must have been misinterpreted by the people at Top Leys, to fit the character they had already cast for Rowland. She interrupted the two children, sitting on their bench, saying, "It wasn't so—it was Adrian who fell through the floor and Colonel Dynham was trying to get him out when it collapsed on him."

The children stared up at her, struck dumb; Nancy's eyes were anxious, even frightened, but she said nothing. Louie felt too tired to go on; as she turned away she heard the boy mutter, "Don't believe it."

Mrs. Cornish offered to keep them all for the night at Top Leys and it seemed the best thing, so that soon there was a great scurrying with jugs of hot water, flannel nightgowns, ointments for bruises, and a warming of beds and then, at last, silence settled down and everyone slept, while the moon went down behind the whitened hills.

Next day the sky was still clear and the sun came up and shone, slanting and cold and bright, across the land. They were to go back to Brentland but they could not ride by cart because of the deep drifts in the lane that went up to meet the road at Moor Cross. Louie was glad of this when she realised that then they would have had to pass over the place where Caroline had met her death, and in Rowland's company. Instead they were to cut across the hillside where he had been the night before when they saw his lantern, and she wondered if he had gone that way to avoid the spot.

Joscelin was going to pull the little boys on the sledge but changed his mind when he saw how painfully his brother was walking, and said he must be the one to ride.

"Nonsense, I'm all right," said Rowland, but before he had gone far he had to give in and allow himself to be made a passenger, though he held Miles in front of him on the big sledge. Miles was far more tired by the events of yesterday than was Adrian, who was once more bright-eyed and rosy-faced, ready for anything. Joscelin and Noah Beer pulled the sledge together.

In spite of the crippling effect of his damaged knee, Rowland had contrived to look, this morning, almost as trim as usual. He had got Beer to shave him, and the plaster on his forehead was half hidden under the brim of his hat. Beer had also been set to brush his clothes and clean his boots, so that nobody meeting him today could have guessed what he had looked like last night, after lying an hour under a pile of rubble.

352

Henrietta even twitted him upon this care for his appearance.

"Colonel Dynham, I declare, it is most ungallant of you to turn yourself out so smart when Louisa and I are forced to look such frights!"

The girls' shoes had gone to pieces as a result of so much walking in the snow and their stockings had been in holes. Mrs. Cornish had provided homely wear of her own and Henrietta did indeed look odd in thick stockings and heavy shoes, though Louie thought she looked charmingly piquante in the country bonnet she had borrowed, her small face looking out, fair and gay.

"It is even more ungallant to ride while you have to walk, Miss Tollington," Rowland replied, with a smile.

"Oh, but it is a great thing to be able to look down on you for once, isn't it, Louie?" said Henrietta, mischievously. "We shall never feel obliged to defer to you again, sir."

And so the journey home was cheerful, Adrian even finding the energy to make snowballs and hurl them wildly about. He did not dare throw one at his father till Rowland flung one at him and then he retaliated with delight, sure that all was well.

When they reached Brentland they found Hilary Tollington there. It appeared that the day before he had walked all the way from Woodford across country, with the messenger, only to find on arrival, that the little boys were lost and everyone out searching for them and the two girls. It had been very late before the Brentland men returned from Top Leys with the news that all was well. Hilary looked tired and anxious. He had heard a muddled account of Adrian's disgrace and running away and in spite of Henrietta's gay greeting, his face remained unusually grave as he watched Rowland come limping in with his hand on Josce's arm.

But he said nothing of what was on his mind till after dinner when the children were sent to rest in the housekeeper's room with Mary Anne, there to tell her all their adventures, while she sat, hugging La Belle, and shuddering at the story.

"How dreadful you must have felt, Adrian," she said, as usual sympathising with both brother and father in their emotional collisions.

In the old wainscoted room, where Rowland was sitting in an upright wooden chair with arms, by the fire, silence fell among the grown up members of the party. With the afternoon, more cloud had come up, but the sleet blowing past the windows had more of water in it than snow and it seemed a thaw was on the way.

Hilary, who had been gazing out of the window with his hands in his pockets, came back to the fireplace and stood opposite Rowland.

"If this frost yields we may soon be able to go back to Woodford," he said. "I think I should take the children with me, Dynham."

Rowland stiffened and his voice was harsh as he replied, "I shall not allow that, Tollington. I intend to keep my children. If you want to fight it out at law, you can be the one to bring the case."

It was Henrietta's advice, but put in the most defiant possible way. Rowland evidently expected an angry answer, but Hilary did not reply angrily.

He paused a moment before saying in his soft lisping voice, "Dynham, do you think you are taking the right way with Adrian? For such a young boy to run away, he must have been pretty frightened."

"Frightened? Nonsense! He was annoyed

because I punished him for misbehaviour," said Rowland. "He thought he would get his own way better with you, I've no doubt."

"I daresay, for he has spirit," said Hilary. "But there must have been fear behind it. And surely you must admit that other people may well fear for him, when they know what you are capable of, once passion gets the better of you."

Rowland did not move but his face went pale. Louie thought it was with anger and was suddenly afraid he was going to hurl himself at Hilary as he had at Caynnes Ridgway. Even in his present crippled state she felt he might seriously injure Hilary, so slight and so lacking in physical strength.

But when Rowland spoke his voice was hoarse with shame, not anger. He did not look at Hilary but at the fire as he said, "I never have felt, never could feel anger against Adrian in that way."

Hilary replied, with more sympathy than contempt, "I do not see how you can be sure of that, Dynham, since on such an occasion you lose control of yourself: that is just the point."

There was a strained silence.

Louie stared at Rowland as he sat by the

fire, too ashamed to look any of them in the face, and suddenly it was as if a spell broke and she saw him as an ordinary mortal, a man afraid of his own passions, cornered by circumstances in a situation where he was about to lose those he loved best, and through his own fault. He looked tired and unhappy, someone beginning to realise the extent of his failure in the inner world of feeling, beginning to be old.

It was a moment of revelation to Louie. Ever since she had first met Rowland Dynham she had unconsciously seen him as a representative man, the figure of the father she had never known, the lover she had scarcely come to dream of, she, a shy girl brought up among women. Because he was so tall, so fine looking, so dominant, he had become for Louie larger than life, whether as hero or villain she had never quite decided. Now here he was, a person like anyone else, not merely vulnerable but defeated.

At last he said, "You may be more fit than I to bring up my children, Tollington, but I cannot give them up."

"No, and you should not—Hilary, this is not right," said Henrietta warmly. "If you had been with us last night you would know that Adrian has nothing to fear from his father and everything to gain by remaining in his care."

"I am glad you think so," said Hilary, looking uncomfortable, as though he found it harder to oppose Rowland when he admitted his weakness than when he proudly stood upon his rights. "But I have to remember that it is those who are nearest to you, Dynham, who have roused this demon before. There it is: I too have a responsibility for Caroline's children."

Joscelin, who had been sitting at the table with his chin on his fist, watching in silence, suddenly looked up, but hesitated.

"What do you think, Mr. Joscelin?" asked Henrietta.

Rowland glanced up. "Oh, Josce knows my temper only too well," he said, bitterly. "He's felt the force of it probably more than anyone else. And, I have to admit it, once already this last summer Adrian took refuge with him, from me."

"But I know you would n-never hurt Adrian," said Joscelin, in his slow, quiet way. "I n-never thought you w-would have hurt C-Caroline either, though that is a different m-matter."

358

"It is something that influences Tollington, however," said Rowland, looking at Hilary, "Is it not so?"

"I am afraid it does, and must," he answered gravely.

There was another silence and then Joscelin suddenly got to his feet. "Then I will fetch N-Nancy after all," he said. "I thought it would be t-too much today, but she's here, and would l-like to get it over."

"Nancy Cottle? What do you mean?" said Rowland, bewildered.

"She has something to t-tell, about the accident," said Joscelin, and he went out, returning in a few moments leading the little farm apprentice by the hand. Nancy looked terrified and stood dumb before them.

"She wants to t-tell it, but she can't help being afraid," said Josce, patting Nancy's shoulder encouragingly. "Such a terrible memory for the child."

"She has nothing to fear," said Rowland. "She told the truth at the inquest. She came out of a gate across the lane and I sent her to Top Leys for help."

"Oh, 'ess, zurr, but I wur there afore that," said Nancy, in a sudden breathless rush.

Louie felt almost sick; now, more than a

year after the event, something was going to come out about Caroline's death.

"I seen 'ee through the hedge, Colonel Dynham, zurr, afore ever missus came, but I hid away, because 'ee looked grim-like." Nancy blushed, overcome by what she had said, but then blundered on, anxious to get her confession over.

"Of a sudden I heard wheels going fast and a lady shouting and I leapt out on the bank to look and there was that high carriage coming into our lane, and the lady driving, standing up I think. Then one horse shied and the wheel went up the bank, and the lady fell out, and oh, she fell down on her head and she never moved more."

They all gazed at the child; Louie felt certain she was telling the truth.

It was Rowland who spoke first. "But you were not there when I came round the corner, Nancy," he said quietly.

"No, zurr, I leapt back over the bank and hid behind the hedge. I wur that scared."

Joscelin said, "Poor Nancy, she thought it was her f-fault, because the mare shied at her. And then, with all the talk later of m-murder and hanging, she thought she'd be hanged, poor child, so she did not d-dare speak up."

"Didn't you think, Nancy, that Colonel Dynham might hang for it, if you did not speak?" said Henrietta gravely.

"Oh no, ma'am, because Colonel Dynham's a gentleman—they wouldn't never hang him."

Rowland gave a wry smile. "She's right—they haven't," he said. "But Nancy, you must not think you are in any sense guilty. Caroline—my wife—was driving like a maniac. She might have killed herself on that turn even had the mare not shied. Be sure it was not your fault, child."

"Thank'ee, zurr," Nancy whispered. "And bean't you angry that I saw 'ee come, crying out to her that was dead, and never told it before the King's Crowner?"

"No, I understand," said Rowland, with a sigh.

"But why did she tell it now?" Hilary asked, puzzled. He had been watching both the child and Rowland closely but now he turned to Joscelin. "And why did she come to you?"

"She came to m-me because she knows me," said Joscelin. "Last night she realised that people were saying Rowland had gone for his son as he had gone for C-Caroline, and she felt sorry for him when she saw him at

Top L-Leys. I d-don't say that her story is the whole of the truth, but it is p-part of it." Joscelin's hesitations seemed to give added weight to his words.

Hilary said, "Well, I must beg your pardon, Dynham, for I confess I believed you had played a more active part in Caroline's death. I am sorry—and I am glad you are not guilty, even though I know she gave you very great provocation."

Rowland's face was still oppressed and he answered slowly, "But as Josce says, Nancy's story is not the whole truth. For there is a sense in which I am guilty of Caroline's death and I shall always feel so. Because if she had not seen me at the cross, waiting for her, she would not have done so mad a thing. She did it to avoid me."

Nancy stared at him, round-eyed, but he did not look at her. He was looking at Henrietta.

She said quietly, "You could not know she would do that."

"No, but I knew I was the last person she would want to see just then," said Rowland. He leant his head on his hand with a gesture of weariness. "I don't know . . . what else could I have done? I could not let her rush headlong into public scandal and ruin without trying to prevent it."

"No, indeed, Dynham, you were right to try," said Hilary. "You cannot be held to account for Caroline's wilfulness, her mad impulses. Poor girl! Perhaps it was better she died then and did not have to endure the effects of her rash actions."

"Perhaps," said Henrietta, dryly, "but she left others to endure them."

"Well," said Hilary, "what can be done to put this right? Can Nancy sign a statement?"

The girl looked terrified and Rowland said at once, "No, no—let us not reopen the case. I was not charged, after all. Besides, as Nancy is so young, I do not know if it would stand, in law. If it convinces you, Tollington, and persuades you that I am not as dangerous as you thought, that is all I care for."

They began to discuss the whole business and Louie, suddenly feeling she could bear no more, slipped out of the room. She went along the dim passage to the breakfast-room, where they had had dinner. There was no candle and the fire was dying but she did not want light, only quiet.

She stood in front of the fire but could not think of anything; only a vague feeling of unhappiness welled up and overcame her, so that she began to weep. She hardly knew why she was weeping.

Presently she heard a door close and then steps in the passage. A band of wavering light ran up the wall on to the ceiling and Hilary appeared in the doorway. He put the candlestick down on the table and came round it towards her.

"Louie? Tears?" he said gently. "I thought you would be so glad to know for certain that your Cousin Rowland had not done what we both feared."

"I am—I am," said Louie, hastily trying to gulp down her sobs. "It's just . . . I was thinking of Caroline, her life—everything wasted. It brought it home, hearing that little girl's tale of the end."

"Poor Louie," he said. "Caroline dazzled you, didn't she?"

"She—she was wonderful in a way," Louie sobbed. "She maddened everybody, me too, with her selfish whims but somehow she was still fascinating. Oh, if only . . . " But she did not know what could have happened to alter that reckless fate. Tears rushed up again to engulf her and the next moment she found herself weeping on Hilary's shoulder and he was murmuring comforting things with his arms round her.

"Dear little Louie, this has all been too much for you," she presently heard him saying. "It is a shame you should have been thrown into such a situation so young. There, don't cry so, it's all over now."

Louie raised her head and looked at him, tears salt on her cheeks. She realised all at once that he was fond of her and that she was crying in the arms of a man who was not even a cousin. "Oh," she whispered, confusion banishing her tears. "Oh, I am sorry."

"What are you sorry for, my dear?" he said, and she saw he was beginning to smile. "I only wish you would let me look after you always, Louie." And he added as if he could not prevent himself, "I suppose you would not consider it?"

Louie gazed at him, trying to grasp what was happening, and he went on recklessly, "I know I am not a fine fellow like Dynham—it's natural you should have been in love with him. But I wish you would not consider whether a lesser mortal might not make for a happier life."

Louie gasped. "I'm not in love with Cousin Rowland," she said.

"I think you were," said Hilary softly.

Louie was wondering if that was what it had been, but no, she felt it was a kind of fascination, not unlike her feeling for Caroline. It was not love, not what she meant by love. As to loving, she did not think it would be difficult to love Hilary, she was not at all sure she did not love him already. She gazed at him and because he was not much taller than herself she was able to look into his eyes, even in this dim candlelight showing bright and alert.

"Hilary," she said, hardly realising she was saying his name aloud, because she was thinking about him, remembering so many little things which now seemed to mean much.

"Yes, me," he said, with a gentle caress. "Try and see if I don't do for a husband, Louie."

His whimsical way of putting it made her smile.

"You don't really want to marry me," she said. "Why, I've nothing—I'm nobody."

"A very dear little somebody to me," said Hilary. "The only reason why I haven't asked you before was because I thought you loved Dynham—though I did not believe it was you he was thinking of."

366

"But your family! Lady Hayford . . ." Louie paused, as the full situation began to dawn on her. "Lady Caynnes!"

"Aunt Caynnes must grin and bear it, if you say yes," said Hilary cheerfully. "I'll protect you from her! Come, Louie, I don't need to marry to please anybody but myself and no one but you pleases me, any longer. Gone are the Julias of yesteryear, tiresome misses! I can't think what made me imagine myself in love with the silly creatures. You were most kind about the last fiasco but now I see how lucky I was to lose that particular Julia."

"Have there been others?" said Louie, suddenly interested.

"Oh, about one every year since I was sixteen—not all called Julia," said Hilary carelessly. "But only one Louie, for ever and a day."

Louie smiled. "You are ridiculous, Mr. Toll—"

Hilary put his finger on her mouth. "Don't—you said Hilary just now, and I shan't let you go back on it."

"Did I?" Louie could not remember. "But I can't decide, all in a moment, such an important thing."

"No, of course you can't," said Hilary, pulling himself up. "But just promise me to consider it seriously. I am serious."

He tried to make his face solemn, but broke into a smile.

"I'm only laughing because I'm invincibly hopeful," he said.

Then the door of the other room opened and Henrietta called for Hilary.

"I'm coming," he replied, relinquishing Louie at last, with reluctance. "Ask Henrietta and see if she doesn't implore you to make me happy," he whispered, pressed her hand and hurried away, leaving the candle with her.

Later that evening, when the girls were in their room together, Louie did bring up the subject, very shyly.

"Henrietta, I hardly like to say this now, after all that has hap-happened today, but Mr. Tollington—your cousin Hilary—he's asked me to marry him."

"At last?" cried Henrietta, running to her with a laughing face. "I thought he would never find the courage!" She embraced Louie. "Oh darling Louie, you will, won't you? Hilary is such a good fellow and yet he has never succeeded in attracting a nice kind girl like you—just what he needs, for he may be merry but he is very affectionate and being an only child who lost his parents early, has had to expend his feelings on mere cousins."

How alike they were, Louie thought, as like as brother and sister; much too alike to marry. "I do like him very much," she said. "More than I realised till he made me think about it."

Henrietta smiled. "Well! Surely that is enough to begin with? He is not the sort to let you down."

"He pretends he has loved me quite a long time," said Louie.

"It is no pretence," said Henrietta. "But he was afraid you loved Rowland Dynham. I told him you had said not, but he would not believe me. I daresay he thought I had a motive in thinking so!" She gave Louie a sidelong glance.

Louie blushed deeply. "I am sure I did not love Cousin Rowland," she said. "But somehow he made me unable to notice anyone else."

"That I can understand all too well," said Henrietta, her hazel eyes as bright and mischievous as Hilary's.

Louie marvelled at her free speaking, even though there was nothing boldly assertive about it.

"Henrietta, do you love him—Cousin Rowland?" she asked with simple seriousness.

"Let us say, as you did, that I like him very much," said Henrietta. "But that does not avail me, since he avoids me—he does, I declare, Louie. And yet I could believe that he . . ." she hesitated and then ended, "is not indifferent."

Louie suddenly decided to tell Henrietta of Tinna's interview with Rowland, which she had interrupted, and the promise extracted from him. Henrietta became quite agitated, wandering restlessly about the room and exclaiming against her sister.

"Oh, it is too cruel of Tinna!"

"But she said then she was sure your heart was not touched," said Louie earnestly.

"She said that to *him*?" cried Henrietta, horrified. "Worse and worse!"

She sat down on the edge of the bed, a slight figure in her thin shift, and after a moment suddenly pressed her hand to her breast and gave Louie a look half comical and half pathetic.

"What a trial they are, these hearts of ours!"

The next moment, with a cry of, "I'm

cold!" she jumped inside the bedclothes and snuggled down. "No, no, let's not talk of it any longer, let's talk of your marrying Hilary. But Louie, I am glad you told me."

Louie got into bed, feeling somehow that she would be marrying Hilary.

9

IN the night the snow turned to rain and by morning patches of grass were showing again and lumps of sodden white were slipping off the roofs with heavy thuds.

Adrian was crestfallen. "Noah Beer says there won't be enough snow left for sledging, not hard enough to slide over," he said at breakfast.

"What, Adrian, haven't you had enough of snow yet?" said Hilary, amused. "But I daresay it will come on again before the holidays are over."

"Must we go back to Woodford?" Adrian demanded.

Rowland corrected him, mechanically. "That is not well said, Adrian, to your Cousin Hilary." Then he realised that it meant his son wanted to stay with him, and glanced across the table at Hilary, half apologetic, half unable to hide the natural satisfaction this gave him.

Hilary smiled. "I don't see why you should not stay here, with your father."

"Me too?" Miles asked, anxiously.

"Why not? It's your home, Miles. But I must take the girls back to Woodford or we shall have Aunt Caynnes driving over to see what has happened to them."

"Today? Must you go today?" said Miles, gazing sadly at Henrietta, his cloudy blue eyes wide open for once.

"Well, if the snow has cleared enough, I thought of going over to Rosewell today," said Hilary. "I've been corresponding with the housekeeper about the damp in the downstairs study room and in her last letter she talked of having the wall mirror unscrewed before the men started work. I would like to see the room myself before they start dismantling it—you know what fools they are about such things. Would you care to come, Dynham, and bring the children?"

It seemed that he had revoked all objections to Rowland's taking up his old position with regard to the children and to the house held in trust for them.

Adrian and Mary Anne at once clamoured to go, but Louie could hardly listen to what was said. At the mention of dismantling the wall mirror she was struck with panic—the letter from Bath would be found, perhaps had already been found by some unsuitable person. Suspicions against Rowland would be revived just when it seemed they could be forgotten, and she was sure he would not allow Nancy to give public evidence even if it proved legally admissible. Louie had already heard him discussing Nancy's future with Joscelin; they planned to buy out her apprenticeship and put her under the supervision of Mrs. Hickman at Brentland. Josce was certain she would like the prospect, for at Top Leys she had been ruled justly but somewhat harshly by Mrs. Cornish.

Louie decided she must tell Hilary about the hidden letter, since he was the one who still had authority over Rosewell. But it was awkward to seek an interview, since he would assume that she was going to give her answer to his marriage proposal.

Trembling with nervous anxiety she went into the drawing-room, cold and dreary, with covers over the furniture, and walked up and down. Before she had made up her mind about anything, Hilary, who had seen her escape from the breakfast room, walked in.

"Louie, my dear, what is the matter? I hope you have not already decided you cannot stand the thought of spending the rest of your life with me? If so, I implore you to wait and see whether a little more time might not accustom you to the idea."

"Oh no, it isn't that," said Louie and then stopped, blushing at her own tactlessness.

But Hilary laughed, if a trifle ruefully. "I might have known *I* could hardly be the cause of such agitation," he said.

"Oh, please, Hilary, I am so worried . . . about the wall mirror."

"The wall mirror?" he repeated in astonishment.

"You see I put it behind there, Caroline's dreadful letter, to hide it from Mr. Ridgway, because he seemed to think it would tell against Cousin Rowland, and it went so far in I could not get it out—oh, suppose they find it?"

Incoherently, the whole story of the letter came out.

Hilary certainly took it seriously. "What a lucky thing I mentioned it," he said. "Well, we may get there before it is discovered."

"But shall I have to tell Rowland?"

Hilary took her hand. "You are frightened of that?" he said, gently.

Louie could only nod, mutely pleading with her large brown eyes.

375

"If he has to be told, I'll tell him," Hilary promised her.

"Oh, thank you!" The brown eyes rewarded him with relief and gratitude. "I can't help feeling he would hate to find I had read what Caroline wrote to Peter Raine—he doesn't even know that anyone else knows there was a letter of hers enclosed in the one from Mrs. Raine."

"Perhaps we need not tell him you read it," Hilary said. "Just that you saw it was the Bath letter and hid it from Caynnes Ridgway."

It was a further relief to Louie, but different feelings came when he added, rather sadly, "I can see he is still your first object, Louie."

And suddenly Louie knew that this was not so; she minded more that Hilary was hurt than anything else. He was holding her hand; now she put the other shyly against his coat and said earnestly, "That is not true, Hilary. Everything to do with Rowland belongs to the past now, for me. The future is . . . with you."

"Do you mean that, Louie?" he asked eagerly. "No, no—don't say, if it's still uncertain. Anything, even days of suspense, is better than *no*."

"Not no, but yes," she said, feeling as if she were jumping over a cliff.

"Oh, you blessed girl!" said Hilary, and in his delight at her consent, to him at that moment unexpected, he caught her to him and kissed her.

And when Hilary kissed her Louie was quite sure she wanted to marry him and marvelled that she had not realised it before. "How blind I've been!" she thought, shyly returning his kiss so that he became even more exhilarated and wanted to declare their engagement at once to everyone.

"No, no, Hilary—only to Henrietta, and to Rowland, I suppose."

"Good heavens," said Hilary, "perhaps I have to ask Cousin Rowland's permission to marry you, Louie!"

This struck him as irresistibly comic and his laughter was so merry that Henrietta came in from the passage and was soon kissing both of them and saying it was just the thing, Louie would stop Hilary being too nonsensical and he would make her laugh more.

"And I am very glad you have managed it before we get back under Lady Caynnes's sway," she said. "*Fait accompli* is the only method with her."

377

When they came out into the hall they saw Rowland standing in the porch, leaning on a walking stick and talking to the coachman about the possibility of driving to Rosewell.

"Heard says carts are going out of Ashworthy to Monkhampton," he said, when he saw them. "They'll be shovelling away any drifts that hold them up. It's the coast road I'm doubtful of, as it's not so much used, but Noah Beer is willing to wield a spade for us if necessary."

His mind was so much on the state of the road that it was only when they were about to separate to get ready that Hilary was able to tell him his news. He looked immediately at Louie and then, reassured by her smiling face, congratulated them both.

"And how pleasant it will be to have you at Woodford, Cousin Louie, acting as liaison between Tollingtons and Dynhams," he said, with a smile.

Louie looked quite alarmed at this view of her new position; she was thinking of Lady Caynnes, and murmured her name.

"Yes indeed, we still have Lady Caynnes to reckon with," said Rowland, "but Tollington seems to think that when he tells her about little Nancy's evidence he will be able to persuade her to leave the children in my care, and not to go to law, provided they may visit her and that he remains their trustee and guardian in the event of any accident to me. And now, Louie, I shall be easy about that, when I think that you will be there too."

Louie saw that Rowland and Hilary had evidently settled it all last night, and were now at last on easy terms with each other. Hilary had liked Rowland better ever since he had lost his temper with Caynnes Ridgway, and Rowland had learned respect for Hilary during these critical snowbound days at the fag-end of the year.

Presently Rowland went on about the day's arrangements. "I had thought you would take Miss Henrietta in your chaise, Tollington, while Louie helped me marshal the children in our old carriage. Joscelin is not coming with us; he is going over to Top Leys to settle things with Mrs. Cornish about Nancy. But now I am sure you will want to travel with Louie, if your cousin can put up with the nursery."

"It is just what I should choose, and nursery maid is about all I am fit for after three days in the same clothes!" said Henrietta gaily.

All the same, she had got fresh muslin frills from Mrs. Hickman and had assisted Louie to arrange hers very prettily. She was deft-fingered and could do her own hair, not lost without her maid as so many young ladies were, waited on from childhood. Louie thought she looked delightful as ever, even in the thick shoes she made such fun over.

Joscelin, with Nancy peeping beside him, came to see them off, looking more cheerful than he had for days, and he smiled at Louie, pleased she was going to marry Hilary Tollington.

The chaise was to go first, the larger carriage following with Noah Beer up on the seat behind and a spade in the boot. Mrs. Hickman had also provided a basket of cold pies and bottles of wine, in case the housekeeper at Rosewell was caught unprepared.

"So if we are marooned again we can make merry and laugh at the storms," said Henrietta, as she prepared to get in.

Adrian was already climbing on to the step when his father pulled him back, gently but firmly.

"You must always let the ladies enter first, Adrian."

The little boy blushed and after Henrietta had got in, handed in his sister, copying his father and doing it very well. He had so much natural grace that as soon as he gave up his resentment against Rowland, his manners improved very quickly. Miles, happy to hold the door for Henrietta, wished he could do things as easily and well as Adrian. But somehow he always blundered or was thinking of something else at the critical moment.

The children found the journey exciting because of the remains of the snow drifts, especially when Noah Beer had to do a bit of shovelling, but he at least was glad when they met a cart coming from Rosewell to Monkhampton, which had cleared the coast road for them.

The housekeeper at Rosewell was new, put in since Rowland had left the place after the accident, and did not know him or the children. She kept glancing at them while she was talking to Hilary, in a great fuss to explain why his instructions about the study had not yet been carried out.

"I was going to get a message to Prust today, sir, to come and remove the mirror. I've lit a fire in there to try to dry out the place, for the melting snow has made everything worse."

As they were talking Louie sidled away, going through the drawing-room towards the study. It was a relief to see the wall mirror still in position. She went up close and peered into the crevice behind it and saw the folded edge of the letters, a thin pale line. She was just wondering if she could draw it out with a hatpin when she heard Rowland's voice behind her, saying in some surprise, "What are you doing, Louie?"

She started as she turned round, unable to conceal her agitation. Somehow she could not make a pretence of looking for signs of damp, faced with those penetrating grey eyes.

"Cousin Rowland, I am afraid you will be angry, but I—I hid the letter—from Bath in there. It is there still."

"The letter from Bath?" he repeated.

To Louie's relief Hilary came in from the drawing-room and seeing that the story now had to come out, he told it as briefly and impersonally as possible. Louie could see Henrietta behind him, sending the children to Noah Beer, who had followed them into the hall. She did not go with them but slipped into the study behind Hilary.

382

"Ridgway frightened Louie into thinking this letter could be used against you, Dynham," he ended.

"In his hands, I suppose it might have been," said Rowland. "But I can't understand how it came to be lying about in here. I am sure I put it in the bureau and locked the lid. I was in a hurry, but it was still locked when I went to look for the letters later in the evening, in order to destroy them."

Hilary went to look at the bureau. "You put it in the top, not in a drawer?"

"Yes, because the key was handy."

"Perhaps it slipped through between the hinges," said Hilary and he took a letter from his own pocket and showed how easily this could happen. "I did it myself, only the other day."

"I suppose that could have been so," said Rowland, "and then one of the housemaids picked it up—none of them could read, fortunately. How careless of me—but Louie, why didn't you tell me?"

Louie looked down, unable to speak.

Rowland immediately guessed the answer. "Of course, you thought then I might have been guilty," he said in his usual cool level tone. He moved to look at the side of the mirror. "Can we get it out, without unscrewing the frame?"

Hilary thought he could and borrowed Louie's hatpin to make the attempt.

"Did you notice, Louie, if there were two sheets?" Rowland asked, leaning on his stick. He spoke quietly but she felt he had become tense once more.

"Yes, I recognised Caroline's writing," she answered, in a low voice.

"Caroline's writing?" said Henrietta, in surprise. It was the first time she had said anything.

"It was a letter of hers to that painter, Peter Raine," said Rowland. "He sent it back to me. That's why I went after her, of course."

"*Peter Raine* sent it to you?" repeated Louie, staring at him. "I thought it must have been his wife."

"I hope his wife, who seems a good, nice girl, knows nothing about it," said Rowland. "No, Raine sent it, to convince me of Caroline's intentions and of his own determination, to stick to his promise, given to me before he left here, not to see her again. To tell the truth, I think that young man was afraid of Caroline's desire to make him play the romantic lover in the drama she designed.

384

In that letter she talked wildly of his genius, of going to America and that kind of thing. What was more, she told him to find her at the White Hart. Imagine how public would be any scene that ensued between them! It would have become the talk of the town within a day."

Hilary had now succeeded in getting the letters, still folded together, out from behind the mirror. He blew off the dust and handed them to Rowland.

"And so Caroline did not know that Raine was not going to receive her gladly?" he said, looking at Rowland with a serious face.

"No—she did not wait for any reply to her own letter," said Rowland, staring down at the faded papers in his hand. "She thought she could make him do as she wished, for you know how she could command people, men or women, by the force of her beauty and her will." He paused and then looked up. "How could I let her rush headlong to such an humiliation? Either she would have carried him with her in some ridiculous travelling odyssey to ruin, or she would have had to endure being repudiated by a third-rate portrait painter in a very public place. I believe she would have gone off alone, had that happened; she could not have borne to return, after that. Either way, what would have become of the children, his and ours?"

He was looking at Hilary, but when he stopped, his glance turned to Henrietta. And it was she who said, "You hoped to persuade Caroline to return, by telling her of Peter Raine's letter? But then, why did you not take it with you?"

"I did intend to," said Rowland. "But then I thought it would be unbearable for her to read his words to me—she thought the man loved her, after all, and she was in love with him, or believed herself to be so. And knew I thought this kind of romantic passion great nonsense. So I imagined I could persuade her to return by telling her of it, since she had never had occasion to disbelieve my word. But I kept the letter, in case she refused to believe me."

He turned away and moved suddenly towards the fireplace where the newly lit fire was burning. But he did not throw the letters into the flames; he stood there a moment and then said, with his back to them, "But I was never able to speak to her again."

There was a moment's silence and then Hilary said, "I must say, Dynham, I cannot see how Ridgway could have used this against you. I think it tells very much in your favour."

Rowland made a weary gesture with his hand but did not turn round. "Probably he would not, had he seen it. Louie feared that, not I. All I wanted was that no one else should read either letter. And now they need not."

His voice was strained, and Hilary took Louie's arm. "Come, let's go and find those children and allow Dynham to have his study to himself," he said. He held out his other hand to Henrietta, and she came out with them into the drawing-room.

The children could be heard running up and down the long gallery, while Noah Beer was anxiously saying, "Now, Master Adrian, take care. Oh, my dear life, you'll have that over."

Louie and Hilary went to see what was happening but Henrietta hung back and when they had gone she walked quietly through the drawing-room once more and paused outside the study door. She saw it was not quite closed and gently pushed it open.

Rowland had sat down on the couch in front of the fire and was holding the letters on his knees, Caroline's uppermost. She thought he had been reading it again. His back was towards her and, most unusually for him, who carried himself so upright, was bowed forward. He had not heard her light tread through the crackling of the fire.

Henrietta walked up behind the couch, which had no back, and said softly, "Burn them." As she spoke, she laid her hand lightly against his shoulder.

Rowland started at her touch and began to get to his feet, but his sprained knee made him slow, and Henrietta came quickly round the couch, saying, "Don't get up." She sat down on the other end but turned towards him and repeated her advice. "Burn them now; it is all finished."

"It will never be finished," Rowland said despondently, though on resuming his seat he was sitting straight again. "And nor will the effects. I am not even sure that Lady Caynnes will be persuaded to leave the children in my care without a fight."

"Well, then, let Hilary use these letters to make her see sense," said Henrietta.

Rowland looked at her with surprise. "How could I? Caroline's so reckless, his so abject? How could you suggest it?"

Henrietta smiled. "I knew you would not—so burn them," she said. "Give them to me, and I will."

She held out her hand and after a moment's hesitation, he put the letters into it. Henrietta got up, crumpling them together, and pushed them between two burning pieces of wood. The paper, rather damp, took a moment or two to catch fire. Rowland sat in silence, staring as Caroline's wild words turned brown and flared and crumbled into ashes.

Henrietta came back and sat down again. "You are still blaming yourself for her death," she said, quietly.

"Perhaps more for what went before," said Rowland. "Perhaps I could have treated Caroline some other way and saved the situation."

"Perhaps you could," said Henrietta, "but Caroline's way of treating you was also part of the situation and one over which you had no control."

Rowland was silent, brooding on the past. Then, as if recollecting himself, he said, "It is very kind of you to take such an interest, Miss Tollington."

Henrietta smiled. In a lighter tone she asked, "What are you going to do next, Colonel

Dynham? Your last move, in carrying off the children, was so sudden."

"The house in Westminster becomes mine again the first of this new year," he said. "I propose to take the children there and install Miss Curtis once more. Even Lady Caynnes could not disapprove of Miss Curtis."

"No, indeed," said Henrietta. "But what you really need to make yourself respectable is a wife. I am almost sorry Hilary has carried off Louie, for she would have been so kind to the children, had you married her."

"Married Louie? My dear Miss Tollington, she is terrified of me!" said Rowland, recovering his ironic smile. "Indeed, you must surely understand that I could not, in my present position, ask any woman to marry me."

"I do not understand it at all," said Henrietta promptly. "That is, if she knew you were not guilty of any crime. You have a profession and Hayford seems to think you will go far in it."

"Does he? I am glad to hear that," said Rowland. "But I could not in conscience ask any woman of means, knowing that her family would consider I wanted her fortune—

it is what they all say about my marriage to Caroline."

"And is it true, what they say?" Henrietta enquired, looking straight at him, with her bright hazel eyes.

"Well, I will not deny that I thought Rosewell a beautiful place as a home for our children," said Rowland. "But Caroline was beautiful herself and I was only twenty-two; I did not at all understand either her character or my own. I doubt if we could ever have been happy together but at the time I did not see why we should not. I believe I imagined that marriage was something that happened of itself. I am sure you must think me extremely insensitive."

Henrietta gave him a sudden, brilliant smile.

"Oh no, I do not! Only a little slow to take up the chances that come your way. After all, you are not twenty-two now."

"And you are not twenty-two yet," said Rowland, sufficiently giving away who was in his mind. Although his tone was light, she saw he was nervously tensed again, on guard against himself.

"But I am twenty-one," she observed coolly. "My sister has no longer any right to order my life for me, though I understand she has tried to do so."

Thus she let him know that she had learned about his conversation with Tinna.

"Louie . . . she told you?" Rowland said, his self-imposed reserve dissolving in relief. "What Lady Hayford said to me?"

"Yes, but she only told me yesterday," said Henrietta. "Tinna wanted me to marry Lord Stanbourne, poor stupid fellow, and so no doubt she persuaded herself that she knew better than I what was good for me." She smiled at him again. "She doesn't, you know."

Rowland's eyes met hers and they sat still, both perfectly aware of each other's feelings.

Presently he took her hand. "Henrietta, I hardly dare to conceive the happiness it would give me if you would marry me but I must confess your sister has reason on her side. It does not seem right for you to be linked with someone like myself."

"What are you talking about?" she said teasingly. "Do you think I care twopence about a high position in society? If I did, I should have accepted Stanbourne. As for your reputation as a cruel husband, I hope we may show the world the contrary."

She was smiling but he could not smile back. He said, "I am thinking of that violent temper, which you know is still there, though I have tried so long to crush it down."

"I am not afraid of you, Rowland," said Henrietta, gently. She slightly pressed his hand, with an affectionate look.

"But I am afraid of *myself*," he replied despondently. "It is terrible to know one can lose all control."

"That has not happened often, has it?" said Henrietta. "Even with Caroline—for you did not go to strike her down but to save her."

"It did come out with her, once," said Rowland, and he dropped his gaze. "When I came back from the war, after Mark was killed, and found our life in chaos and Adrian's inheritance half gambled away. And then too, just as with Ridgway, it was some quite trivial taunt which seemed to snap one's control. Yes, *then* I might have done her an injury."

"But you did not," said Henrietta quietly, still firmly holding his hand. "What did you do?"

"I hardly know what I *began* to do," Rowland said, in a tone of such deep self-disgust that Henrietta realised that to him, who set so much store by right conduct, it was intolerable to be driven by blind rage into physical violence against a woman. "Fortunately, someone came into the room and I managed to get out of it before I had done more, I think, than . . . push her against the wall."

The last words came out very low, in a tone of shame and distaste.

"And then," he went on hastily, "I walked out of the house and just went on walking till I was too tired to feel anything at all. But after that, I was even more afraid of losing control."

"Caroline did not make it any easier, trying to provoke you as she did," Henrietta said. "But I do not think you should feel so desperately ashamed of this violent temper, Rowland, since it was something you were born with—we all have some weakness."

"Weakness!" he said. "It is like knowing you have a wild beast inside."

Henrietta felt that one cause of his rare fits of violence might well be his own fear and disgust of it and she chose to alter the tone of their conversation.

"I am not sure that crushing down that monster by main force is the best way of taming it," she said. "I propose we try a new way."

Rowland, who had looked away while he spoke of what most shamed him in the past, looked back at her again. "What is that?" he asked, wonder at the resourceful spirit of this lively and exquisite little creature beside him showing in the softened expression of his usually keen and guarded grey eyes.

For answer Henrietta held up their clasped hands and smiled.

"Oh, I dare not say the word, for you would call it great nonsense," she said. "But still it is a very proper feeling for married persons. I always told Louie I did not intend to fall in love but that of course I would love my husband. Don't you consider that quite a correct attitude, Colonel Dynham?"

"My dear girl, I can't consider anything rationally when you look at me with those beautiful bright eyes," said Rowland, putting his other hand up to her shoulder but still hesitantly, as if he felt he ought not.

Henrietta at once drew to him so that he should have no chance for further rational consideration; in the kiss she returned for his, Rowland was able at last to find the conviction that happiness was, after all, a possibility.

They were not left very long alone, for steps and voices in the drawing-room announced the approach of the housekeeper and one of the Prust family, who was to take down the wall mirror. He greeted Rowland not with mere respect but with a smile of pleasure at seeing him again.

"So you'm back from furrin parts at last, Colonel zurr?" he said. "And Master Adrian, hasn't he growed? He's a fine young b'y, to be sure, just like Lord Caynnes, his grandfer that was—a fine gentleman he were, my father do say, when he were young."

"I hope my Adrian will turn out a finer character than his namesake was said to be," said Rowland, with a smile and went on to enquire after Prust's family, and then to give directions about the mirror and pictures.

As he and Henrietta went through the drawing-room again, Rowland remarked that he was afraid her choice would not be welcomed by any of her family, except perhaps Hilary.

"Tinna will like you when she knows you better," said Henrietta, confidently. "And I hope you will like her too. I do not care what anyone else may think."

"What about Lady Caynnes?" said Rowland. "For I do not think she will consider you are making me respectable by promising to marry me; she will merely conclude that I have proved my villainy by beguiling another young lady of fortune into matrimony."

"Oh my dear Rowland," said Henrietta merrily, "Lady Caynnes will have the pleasure of being confirmed in her opinion that I am a bold flighty girl who was determined from the start to capture the monster and deserves all she gets in consequence."

Rowland laughed aloud, they were both laughing as they came together into the gallery and Hilary at once guessed the reason, and offered warm congratulations to them both, while Louie smiled happily, even though she still found it difficult to imagine Rowland married to anyone but Caroline. And she glanced at the tall picture on the shadowy wall between the windows of Caroline young and beautiful and unconscious of her fate.

The picnic meal at Rosewell was a cheerful one, but nevertheless most of them were glad to be once more on the road to Brentland, hoping to get home before darkness altogether closed in.

Hilary, with a sly look, asked if Henrietta would like to ride home in the chaise with Rowland, but she jumped, laughing, into the bigger carriage. "No indeed, I can't do without my two little cavaliers," she cried, as Miles and Adrian ran to assist her. "And my pet, Mary Anne."

"And La Belle?" said Mary Anne, climbing in with that beauty clutched in her arm. La Belle had worn her new hat that day and it was over one eye.

"Of course La Belle is above suspicion," said Rowland, "or else I would say she had been merrymaking a little too riotously."

"Oh Papa!" cried Mary Anne in shocked tones. "What a very naughty thing to say about La Belle. Henrietta, what are you laughing at?"

"I am laughing because I am happy," said Henrietta, as Rowland sat down beside her and the door was closed.

He took Mary Anne on his knee because she did not like travelling back to the horses. Nor did Miles, who was squeezed in beside Henrietta.

"What about me?" Adrian demanded. "Have I got to be all by myself out here, just because I'm not sick? It's not fair!"

"There's room for you too. Come on," said Rowland, pulling the little boy on to his other knee and looking over his dark head at Henrietta's fair one, curls bobbing at the edge of her green bonnet, and his eyes were full of contentment.

Miles was staring out of the window glass into the murky winter afternoon.

"Goodbye to the sea," he murmured to himself.

"It's the only thing we haven't got at Brentland," said Mary Anne, with some regret.

"We can see it from the top of the house," said Rowland. "It's not very far away."

Curiously enough, in the chaise ahead, Louie was thinking of the same thing. There had been no time, while they were at Rosewell, to walk out to the sea but as they drove away she caught sight of its grey heaving field stretched to the horizon and remembered the attic at the top of Brentland House, where Rowland had slept with his brothers when they were boys, and she thought of the time, the summer before last, when he had lifted up Adrian to look at the sea. Even ten miles off, the great ocean ruled all that windswept country.

Louie's arm was in Hilary's and she was leaning against him.

"Don't look so sad, my sweet Louie," he said, thinking her mind was on Caroline still. "Life has to go on, and we can't help hoping it will go on better for us."

"I am not sad," said Louie, surprised. "No, but I was thinking how little I understood when I first came here. People are not so strong, so unchangeable, as I thought. We are always moving on. Even the places change."

"I like changing places," said Hilary cheerfully. "What do you think of putting bay windows into the drawing-room at Woodford?"

Louie let the past fall behind and began to look forward.

THE END

THE SHADOWS OF THE CROWN TITLES IN THE ULVERSCROFT LARGE PRINT SERIES

The Tudor Rose
Margaret Campbell Barnes
The King's Pleasure   *Norah Lofts*
Brief Gaudy Hour
Margaret Campbell Barnes
Mistress Jane Seymour   *Frances B. Clark*
My Lady of Cleves
Margaret Campbell Barnes
Katheryn the Wanton Queen
Maureen Peters
The Sixth Wife   *Jean Plaidy*
The Last Tudor King   *Hester Chapman*
Young Bess   *Margaret Irwin*
Lady Jane Grey   *Hester Chapman*
Elizabeth, Captive Princess   *Margaret Irwin*
Elizabeth and the Prince of Spain
Margaret Irwin
Gay Lord Robert   *Jean Plaidy*
Here Was A Man   *Norah Lofts*
Mary Queen of Scotland:
  The Triumphant Year   *Jean Plaidy*
The Captive Queen of Scots   *Jean Plaidy*
The Murder in the Tower   *Jean Plaidy*
The Young & Lonely King   *Jane Lane*

King's Adversary   *Monica Beardsworth*
A Call of Trumpets   *Jane Lane*
The Trial of Charles I   *C. V. Wedgwood*
Royal Flush   *Margaret Irwin*
The Sceptre and the Rose   *Doris Leslie*
Mary II: Queen of England

        Hester Chapman
That Enchantress   *Doris Leslie*
The Princess of Celle   *Jean Plaidy*
Caroline the Queen   *Jean Plaidy*
The Third George   *Jean Plaidy*
The Great Corinthian   *Doris Leslie*
Victoria in the Wings   *Jean Plaidy*
The Captive of Kensington Palace

         Jean Plaidy
The Queen and Lord 'M'   *Jean Plaidy*
The Queen's Husband   *Jean Plaidy*
The Widow of Windsor   *Jean Plaidy*
Bertie and Alix *Graham & Heather Fisher*
The Duke of Windsor   *Ursula Bloom*

ROMANCE TITLES IN THE ULVERSCROFT LARGE PRINT SERIES

Hospital Circles	*Lucilla Andrews*
A Hospital Summer	*Lucilla Andrews*
My Friend the Professor	*Lucilla Andrews*
The First Year	*Lucilla Andrews*
The Healing Time	*Lucilla Andrews*
Edinburgh Excursion	*Lucilla Andrews*
Highland Interlude	*Lucilla Andrews*
The Quiet Wards	*Lucilla Andrews*
Carpet of Dreams	*Susan Barrie*
The House of Conflict	*Iris Bromige*
Gay Intruder	*Iris Bromige*
Be My Guest	*Elizabeth Cadell*
The Haymaker	*Elizabeth Cadell*
The Past Tense of Love	*Elizabeth Cadell*
The Bespoken Mile	*March Cost*
The Hour Awaits	*March Cost*
Island of Mermaids	*Iris Danbury*
Penny Plain	*O. Douglas*
The Post at Gundooee	*Amanda Doyle*
My Friend Flora	*Jane Duncan*
Journey from Yesterday	*Suzanne Ebel*
The Half-Enchanted	*Suzanne Ebel*
The Doctor's Circle	*Eleanor Farnes*
The Constant Heart	*Eleanor Farnes*

THE WHITEOAK CHRONICLE SERIES TITLES IN THE ULVERSCROFT LARGE PRINT SERIES

by Mazo De La Roche

The Building of Jalna
Morning at Jalna
Mary Wakefield
Young Renny
Whiteoak Heritage
The Whiteoak Brothers
Jalna
Whiteoaks
Finch's Fortune
The Master of Jalna
Whiteoak Harvest
Wakefield's Course
Return to Jalna
Renny's Daughter
Variable Winds at Jalna
Centenary at Jalna

FICTION TITLES IN THE ULVERSCROFT LARGE PRINT SERIES